C000284328

*The Keeper of Secrets*

a&b

# *The Keeper of Secrets*

JUDITH CUTLER

Allison & Busby Limited
13 Charlotte Mews
London W1T 4EJ
*www.allisonandbusby.com*

Hardcover published in Great Britain in 2007.
This paperback edition published in 2008.



*All characters and events in this publication,
other than those clearly in the public domain,
are fictitious and any resemblance to actual persons,
living or dead, is purely coincidental.*



A CIP catalogue record for this book is available from
the British Library.

10 9 8 7 6 5 4 3 2 1

ISBN 978-0-7490-7912-3

Typeset in Sabon by
Terry Shannon

Printed and bound in the UK by
CPI Bookmarque, Croydon, CR0 4TD

Prize-winning short-story writer JUDITH CUTLER is the author of over twenty novels, including two acclaimed crime series set in the murkier depths of Birmingham. Her latest stand-alones show there's no escaping crime in the countryside either. Judith has taught Creative Writing at Birmingham University, and has run writing courses elsewhere, including a maximum-security prison and an idyllic Greek island. Having nurtured colleagues as the Secretary of the Crime Writers' Association, she now devotes her free time to growing organic vegetables.

Find out more about Judith Cutler by visiting her website at *www.judithcutler.com*.

Available from
ALLISON & BUSBY

**In the Chief Superintendent Frances Harman series**

*Cold Pursuit · Life Sentence*

**In the Josie Welford series**

*The Chinese Takeout · The Food Detective*

**Stand-alones**

*Drawing the Line · Scar Tissue*

Also by Judith Cutler

**In the Sophie Rivers series**

*Dying to Deceive · Dying in Discord*
*Dying by the Book · Dying by Degrees*
*Dying to Score · Dying for Power*
*Dying for Millions · Dying on Principle*
*Dying to Write · Dying Fall*

**In the Kate Power series**

*Power Shift · Hidden Power*
*Will Power · Power Games*
*Staying Power · Power on her Own*

**Romances**

*Head over Heels · Coming Alive*

*For Richard Hoggart,*
*whose inspired teaching changed my life and that of every other student who was fortunate enough to come under his influence.*

# PROLOGUE

*Spring, 1810*

*The bird I was watching, flitting to and fro through the woodland to her unseen nesting place, was one of the genus Sylviidae, the warblers. I could not tell in the dim light that was all the noble trees permitted whether she was a sedge-warbler or a whitethroat. I resolved to tread softly in the hope of seeing her more closely – perhaps even finding her nest.*

*There! I was almost upon her! A whitethroat, surely, with the building material of her nest in her beak – soft, delicate threads, blowing in the breeze as she darted with purpose into a rowan tree. The thread was red.*

*Dared I tiptoe closer?*

*Now, while the bird was on another foray, I reached my target, her nest. A miracle of workmanship, it was even lined to protect the eggs and then the young. That much I had expected. Now I saw what I feared, that the lining was not grey-green grass, but that it was all a soft red. I reached to touch. Alas, yes – it was as soft and fine as hair. It was hair.*

*Whence had it come? I reached and plucked a single fibre. Surely I could not fail to recognise that glow, that lustre? Did that mean—? As realisation dawned that it was hers, hers indeed, I threw back my head and howled like the most primitive animal till the spring's blue firmament rang with my pain.*

# CHAPTER ONE

I was musing on my future, seated in the room I had been kindly allocated in the east wing of Moreton Priory, when I heard the scream of terror. Bursting out into the corridor, I saw a copper-gold waterfall of hair, spotlit by the late afternoon summer's sun, tumbling straight to the floor. Cruel male hands were gripping it, as the girl tried to evade her assailant's unwanted embraces. Even at this hour, he was jug-bitten, already too foxed to heed my urgent remonstrations, or to loosen his grip when I tried to tear the poor girl free. There was only one thing to do. I landed him a facer, all the science that Cribb had taught me in that single blow.

He fell senseless, or near enough, at my feet. The girl – a housemaid, already trying to gather her hair back under an ugly cap – now cowered as far from the wretch as she could, pressed against the ancient wainscoting. Her slender body was wracked by great dry sobs. I feared an attack of the vapours, and would have run to summon another servant had she not piteously grasped my hand.

'You're safe now,' I reassured her, pointing to the prone youth, who was much younger than I'd realised.

'You've killed him, sir. And you a parson!' she cried.

'Dead! He's not dead, the ill-bred oaf. Look, he's moving already. Which is his room?'

She pointed. I shouldered open the door, and gathering the creature by the scruff of his neck and the seat of his breeches I heaved him bodily away from her. He was by now conscious enough to kick it shut behind him.

'He'll lose me my place!' she whispered.

'Did he hurt you?' I helped her to her feet.

She modestly rearranged the neck of her gown, and smoothed her apron. 'What if he complains to her ladyship? I shall be sent packing! And then what will become of me?' she ended, close to tears.

'What's your name?' I passed her my handkerchief, as she brought the hem of her apron to her eye.

'Lizzie, sir.' Fingers touching her clothing as if she were still troubled by her state of dishevelment, she sketched a curtsy. She was tall for a woman, but neither willowy nor Junoesque. Indeed, her figure was perfection itself; the plain clothes of her household uniform could not deny it. Her complexion was pale, as you often find with hair the shade Titian would have been proud of. Her eyes were the blue-green of the far-distant sea and, despite her lowly station, her voice as sweet and low as the Bard himself would have liked.

'Nothing will happen to you. Because I shall speak to Lady Elham and explain what I saw. And if that young cur—'

'Lord Hednesford, sir—'

'Should he ever lay a finger not just on you but on any other young woman here, he will answer to me. Do you understand?'

Understanding me was one matter, believing quite another.

And here I came to a stand. What should I do next? Six months ago I would have slipped half a guinea into her hand and sent her on her way, adjuring her to think no more about it and taking my advice myself. That would have been all she would have expected. But now I stood before her an ordained clergyman, as my neckbands had plainly declared. Did a parson in his first evening in his new parish bless her? Or ask if she went to church regularly? What I should certainly not be doing was standing transfixed by her beauty. I swallowed.

'Yes, sir. Thank you, sir. Can I go now, sir?'

'Of course, Lizzie. But tell the housekeeper to send someone else up to light Lord Hednesford's fire and bring his water in future. Ask her. Tell her I told you to ask her.' By now I was almost as embarrassed as she was, and tried to redeem the situation by bowing to her as if she were a lady with whom I'd just stood up to dance.

Turning, she fled down the corridor, and thence the backstairs.

I returned to my room, closing the door quietly behind me, and sat with my head in my hands. Had I done wrong? Should a man of the cloth ever resort to violence? The smarting of my knuckles testified to the force of my blow.

There was a tap on my door.

'I thought you might want this, sir,' a wooden-faced manservant announced, producing a jug of hot water. 'Will you be needing basilicum powder, sir?'

'I think not.' But I could scarce forbear to wince as I sponged my hands. 'Is someone attending to Lord Hednesford?'

'I should think he might be left to the ministrations of his man, sir. Do not you?'

Despite my protestations, he dusted the raw areas with the powder with which he had provided himself. 'The maid insists that his lordship – a friend of Lord Chartham, his lordship's heir, sir – behaved in a far from gentlemanly way, sir, and that you rescued her from his clutches.'

'She tells the truth, no more, no less. I trust no one will doubt her word?'

'I will inform Mr Davies, sir, of the truth of the affair.'

Davies was the Elhams' steward, who had put in train the arrangements for the living here in Moreton St Jude. The gift was in the hands of Lady Elham, a distant but generous cousin of my mother.

'Thank you.'

'I understand that your effects have had a mishap, sir?'

'Indeed they have – if the complete disappearance of two baggage carts laden with furniture, clothing and books can be called a mishap.'

'No doubt an accident with an axle or a wheel, sir.'

'No doubt. Meanwhile, I have had to throw myself on Lady Elham's hospitality, as you can see. Fortunately I had my valise with me in my gig.'

I could have ventured into Moreton St Jude's wretched-looking village inn, the Silent Woman, slumped across the village green from the rectory, my new and empty abode, but my experiences at a similar hostelry the previous night had deterred me.

Travelling for the first time without all the uproar attending my family's journeys, and no longer enjoying my own bed linen in the finest of coaching houses, I had realised for the first time at least one of the consequences of my decision to eschew the leisured, moneyed existence of the rest of my family and to take holy orders – lack of readily available comfort. My bedchamber, directly above the taproom, was filled with the sound of rustic conversation and the stink of the cheap tobacco with which the drinkers filled their pipes. When all had become quiet below, the noise began above, was the servants clattered around above me in their attic room. When sleep had at last become possible, I found I was not alone in the vilely lumpy bed, but that I shared it with a variety of viciously biting insects.

'If you would permit me to unpack, sir?'

'Thank you.'

'One presumes that your manservant has been mislaid along with your other effects, sir?' Shaking out here and smoothing there, he padded silently backwards and forwards, disposing of all my apparel, although I intended to take advantage of the Elhams' hospitality for no more than one night.

I looked at him sharply. He was not many years my senior, perhaps in his early thirties, but had already cultivated the impersonal demeanour of a good valet. To my chagrin I did not know his name.

As reading my mind, he bowed, but not obsequiously. 'Sutton, sir.'

'Alas, Sutton,' I smiled, 'my valet and I had to part company. A country parson needs a man – or rather, woman – of all work, rather than someone to devote himself to the care of his garments. So all I shall need is a housekeeper-cook.'

'And a little maid? And a groom?'

I could not refrain from laughter. 'Sutton, you wish to fill my humble dwelling from cellar to attic. However, I am not in need of a groom, at least. Jem Turbeville is even now enjoying the hospitality downstairs.'

He nodded tepid approval. 'A gentleman has his position to maintain, sir,' he insisted.

For a moment I thought he was going to say something more, but he occupied himself with gathering some sadly crumpled neck cloths. 'If that is all, sir, I will see to these and return them in time for you to dress for dinner. I take it you will not be wearing your bands, sir?'

Cravenly, I shook my head. I would be wearing full evening dress.

Sutton seemed relieved rather than shocked. 'We keep town hours, here, sir. Her ladyship receives her guests in the Green Saloon at seven. Dinner is at seven-thirty.'

'Thank you, Sutton.'

'Thank *you*, sir.'

Sutton's ministrations stood me in good stead as I joined my fellow – but in their case, *invited* – guests in the Green Saloon, a room of perfect elegance dominated by family portraits.

Lady Elham received me graciously, as I made my bow to her. She was a very handsome woman, though it would have taken one of my sisters to tell me if the flaming locks of her hair, partly concealed under a dark brown turban in homage, I fancied, to Lord Byron, owed more to art than to nature. She dressed in a dark green evening dress with an overtunic of silk the exact green of the wall hangings, set off with a heavy emerald necklace. She bore an uncanny resemblance to a portrait on the wall behind her – an enchanting damsel well caught by Lely at his most sensuous.

'Now, Cousin Tobias – for I decline absolutely to call you Dr Campion, lest anyone confuse you with a physician, and Rector is altogether too formal and as for Parson...' I rather liked being called Parson, and resolved to keep to myself the secret of my doctorate. 'Cousin Tobias,' she continued, 'may I present you to my husband?'

With little enthusiasm, I fancied, on his side, Lord Elham and I bowed to each other. Like me he was in evening dress, as were all the older men present. Only his son, Lord Chartham, wore pantaloons. He was a sulky youth who tried to outstare me, wondering, no doubt, whether he could refer to what he probably considered my ill-treatment of his friend, Hednesford. Of Hednesford himself there was no sign.

When we took our places in the lofty dining room, complete with huge Tudor fireplace, I hoped that the occasion would offer me the opportunity to meet some of my new parishioners, but the young ladies either side of me at dinner were also visitors, Lord Elham's Cornish cousins. Both found my choice of career sadly unromantic, not to say unpromising financially. Clearly both wished to marry well, and since I was careful not to disclose the identity of my own family they cared do no more than practise their flirtation skills upon me. Conversation with the gentleman opposite me, Squire Oldbury, was limited by a huge and extremely ugly epergne, the sort my mother had long since banished to a distant attic. He barked an enquiry about hunting, and whether I intended to keep a pack of hounds, but lost interest the instant I answered in the negative.

My cousin kept a very good table. The young lady to my

right confided in a stage whisper that her ladyship employed a French chef, at goodness knew how many pounds a year. The three courses set before us gave veracity to the theory, with the estate and the succession houses providing an array of delicacies, including Davenport fowls, salsify fried in butter and a Rhenish cream, that would not have disgraced my family's kitchens even on the most formal of occasions and would certainly not have been offered to the mere twelve couples now sitting down. No doubt her ladyship had sighed hugely with relief when she had learnt that Hednesford was indisposed, or she would have had to sit down with uneven numbers, not a solecism to appeal to her.

Left alone, the gentlemen did not sit long over port, to my great relief. It inescapably dawned on me that my host was decidedly lacking in understanding, incapable of discussing anything except the hunt or gunsport. His son, still smouldering with resentment against me for what he presumably saw as my officiousness in the matter of his friend and the maid contributed even less to the conversation. His father said in a brusque aside that the lad's less than robust health was the excuse for his having been tutored at home. In my experience, that often meant a youth was beyond control. Whatever the reason, Chartham lacked the social skills and ease with one's peers that a spell at school imposes. Much as one strives to love all one's fellow men, I confess to having it found hard to be attracted to this ginger-haired, loose-lipped, ungainly young man, whose ease in ferreting out his interlocutors' weaknesses was matched only by his enjoyment of exploiting them. An aristocrat he might be by birth, but a gentleman in behaviour he was not.

The other gentlemen were arguing over the points of a horse I had never seen. I was delighted, even though it was a clear breech of manners, when Squire Oldbury heaved himself to his feet with the proclaimed intention of joining the ladies. Chartham announced he was going to make himself scarce for the rest of the evening. He had enough time, however, to jostle with me in the doorway as we left.

'Mighty fine guest to strike my friend!'

I wanted to reply, schoolboy-like, 'Mighty fine friend!' But I restrained myself. Instead I said quietly, 'Sir, your friend went so far as to forget himself. I'm sure in the morning he will wish to apologise to the young lady concerned and possibly make some financial reparation.'

'Pay for squeezing a skivvy!' He pushed past me, and that was that.

The ladies awaited us in the crimson drawing room. I must confess to being unnerved by the effect my entrance had upon them. It was as if someone had put a large pot of honey near a bees' nest. Suddenly the room was abuzz with feminine voices. A harp was dragged forward, a piano opened, there was a veritable flutter of sheet music. Even when the word went round that I was no more than a country clergyman, some damsels persisted with their inviting smiles and fluttering lashes.

My inclination would have been to read aloud, as her ladyship indeed invited me to do, despatching the butler to locate her favourite volume of Cowper. 'Quite an unexceptionable poet for a clergyman,' she added archly.

The mood of the young people, however, was not for pastoral verse, but for country dancing, and it would have been a hard heart indeed that could have withstood their pleas to form a set.

When her ladyship judged we had made merry long enough, she called for tea, soon afterwards dismissing the younger sort to their bedchambers. I was permitted to seek the masculine entertainments on offer from his lordship, grumbling away over cards in the library or billiards. No card lover, I sought the billiards room. One glance showed me Chartham and Hednesford in occupation. Half of me wanted to remonstrate further with the latter, but I must try for a more private occasion, since I had no wish to antagonise my young cousin further.

No sooner had I made my way upstairs than there was a discreet tap on my door and Sutton appeared.

Assured that I needed no help undressing, he prepared to withdraw.

'That maid, Sutton – has she recovered from her ordeal?'

'I believe so, my lord. I presumed to suggest to Mrs Beckles, the housekeeper, that she might in future carry out her duties in another wing. It seems that Mrs Beckles had already resolved on such a move. She has been sufficiently conscientious in her duties, sir, to become lady's maid, whenever a visitor does not bring her own servant. Mrs Beckles will instruct her fully.'

Satisfied on that score I should have slept the sleep of the just. But at one point I woke sharply, my heart beating with violence. Had I heard a scream? I sat up, straining my ears to hear more. But there was nothing but the creaks and groans of the aged timbers settling for the night, and at last they lulled me to slumber.

* * *

I did not expect my hostess to be at the breakfast table the following morning, and Lord Elham had clearly sunk too much port the previous evening to incline him to conversation now.

As I helped myself to a slice of very fine ham, I summoned Corby, the butler, to my side. 'Tell me, was there any disturbance in the night? I thought I heard something – a shout, a scream – I know not...'

I would swear I saw panic in his eyes, but he said bracingly, 'Sir, next you will be telling me you peered out of the window and saw a headless rider galloping into the courtyard! Why,' he continued, his eyes a-twinkle, 'I recall a footman saw the hooded figure of a friar being hauled down the main staircase only a month or so ago. Regrettably he had made such inroads into his lordship's port that I had to dismiss him on the spot.'

Certainly Corby would not venture to accuse me of having been top-heavy, but I took his drift.

'Now, sir,' he continued, 'I understand from Mr Davies – his lordship's steward, sir – that the carter has at last reached the vicarage. He himself will supervise the unloading of your effects, but requests the pleasure of your early presence. Naturally he would not want to install furniture in the wrong rooms, sir.'

'Naturally. Will you have my gig brought round in – say – half an hour? And have Sutton apprised of my move?'

As he bowed himself away, another pang struck me. All my life I had had but to raise a finger and my orders were obeyed. Now I would have to do simple errands like that for myself.

* * *

Scarce was the last stick of furniture in place, and Jem, my groom, inspecting the stabling, than there was a knock on the back door. Hurrying through the still unfamiliar territory, I found before me a comely woman in her forties. Although very plainly and respectably dressed, she was as elegant in her way as Lady Elham. She carried a basket covered with a white cloth, as if an alfresco repast were planned.

Curtsying slightly in response to my bow, she said, 'Mrs Beckles, at your service, Parson Campion. I have the honour to be housekeeper up at the Priory. I hope these few offerings will make life more tolerable for you until you have your own staff.'

'Why, thank you, Mrs Beckles. That is more than kind of Lady Elham—' I stopped. 'I do beg your pardon, Mrs Beckles. These come from you, not her ladyship, do they not?'

She smiled dismissively. 'A man needs his comforts, sir. Shall I dispose of them in your kitchen for you?'

'I hardly like—' Nonetheless, I stood aside.

'When did any man know his way about a kitchen, sir? Let alone a gentleman.'

Her honest face made me trust her. 'Mrs Beckles, here in Moreton St Jude I am a gentleman no more.'

She lifted her chin. 'With respect, sir, being a gentleman has less to do with birth than behaviour – if you'll pardon me for saying so,' she added quickly. But encouraged by my smile, she continued, 'Up at the Priory I see fine lords behaving like savages, and working men as charitable and gracious as if they had been born with a whole canteen of silver spoons.'

I hung my head, but lifted it to say, 'Mrs Beckles, I think

you have just given a better sermon than I shall ever hope to do.'

'Nay, sir, each to his or her trade. And mine is to tell you that one of the first things you must do is to install a new closed range for this kitchen.'

Extending her attentions to the rest of the house, she hung curtains and stowed linen with the brisk efficiency of Sutton, but more conversation, though none as controversial as her comments about gentility. I tried to draw her out about my new neighbours, but she looked me straight in the eye. 'That would be gossip and hearsay, Parson Campion. You must make your own judgements. You'll make some mistakes – every young man does that – but I doubt that you'll make many. There now, at least you'll have a shirt to your back in the morning,' she said, closing the last drawer. 'I'll arrange for old Dame Phipps to come and wash for you, shall I? Every two weeks? Or every month?'

I shook my head. 'Mrs Beckles, pray arrange what you think best. If you can run a house the size of the Priory, I dare swear you know what is best for this.'

Her laugh showed her excellent teeth, of which her ladyship must have been very jealous.

At last what I had wanted to know all morning. 'Might I ask, Mrs Beckles, how young Lizzie fares this morning?'

'Indeed you may. She is shaken, a little inclined to weep, so I have kept her busy with tasks in my room.' She smiled. 'I honour you for what you did yesterday, Parson. Many another young man would have looked the other way. But you did right. I should be glad for Lizzie's sake if she could find a position in another house, but wherever she went she would have young bloods thinking she was there for their pleasure, and at least here I can keep an eye on her. But a word of advice, Parson. When you chose servants, let your head do the choosing, not your heart. Many a plain girl works harder than a pretty one.'

'I suppose, Mrs Beckles, that you would not be able to recommend one?'

She shook her head firmly. 'It is your new housekeeper-cook you should consult. It is she who will have the training of her after all.'

'And where would I find a housekeeper-cook? Should I ask Mr Davies for advice?'

We both knew what her answer would be. 'I think I can find you just the lady,' she said.

For all its curtains, carpets, tables and chairs, the house felt very empty when she had left.

I repaired to the obvious place – to St Jude's, there to offer belated morning prayers in the ineffable peace of the ancient building and then to become acquainted with its fabric.

At last rising from my knees, I looked about me. From the shape of the arches and the windows, I judged the building to date from Norman times. There were brasses aplenty, and some grandiose tombs holding the earthly remains of the family who held the benefice, with Latin inscriptions testifying to the excellence of their lives. *Nil nisi bonum,* I supposed. The choir stalls looked as old as those in the Chapel of King's College, in Cambridge, where I had taken my degree and later been ordained. I sat in one for a moment, feeling a sense of home there that I had yet to feel in the parsonage. As if in greeting, coloured light danced on my hands with the sudden illumination of the stained-glass windows.

I had hardly closed the heavy door behind me when I realised I was not alone. Rake in one hand, shapeless hat in another, a man in his thirties greeted me. Though much the same age as Jem, he was spare to the point of emaciation, whereas Jem was broad and enough to carry me – as on occasion he had had to, when I had dipped far too deep. His thin face contrasted with Jem's manly features.

'Simon Clark, your honour,' he greeted me. 'Your verger, your honour.'

Could this man dig a grave a full six feet deep? I doubted it, but little knew how soon he would prove my doubts unnecessary.

'Call me Parson Campion, Mr Clark. And carry on with your excellent work.' Now I looked about me, I could see how neat and trim the graveyard looked, barely one weed daring to show its head in the immaculate grass. When he stood where he was, still smiling, I added, with perfect truth, 'Rarely have I seen so beautifully tended churchyard. Is this all your work?'

Eyes huge and round, he nodded convulsively. 'Thank you, your honour!'

I shook my head. 'No, it is I who must thank you. It is you who cleans the church?'

He swallowed hard. 'That be my good wife, your honour. She does her best, your honour.'

'Then pray thank her on my behalf.'

'Thank you, your honour.'

Clearly he could not move until I did, so with another smile, I turned and walked to the lych-gate.

I came face to face with two stolid countrymen, one ruddy and broad, the other as pale and thin as Simon Clark. Neither evinced any immediate signs of friendliness.

'And who might you be, young sir?' the red-faced one demanded.

'Nay, it's the new rector!' cried his companion, at last perceiving my white bands, tearing off his hat and bowing.

I thrust out my hand. 'Parson Campion it is,' I declared, smiling.

By now both men were bare-headed and ready to be servile, an improvement on truculence, perhaps. In turn each wiped his right hand roughly on his breeches before proffering it to me.

'Begging your pardon, sir, we weren't expecting you yet a while.'

'And not so young, neither, not with so many fine men going for to be soldiers.'

I said nothing.

'We're the churchwardens, sir. This here is Farmer Bulmer.'

The red-faced man bowed again.

'And I be Dusty Miller,' the pale one added, laughing almost toothlessly at his appellation. He patted his coat by way of explanation. It rewarded him with a puff of white dust. He coughed, though more as a preface to a well-rehearsed speech than in response to the flour. 'Welcome to your new cure of souls, Mr Campion. We hope you find all as you expect it to be, but if you do not, rest assured we will do all in our power to set it right.' How many hours, how many scribblings and crossings out had gone into that utterance before he conned it by heart?

'Thank you, gentlemen. I'm sure we will work together very well.'

'We hear you haven't any furniture yet, Parson,' Bulmer said.

'Nay, nor any servants, neither,' Miller added.

I smiled. 'Thank goodness the carter brought all my effects this morning. As for servants—' I would rather trust Mrs Beckles' advice than theirs, but listening would do no harm.

'You'll be wanting a good serving-wench,' suggested Farmer Bulmer, with what I thought might have been the ghost of an unseemly wink.

Sensing a trap, I added firmly, 'My new housekeeper will select the staff.' Thank goodness for the prescience of Mrs Beckles.

They exchanged a glance. Miller sucked his few remaining teeth, the pressure putting them at imminent risk.

'Were there no servants at the parsonage before?' I pursued.

'Bless your life, there was just the one. And she went with the last vicar to his new place near Bath.'

'Such loyalty is commendable,' I remarked, perhaps wishing that she had had stronger ties to her home village.

My naivety produced guffaws of laughter, not soon enough suppressed. 'Why, bless your heart, of course she's loyal! She's the old vicar's wife, now, see. And they do say there's like to be a new arrival in their family soon.' This time his wink was unmistakable.

'And him a man not seeing sixty again,' Mr Miller added, his tone a mixture of admiration and envy.

'And her not turned twenty-five, I dare swear. Yes, we must find such a housekeeper for you, Parson Campion. Likely you too will want to see if you've got a breeder before you tie the knot!' His bawdy laughter rang across the green.

'I understand that that is the way of those who know no better, but it is my belief, gentlemen, that it is not the way of a true man of God.'

'Don't 'ee go complaining of Mr Hetherington,' Miller said sharply. 'A fine man he was, the keenest after a fox you ever did see. Three times I saw him brought home on a gate, and like to breathe his last. But next season he was up and doing, just as a man should.'

I bowed silently and coldly. 'I believe my presence is needed at the parsonage. But I will be reading morning service again tomorrow, and hope for your presence. Good day to you, gentlemen.'

Helplessness was a sensation quite new to me. At Eton I had gone well prepared with my elder brothers' advice, and at Cambridge I had found my school friends ready to greet me. Here there was no one, and though I supposed that preparing a nuncheon with the contents of the kind Mrs Beckles' basket should not be beyond my powers, I found myself waiting for a servant to unpack, to find me plate and knife, even to pull out my chair for me.

Now my only servant was Jem, still toiling in the stables, Augean in their condition. It was only right that for once I should serve him. How might I do so without causing him embarrassment? At last it occurred to me that we could sit together in the yard, perhaps on a convenient hay-bale, and have a truly rustic picnic. I carried a basket outside and summoned him. Awkwardly, first sluicing himself under the pump, he pulled over three bales – it was clear that the third would make a good table. From the embarrassed way he rubbed his hands on the straw, he felt unequal to the task of being our ad hoc butler, so I myself placed the cloth on the spare bale and laid out the basket's contents on it. Mrs Beckles had provided a good jug of ale, a selection of cold meats and two handsome pies. There was cutlery aplenty in the kitchen, stowed so dexterously by Mrs Beckles, but I knew not where. Without a word, Jem produced a haft-knife, and cut two huge slices of mutton pie.

My appetite assuaged, for food if not for conversation, Jem being ever taciturn, and now completely silent, except for two or three brief utterances on the subject of the horses, I had the rest of my day to fill. Mrs Beckles' kind ministrations had not extended to my study. My books – quite rightly – awaited my attention.

Installing the last volume in the handsome new bookcase, I felt at last that I might be at home here, my old friends with their worn spines but perennially fresh interiors about me. But I was so filthy the only option open to me was the pump Jem had used earlier. So I was dripping wet when I heard a distant ring on my new doorbell. Of course, there was no servant to respond, and I was loath to miss a visitor. Pulling on my shirt, I almost ran through the house.

'Hello? Hello there?' Whoever it was did not wait, but stepped inside, his broad frame making a silhouette against the bright afternoon sun.

Still in my shirt-sleeves, I stepped forward, hand

outstretched. If my guest did not stand upon ceremony, neither would I.

'Edmund Hansard at your service, sir,' he greeted me, pulling off a shapeless hat to reveal an old-fashioned wig atop the face of a man in his early fifties.

'Tobias Campion at yours,' I responded with a slight bow. My hand was enveloped in his.

'I have the advantage of you,' he laughed, bright blue eyes a-twinkle. 'I know that you are the new parson, but you cannot know that I am the doctor. And I come not to treat any ills – for you look a healthy enough young man – but to bid you come and share my board this evening. Aye, and bring your man too. I have no doubt my servants will look after him.'

'This is most kind—' I began.

'Did I not read somewhere that you should do unto others as you would they do unto you? Well, man, someone must needs feed and water you. I keep a plain table, mind you. And country hours. Would six be too early for you? You'll find me at Langley House, out on the Leamington Road. Till six, then. No need to dress.'

'Till six,' I agreed.

He left without further ado, leaving, as Mrs Beckles had done, a house feeling the lack of his presence.

'Langley House,' I repeated to Jem, as we trotted side by side through the village, the westering sun bathing it in a golden glow.

On the green a few very young boys, no more than five or six years old, played with a bat and ball. Beyond the green was a duck pond, with St Jude's the far side of the graveyard to my left. The Silent Woman, so old that Shakespeare might have drunk there, sank down on its knees opposite. On the outskirts of the village a coaching inn was being built, to celebrate the arrival of a turnpike road, no doubt. It would be the only building of note, St Jude's apart. The rest of the village comprised picturesque thatched cottages, haphazardly arranged in a verdant innocence so beloved of our poets.

We were heading in the opposite direction from Moreton Priory, into neat and I hoped prosperous farmland. Jem rode alongside me, as he'd done from the days he taught me to ride. It was the only time he permitted me to treat him as my friend.

'And what sort of place are we looking for?' he asked.

'Do you know, I've no idea.' I scanned the scattering of cottages we passed, greeting the shirt-sleeved men toiling in gardens crammed from corner to corner with bright flowers and anomalous vegetables. 'Surely they cannot feed a family from so small a plot,' I exclaimed. 'My father's estate workers have allotments three or four times this size.'

'Not all farmers are as generous as his lordship,' Jem replied, eyeing the half-naked children as if they were savages. Their filthy hands shot out as we passed. I scattered a handful of pennies and resolved to do something of more long-term benefit, God willing.

At last we had fairly left the cottages behind. A high stone wall ran parallel with the road. After half a mile or so, it was broken by a handsome pair of gates, and a gravelled driveway led up to a house some thirty or forty years old, elegant in its proportions.

'Can this be it?' Jem asked. ''Tis a mighty fine place for a country doctor.'

And so it was. The rosy brick-built house glowed in welcome. Three storeys high, its symmetry was more than agreeable to the eye. Perhaps it reminded me of the doll's house my sister once cherished.

Two lads dawdling home assured us, when prompted by a penny from me and a scowl from Jem with an adjuration to watch their manners when the parson was speaking to them, elicited the information that this was indeed Dr Hansard's home. Exchanging amused and rueful grins, we set our mounts in motion once again, to be greeted by our host himself on the front steps, deep in conversation with his groom.

As he glimpsed us, he broke into a broad smile. 'Welcome to Langley House,' he said.

The evening went with enormous speed. At some point, perhaps as we supped in leisurely fashion, perhaps as we sipped our port afterwards, Edmund Hansard and I progressed from being sympathetic acquaintances to men likely to become friends. It may have been when he showed me his experiment room, where he explained his aspiration to grow pink hyacinths from blue stock, or his curiosities collection, or even his library, where he had had a small fire lit, to take off the chill of the evening. Without exchanging the sort of personal confidence my sisters pressed on their bosom bows, it was clear we saw the world from a similar position, though I would have been hard pressed to recall a single instance where we had formally exchanged opinions.

He pressed a final glass of brandy upon me.

'So you see,' he said expansively, 'the neighbourhood does

not know what to make of me. They see this fine house, and from it emerges an old country doctor. Should they admit me through their grand front doors – which, to be fair, Lord and Lady Elham have come to do – or send me, tail between my legs, to the servants' entrance?'

'A man of your learning—' I began.

'Is less respected for what lies between his ears than for his land, just as any other country gentleman is. Do you think I would have been appointed as a justice of the peace had it not been for my acres? Would my library, my travels, my learning, as you put it, have entitled me to such a responsibility? I think not, my friend. And indeed, if they knew how I had acquired my land and my house, I might not have—' He broke off as a peal from his doorbell, veritably loud enough to waken the dead, rang throughout the house. He was on his feet in an instant. 'At this time of night that can mean only one thing – a hatch or a despatch,' he said with a rueful grin. 'My young Tobias, I am sorry to bid you such an unceremonious farewell. But I have a feeling we shall deal well together.'

With that he bustled me out, grabbing his hat and his bag from a servant already holding the front door ajar. A man was running his horse round even as we passed through it. Throwing the farm lad messenger up before him, Dr Hansard was on his way.

Jem had brought Titus round at a not much slower pace.

'Seems he has the bell connected to his kitchen and to his stable, too, so George – that's his groom – always knows when he has to saddle up,' he said. 'Do you want to follow him, Master Tobias?'

I pondered. Once again, a deep longing to be told what to

do possessed me. But I had not so much as a tutor to guide me now. 'If it's a "hatching" I shall only be in the way,' I mused. 'And I know that if mother or baby ails he will send for me.'

Jem frowned. 'But it might be a deathbed he's called to. And there, I tell you straight, Master Tobias, you should be.'

To be shamed thus by my own servant! In silence, I let him heave me into the saddle, and within a minute we were following the good doctor's tracks.

# CHAPTER TWO

As I stood beside the grave, I thanked the Almighty that the first deathbed I had had to attend in my new cure had been such an easy one. Old Mrs Gates's passing had been entirely peaceful with, not so much as a backward glance. Indeed, even Dr Hansard had found it hard to pronounce the absolute moment of death, it was so gentle.

Her family, farmers comfortably ensconced in a house the origins of which must have been at least as old as those of Moreton Priory, had surrounded her, repeating after me the appropriate prayers. Perhaps they had been surprised to see me, but their welcome, once I had introduced myself, was gratifyingly warm. Only Dr Hansard allowed a gleam of surprise, then amused approval, to flicker across his face. I had had the grace, I believe, to blush. I trusted Jem far too well to fear that the reason for my presence would ever become public knowledge.

It seemed that in this part of the kingdom it was not considered seemly for women to attend the final obsequies, and so it was only men gathered round the graveside to hear – and, I hoped, be consoled by – the solemn grandeur of the burial service. They stood in the late summer sun, their heads bowed in a final farewell, in this world at least, but in sure hope of a reunion in the next.

'Thank you, Parson Campion,' said Farmer Gates as I signified the proceedings were over. 'Now, let me press you and Dr Hansard here to join the mourners back at the farmhouse for a glass of sherry before the old lady's will is read.' He clapped me familiarly on the shoulder.

Two years ago I should have shuddered at the touch and at such an invitation. Now I would accept them both, for two reasons. The first was to keep Jem's good opinion, so very nearly lost the other night; the second was that I rattled round my empty house like an egg in a bucket, to use his phrase, and however I tried to fill my hours of leisure with study and prayer, I felt at times a quite desperate need for the company of my fellow men – even if they were, like Farmer Gates, huge, red-faced yeomen, clothes straining at the seams and great hams of hands dealing greasy cards for whist: people, in short, to whom my family would scarcely have bowed from their carriage.

However, even as I smiled my acceptance, Simon Clark, the verger, scuttled across the greensward with a far from reverent haste.

'Simon,' I began to remonstrate, in a serious voice.

'Begging your pardon, your honour, and yours, Dr Hansard, but the doctor's wanted,' he panted. 'Real urgent, they say. Down in Marsh Bottom. Young Will says it's bad, desperate bad he says.'

'Is William waiting?'

'No, Doctor. He's run straight back, fast as if his life depended on it.'

'How fortunate you left your gig at the parsonage,' I said to Hansard. 'Let me apologise to these good people and I will accompany you.'

'To Marsh Bottom?' Simon demanded incredulously. 'That's not a fit place for such as you, your honour!'

'Anywhere on God's earth is fitting for His servants,' I said as mildly as I could.

'Not even a pig would want—' he persisted.

'How fortunate I am not a pig. Enough of this, Simon.' I turned to Farmer Gates. 'It seems I cannot accept your kind invitation. Pray forgive me.'

He nodded, apparently bemused. I fancied, however, that even if he had not taken offence, my churchwardens had. Mr Bulmer's complexion was dark with anger, and Mr Miller's eyes narrowed. But from the expression on Dr Hansard's face, this was no time for doctrinal or social argument, so, with a final shake of Mr Gates's hand, I turned towards the parsonage.

Shedding my surplice with more haste than dignity, and providing myself, on impulse, with the requisites for both communion and infant baptism, I bade Jem, busy with a hammer and some long nails, bring the gig round immediately. Even Jem looked solemn when I mentioned our destination, but he gave a grim nod, as if approving despite himself.

'What is Marsh Bottom, that no one wants me to see it?' I enquired lightly, as I took my place beside Dr Hansard. 'Or is it my solecism in declining to partake of the funeral baked meats that gives offence?'

'I know not why Bulmer and Miller are so hostile,' he said thoughtfully, whipping his horses into a brisk trot. 'They dealt extremely well with your predecessor, but that in itself is no commendation, not in my eyes at least. Simon Clark, however, is a decent man, who – not to wrap it up in clean linen – fears for your health as much as for your sensibilities. I doubt you'll have seen much to prepare you for the Bottom, not unless you have seen military service abroad.'

Although I felt his eyes upon me, I declined to respond. Although one day I had no doubt I would open my budget and be fully frank with him, this was neither the time nor the place, and, were I honest with myself, it was still an episode painful to refer to. 'My health?' I prompted him at last.

'A foul, miasmic place,' he said. 'And Simon was right; no decent farmer would want to house his pig in such a sty. But labourers are not pigs, Tobias, and neither are their families,' he added grimly. 'I often think they are not valued so highly.' He slowed his horses to a funereal walk, the lane being so deeply rutted that I would imagine it impassable after rain.

'The landlord—'

'—Is so busy improving his lands after at last enclosing them that he has no time to care for his workers' accommodation. He would probably assert that he has no money, either, for putting land into good heart is not to be undertaken lightly. But soon you may judge for yourself. I normally come to such places on horseback,' he added grimly, struggling to keep the gig upright.

At last, the gig came to a halt – for the life of me I could not see why – and, reaching behind him for his bag, Hansard jumped down. Nothing loath I followed suit. 'We have to walk from here?' I ventured.

'We are here, man,' he declared, his voice rough with an emotion I eventually deduced must be anger.

'But I see nought but a haystack,' I protested. 'And a damned poor one to boot!'

'You see Marsh Bottom,' he said dryly.

He strode along what might have been a path, his boots leaving phosphorescent puddles in the ooze. I followed in an altogether more gingerly fashion, still wondering whither he led. At last I perceived two or three holes in the side of the stack, which might be doorways, with further holes emitting a quantity of thin smoke.

'Can it really be that someone lives here?'

'Three families,' he threw over his shoulder. 'One in each hovel. Now do you see why people doubted the wisdom of your venturing down here? Continue at your own risk, Parson Campion.'

I fear that even at that moment I might have turned back, had I not heard a hideous sound, midway between a groan and a scream, issuing from the middle hole.

We plunged within. It took me all the willpower at my disposal not to retch and recoil at the stench of a veritable charnel house. I could not but reach for my handkerchief, pressing it hard against my nose and mouth, however that might diminish me in Hansard's opinion.

At last my eyes accustomed themselves to the dimness within. The only light came from the doorway – there was no door that I could see – and from the hole supposedly acting as a chimney. There was a pallid glimmer of flame from a fire, but I did not think it would survive much longer. Three or four shapes cowered in the furthest corner. It took me moments to realise that they were children. To my left a woman leant over another figure on a heap of straw that was the sufferer's only bed.

'How long has Luke been like this, Mrs Jenkins?' Dr

Hansard asked, as courteously as if he had been addressing Lady Elham.

'These three days, Doctor. And getting worse.'

'And why did you not call me earlier, my dear lady?'

A groan and a wringing of hands told him what he needed to know.

'You must know that in cases like these I never ask for a fee. I might not have saved his leg, or even his life, but I would have spared him pain.'

Another terrible scream rent the air.

'Parson Campion, pray, take those children outside. This is not a sight for their eyes.' He might have added, 'Or yours.'

I did as I was bid, holding out my hands to encourage them. They cowered further into their corner.

'William, go with my new friend,' he said, over his shoulder. 'You know what you will find in my gig.'

I moved to the door, hoping with all my heart that they might follow and knowing that when they were safely outside I must return to pray for the dying man.

'What will you find in the kind doctor's gig?' I asked, my voice falsely bright. 'Come, let us find what he carries.'

'Apples,' hissed Hansard, whether for my benefit or theirs I could not tell.

The urchins – more wild animals than humans, with their bodies ill-concealed in rags – erupted, shooting past me and lurching towards the gig, as if their legs were not sturdy enough for the business of running.

I wondered at the doctor's wisdom in encouraging them to eat fruit, but he must know best. I reached for the bag, allowing but one apple for each grasping hand, and fed one to both horses. The contrast between the animals and the humans shocked me. Never had those childish heads been subjected to brush or comb, never had their hands been washed or the nails pared. I judged not one of them to be more than six years old.

The apples were devoured, stalks and all. I feared to distribute more, but spied another paper-wrapped parcel. Doctor Hansard had provided himself with bread as well. Whatever he had intended this for, I could not restrain myself from breaking it, with a silent blessing, in some strange but not irreverent parody of the Holy Communion. Had I had wine, or better, good milk, I would have administered that too.

Another scream tore through the comparatively peaceful air. This was no place for the children. Approaching William, the eldest, I bent down and asked quietly, ' Do you know the parsonage, my child?'

'Where Parson Hetherington lives?'

'He lives there no longer. I live there now, with my groom, Jem. Pray you, take your brothers and sisters and go to find him. He will find you more food and drink. Ask Jem particularly for milk, mind. And stay with him till I come back. Do you understand that? Tell him Parson Campion sent you.' As an afterthought, I added, 'And ask him to send for Mrs Beckles. Do you understand? Mrs Beckles.'

The straw on which the dying man lay was soaked with blood and worse. The stump of one leg jerked frantically in its own dance of death as his body arched and writhed. I swear he had bitten his own arm to the bone in an effort not to call out.

'Is there nothing you can do?' I whispered.

'If I administer enough laudanum to ease his pain it will speed his death, Parson,' Hansard said. 'And would you want that?'

It was not a question that my tutor had ever propounded. I had been taught precepts and precedents, rules for a better life on this earth.

I bit my lip. 'I believe God would want you to ease his pain. If He chooses to call him to Him, then that is His Will.'

He nodded. 'Good. That is what I have already done. He will soon be quiet.'

What of the sobbing woman even now clutching the poor sufferer's hand and calling his name? 'What can you offer to ease her pain?' I asked.

'I think that that is for you to do. She may not understand all the words of your prayers but she will know that they are being said.'

At last the broken man fell quiet. It might have been a deep slumber, but for the great gasps for breath that seemed to tear his chest.

'The death throes,' Hansard murmured. 'Pray God it is not long now.'

For with each gasp the woman wailed anew.

'Madam,' I said softly, 'will you join me as I pray?'

To my horror, she stared at me, eyes wild. She raised her hand, pointing a finger in veritable accusation. But then she dropped it, and looked in bemusement at Hansard.

'Our new parson, Maggie. Parson Campion. I think your good man needs all the help he can get, don't you?'

'He ain't never been to church, not his whole life, I doubt.'

'Not even to be baptised?' I asked.

'Does that count now?' was Hansard's swift rejoinder.

'Find me a little water, Mrs Jenkins. Go, now, quickly. I will get my bag.' It could only be an *ex tempore* baptism, but it was the best I could do.

The little ceremony did not last long. Perhaps Luke Jenkins was quieter, more serene, as I read the fearsome but hope-giving words, Dr Hansard making the responses on his behalf, as if he were an infant. And then, in a request that brought tears to my eyes, Mrs Jenkins begged me to wed them on the spot. Such a rite demanded licence, witnesses – aye, and the consent of the poor dying man – for it to hold any legality. But how could I deny her at least an attenuated form of the service? It would bring her some solace in the black days to come. But still I doubted.

Mr Hansard said in an urgent undervoice, 'You have little time for quibbling, man.'

I swallowed my fears. 'Provided that you promise to come to church – soon – and let me baptise you and your children, then yes, Mrs Jenkins, with all my heart.'

The children had had an earthly baptism by the time I reached home, Dr Hansard leaving his gig with Jem while he spoke to Simon, the verger, about the burial. Jem paraded them in front of me. They were all clean, all had had their hair trimmed or tied back, and their claws had been returned to the state of nails. They were wrapped in towels, like veritable Hindoos. But even as I stared, the smart clatter of horses' hooves announced the arrival of another gig, capably turned into the yard by Mrs Beckles, a large bundle at her feet. To my delight she was accompanied by none other than Lizzie, the maidservant whose acquaintance I had made at the Priory. In the midst of our darkness was sudden light, as the sun spun her hair into a veritable halo. Even as her lips parted in a shy smile, her eyes caught something beyond me, and her face was transfixed.

Involuntarily I turned. Jem's eyes were locked on hers. Slow flushes rose on both sets of cheeks, his turning his weather-beaten features russet, hers a delicate rose. But perhaps I imagined all, for in a second, Jem was assisting Mrs Beckles from the gig, and I was handing Lizzie down, rewarded for my pains by a shy smile and modestly lowered eyes.

Jem was all a-bustle with the horses, while Lizzie, seizing a familiar covered basket, ran to the tongue-tied children as if to gather them to her. Mrs Beckles was not far behind, soon delving into her bundle, and producing a variety of small garments, with which they covered the children's limbs.

So engrossed were they in their task, they did not notice the approach on foot of Dr Hansard, looking inexpressibly weary. But he straightened at the sight before him, and a smile softened his features. Still the figures in the tableau were unaware of him.

'From the poor basket,' Mrs Beckles explained, with what seemed a conscious glance at him. 'The maids practise their plain sewing on garments which they pass to the poor. I cut the fabric myself, Mr Campion, so each item should have the requisite number of sleeves and legs, but I cannot vouch for the straightness of seams.'

'Whatever the state of the needlework, I doubt if they will ever wear better quality clothes however long they may live,'

Hansard grunted. 'Or, ma'am, eat better food.'

Mrs Beckles turned swiftly, dropping into a half-curtsy.

Dr Hansard responded with a bow, but then held a hand outstretched as if to warn us off. 'I too must have recourse to a pump, I fear.' Indeed, his attire was covered in blood and other matter. 'Jem, will you convey the youngsters to the workhouse? And later I will take their mother there,' he added, in a voice blending anger and despair.

Mrs Beckles stepped forward, as did I.

'Surely, Dr Hansard, the mother—' I began.

'May they not spend just one night together, she and her children?' Mrs Beckles urged. 'Even Mr Campion's stable would be a more comfortable place than the workhouse. And we can find female clothes from somewhere – I doubt the poor creature's garments will be any more decent than the children's rags.'

'Indeed, with all my heart! But must it be the workhouse?' My impulse, like Lizzie's, was to embrace the children. I sank to my knees beside them.

'Let them for tonight be reunited with their mother,' Hansard decreed. 'For modesty's sake, Campion, we must leave Mrs Jenkins to the ministrations of these kind ladies. Jem, will you bring the poor creature here? Nay, I'd best come with you.'

Mrs Beckles nodded approvingly, watching him, a warm smile on her face, until he was out of sight. I stole a glance at Lizzie, but she was coaxing the hair of the eldest girl into a semblance of order, and did not appear to be interested in anything else.

* * *

The little family at last touchingly reunited, Mrs Beckles shooed away Jem, Hansard and myself, like so many chickens, so that Mrs Jenkins could be persuaded under the pump.

The doctor declined to enter my house. 'Not in all my dirt, man. Naturally you and Jem will both be eating at Langley House,' he added, as he turned to leave. 'But I'd advise a session under that pump for both of you before you come. And a bonfire for all of your clothes.'

Neither of us argued.

'There is absolutely no alternative?' I demanded, as Dr Hansard and I sipped a restorative sherry in the comfort and warmth of his study before supper, the aromatic precursors of which were emanating enticingly from behind the green baize door.

'The workhouse it must be. And, grim and inhumane as such a refuge is, it cannot be worse than the circumstances in which the family now finds itself. It was a tied cottage—'

'*Cottage!*' I repeated derisively.

'—And as such it must be vacated once the labourer is an employee no longer. That is the law, and as a justice of the peace I must enforce it. But at least under the parish Maggie Jenkins and her little brood will get some food, and better shelter than they have been used to.'

'Is there nothing else I can do?' I thought of my new home, with all its empty rooms.

As if he read my thoughts, he gave a kind but dismissive shake of the head. 'Maggie is completely unlettered, her children little more than savages,' he explained. 'With luck not all of them will die, and with yet more luck they will be taken into apprenticeships by decent masters. Do not think you can adopt all paupers who come your way, young man, for you cannot.'

'But I have so much...and there are other families at Marsh Bottom—'

'Who are still the farmer's responsibility. And however much you have, my friend, you do not have enough to change the world. The best you can do – the best any of us can do – is improve your own little corner. Jem, for instance: can he afford to replace the shirt, breeches and waistcoat I hope he has burnt?'

I blushed. How easy it was for me to reach for fresh garments. And how easy to forget that while Jem might be well paid for his services compared with others in his position, he could ill manage an extra expense, a sum of money that my father would not hesitate to spend on a single supper for one of his high-fliers.

'Do not worry, Tobias. You will learn in time.'

Perhaps he was right. 'But there is something else I need to learn, Dr Hansard. You have not told me yet how Jenkins came to have such a terrible injury. Or why his... the lady now his widow...looked at me with such hatred.' As he hesitated, I added, 'I am not a child to be protected, you know.'

His laugh was indulgent, but his voice hardened as he told the tale. 'Very well. I hoped to spare you until at least we had supped. Jenkins was poaching. His leg was caught in a man-trap. He hacked it free himself and dragged himself home, fearing that if one of his children came a-looking, he might suffer the same fate. And then he took three days to die.'

For minutes I could not speak, and paced about the room

in an effort to regain control over my emotions. Such heroism, such suffering, were beyond my comprehension. I came to a halt by the window, overlooking Hansard's peaceful garden and parkland, hoping the verdant scene would ease away the recollection of the man's sufferings. At last Hansard joined me, laying a consoling hand upon my shoulder.

'And why did his wife blame me?' I ventured.

'Because the trap, my friend, was on your glebe land.'

I was afflicted with such shame that none of Hansard's words over supper, nor the excellent repast with which he regaled me, could lift my spirits.

At last, perhaps attributing my want of conversation to fatigue, he bade me a hearty goodnight, handing me over to Jem's care, as he put it.

Through the pitch-black night – clouds had by now obscured the moon – we rode in silence towards the village. We knew each other well enough never to interrupt each other's thoughts with idle chatter.

'Hark! What on earth is that?' I demanded.

'A carriage moving very fast,' Jem had time to reply.

Before I knew it, he had grabbed my reins and yanked Titus into a gateway just deep enough for the two trembling horses. Barely had he done so than an unlit chaise shot by.

'Why did we not hear them before?' I asked foolishly.

'The horses' hooves were muffled in felt,' Jem responded thoughtfully. 'Now why should anyone go to the trouble of doing that?'

I shrugged. After the tribulations of the day I had no answer and neither, it seemed, did he.

# CHAPTER THREE

If my first sermon at St Jude's, delivered to a congregation I could count on my fingers, had been as bland as buttermilk (though at least, I protest, the product of my own labour, not taken from another's book), my second would certainly cause offence. My subject was our duties to the poor. I had prayed long and hard, but the answer always came that I should and must deliver it, offend whom it might.

Nonetheless, I felt unwonted tremors of apprehension as I climbed into the pulpit to face – why I knew not – a much larger congregation. Looking up at me were the narrowed eyes of my churchwardens, the watery ones of Simon Clark and the astonishingly dark brown ones of an otherwise faded lady I presumed to be his wife, whose efforts to keep the church clean had noticeably waned. Also there were Mrs Beckles and a flock of servants from the Priory, including Lizzie, whose turquoise eyes almost dazzled in the darkness, as she sat with lips slightly apart, as if to drink in my words. Gazing at her, not me, with unabashed longing, was a sturdy young man I did not recognise, who clearly led an outdoor life. If I had wondered what a well set-up young man was doing here at home, not earning the King's shilling, in Lizzie, I suspected, lay the answer.

Squire Oldbury and Farmer Gates were stolid in their churchwardens' pew. The rest of the congregation were labourers, tricked out in what little they could call their best, and a pew devoted to the preternaturally smart Jenkins family. Mrs Jenkins, eyes still red from her bereavement, raised her face to me with the sort of adoration seen on the features of Mary Magdalene, as depicted by the Old Masters. The family's sartorial good fortune brought forth one or two nudges and winks, as if the neighbours envied them their still miserably straitened existence.

One who did not raise his head, or attempt to meet my gaze, was Mr Ford, the steward who had overseen the glebe for my predecessor. Our encounter, the day after Dr Hansard's disclosure, had not been pleasant, not just because the fire in my study would not draw and smoke was seeping into the room.

'If the traps were good enough for Parson Hetherington, I don't see why they aren't good enough for you,' he had muttered. He was a small man, and his long features irresistibly reminded me of a ferret's.

'I'm sure the traps are perfectly good,' I had assured him. 'But I do not want traps of any kind upon my land.'

'Not gins, even, to catch rabbits?'

Perhaps his understanding was weak. But until I could replace him with a better, I realised with horror, I could not afford to dismiss him from my service.

'Nothing that can harm a human, adult or child,' I had said firmly.

His mean eyes regarded me curiously, and I sensed that he held me in at least as much contempt as I held him, but he had said nothing.

At last I tried for a magnanimous ending to our uncomfortable conversation. 'Now, Mr Ford, how are your wife and children?'

'They all have their health, the Lord be thanked.'

'Good. Now, could you put a man on to deal with my chimneys? And Mr Ford,' I said, in a tone reminiscent of my old headmaster's, 'I hope that I will never again have cause to be displeased with you.'

He had scuttled out with what I fear was a resentful look.

No, today I did not expect a reassuring nod from my steward.

I received one from Jem, in his Sunday best, a clean kerchief at his neck, who sat stolid in the rectory pew, powerful hands folded meekly in his lap. He resembled nothing so much as a gentle guard dog, as he shot a careful glance over his shoulder at each newcomer. Was it my imagination that his eyes had lingered longest on Lizzie, and then on the smitten suitor?

I prayed in silence for a moment, and commenced my sermon.

Our Lord, I said, had always fed and healed the poor, and though he advised people to render unto Caesar the things that were Caesar's, nowhere in the New Testament was there any suggestion that he would approve of mantraps. I confessed my own part in the death of poor Luke Jenkins, vowing publicly that never again would I permit such a vile instrument to appear on my glebe land.

In conclusion, I urged all the landowners and tenant farmers present, and those who would only hear what I had said at second hand, to rid their acres entirely of the foul machinery.

If the murmur greeting my words was largely of approval, I fear it reflected the status of the congregation; it was clear I would have to carry my message in person into all the great houses of the district. I trust that my anxiety did not show as we sang our hymns and I said the remaining prayers.

At the conclusion of the service, I reminded my flock that the following week I would be celebrating Holy Communion following the baptism of all the Jenkins children and poor Widow Jenkins herself. Then I posted myself at the door, to shake the hand of each and every person in my congregation.

Mrs Beckles had tarried in the church, but now she too came to bid me good day. 'I was glad to see the Jenkins brood here today,' she began, 'and glad to hear your sermon. I tell you straight, that Mr Hetherington would never – could never – have said such things.'

'You think I have – to use a cant phrase – led with my chin?'

'You will not have pleased everyone, that is certain. But I do not think you wanted to.'

'I would not be doing my duty if I did. But Mrs Beckles,' I continued, noticing for the first time that she was not in her best looks, 'you look...'

'Fagged to death,' she said, obligingly finishing my question for me. 'Indeed, the Jenkins adventure apart, I have had a busy week. Have you not heard of the goings-on at the Priory?'

'Alas, I am not yet deemed to be sufficiently part of the village to be admitted into everyday gossip.'

'I am sure you will not remain a stranger for long,' she reassured me. 'And perhaps a change of butler is not of such moment, after all – except to his fellow servants.'

'The butler! Corby?' Well trained and discreet, the butler was the keystone of every great house. 'That kind old man who was in place when I stayed at the Priory?'

'The very same. Mr Corby. For no reason he ups and offs, leaving no more than a letter to Mr Davies, the steward, to say that he has come into a small legacy and proposes to set up a boarding house at a seaside resort in Devon. Did you ever hear the like?'

'Indeed I have not.'

'And him, the most meticulous of men, to leave his room like a pigsty. How mistaken one can be in one's fellow men.'

I nodded in commiseration. 'But such a household as the Priory must have a butler.'

'Indeed. And at last Mr Davies is satisfied that he has found a replacement – Mr Woodvine – who will match her ladyship's exacting standards.' As if reflecting on those standards, she nodded in the direction of the moonstruck youth still gazing upon Lizzie. When she spoke, however, she made no direct reference to him. 'I believe that Lizzie, with her industry and ability, could do very well in life.' It was implicit that were her life to be linked to the young chawbacon's, Lizzie would not do very well at all. 'I have spoken to her ladyship about her, and we both agree that she deserves a chance to better herself – perhaps she might become her ladyship's own maid. At one time your predecessor spoke of teaching some of the lower servants to read and write, though for some reason his plans came to naught. Would you, Parson Campion, share some of your learning?'

'Nothing would give me more pleasure, Mrs Beckles,' I said truthfully. 'Will you arrange a time when the young men and women can best be spared from their duties? And find me a suitable room?'

'Of course.' She nodded briskly and looked about her for her charges, all enjoying rare moments of freedom in the still-warm sun.

I resolved to indulge them a few minutes more. 'Mrs Beckles, I have it in mind to start a school for the children of the parish. In fact, I have already told the master of the workhouse that I intend to instruct all his young inmates.'

'"Told?"' she repeated, amusement lighting her eyes.

'I suggested they could more easily become apprenticed, if they knew their letters and their numbers. As for the parish itself, it would be a shame if only those incarcerated in the workhouse could benefit. Hence my hopes for the labourers' children.'

She looked at me shrewdly. 'And will there be a charge for this schooling?'

'Heavens, no! How could I ask such poor families—'

Shaking her head, she said slowly, 'If you give them something for nothing, they may not value it. Why not ask for a farthing for each child?'

'But I would not want to stop anyone coming for lack of money!'

'Allow them to pay in arrears. If some debts are never paid, no one need know, and honour will be satisfied – yours, Mr Campion, and the parents'. Where would you hold the classes?'

'There are rooms aplenty in the rectory.'

She nodded, but wrinkled her nose, as if she were twenty years younger. She must have been very attractive then.

'You disagree?'

'Even a parson,' she said slowly, 'might need a woman to give him countenance.'

I thought of my predecessor's pell-mell marriage. Perhaps she did too. 'Mrs Beckles, the best person to chaperone the children would be my wife, did I have one, and failing that, my housekeeper. I suspect it will be easier to obtain the latter than the former.'

She threw back her head and laughed. 'My dear Mr Campion, were you to drop your handkerchief, I can think of forty young ladies all too ready to pick it up for you! But as to a housekeeper, you are right. You asked me to find you one, and at last – with my apologies for the delay – I have two ladies to propose. Would you care to speak to them yourself? If so, I will bid one to present herself tomorrow morning, at eleven, and the other at noon.'

I suspected she was setting me a test. 'Are the ladies in every way equal?'

'They are. Both Mrs Trent and Mrs Wallace can cook and sew and could easily run a household rather larger than yours. But since the one you select will have to live under your roof, Mr Campion, it is important that you like her – and,' she added with a decided twinkle, 'it is important that she likes you.'

'Or can at the very least tolerate your foibles, ecclesiastic and otherwise,' Dr Hansard added, coming on me unawares. 'I'm sorry I missed the service, Parson. My horse cast a shoe, and I was obliged to walk home. But at least there is a lusty boy to show for my night's endeavours. Mr and Mrs Hall – their third, Mrs Beckles.'

'In as many years,' she exclaimed, though more in sorrow than in anger.

'Your pardon, Parson,' Mr Miller interrupted. He had left with the others but now came back to the porch. I turned to speak to him, leaving my two friends to each other's company, something that did not appear to displease either.

'Good morning, Mr Miller.'

'That sermon, Parson. We don't want no politics from our pulpit.'

'What do you want?' I parried.

He flushed a patchy pink. 'Things what's proper,' he said. 'Minding your betters, knowing your place and suchlike.'

I permitted myself a cold smile. 'Keeping the Ten Commandments, perhaps?'

He nodded.

'Observing the Sabbath, and so on?'

He shuffled.

'Good. Now, recall, if you can, the sixth commandment. You are unable to do so? Pray, Mr Miller, step back into church for a moment, and I will point it out to you from the Bible itself.'

As I expected, he declined my offer. 'One day you'll go too far, Parson, that's all I can say. And then we know who'll be sorry.'

Before I could ask him to expand his threat, Jem presented himself at my shoulder, and Miller melted away like dew under the sun.

'Churchwarden he may be,' Jem murmured as we walked back together, 'but I don't like him. And I wouldn't trust him further than I can throw him.'

* * *

Once again, my appearance at dinner later that week at Moreton Priory provoked a very strong response amongst the younger females. I could only attribute their interest to the dearth of eligible males in the area and a heavy preponderance of daughters in the local gentry's families. For the sake of my self-esteem, however, it was fortunate that I had such fair companions. Although the previous Sunday's service had been but ill-attended, what I had said in my sermon had obviously been widely reported. As a consequence, many of the men were offering, if not the cut direct, a politeness so cool it was barely politeness at all.

'Bad business,' Lord Elham growled, digging again into fine Stilton. 'If a man can't have mantraps, how may he protect his coverts? You tell me that, young fellow-me-lad.'

'Sir, I—'

'See, you've no answer, have you?'

I had many, but none suitable for conversation over the port. However, I persevered. 'Sir, if families had enough to eat, men would not need to poach other's game.'

'If they want to eat more, they should work harder. Aye, and have fewer mouths to feed. They breed like rabbits.'

'And don't taste so good in the pot,' Lord Chartham sneered, jostling my elbow so that my port slopped.

Squire Oldbury nodded. 'And if they weren't trespassing, they wouldn't get hurt, would they?' he added, with the conviction that he had uttered a clincher.

Perhaps he had. Lord Elham heaved himself to his feet; we were to join the ladies at last.

'Not if they knew their place,' Chartham agreed, tripping me hard so I veritably tumbled into the saloon.

But my denunciation of the evils of such instruments had appealed to others. As I looked about for a suitable seat, I found myself greeted by a violet-eyed young damsel, who, as she whispered confidingly, was not yet quite "out".

'Parson Campion, I hear that you have been perfectly heroic!'

This was a notion of which I was quick to disabuse her. 'Indeed, I am no hero. Those young men called to defend our shores or fight overseas are our heroes. Mine is an altogether calmer, even sedate existence.'

'Not,' she said, with an emphasis that surprised me from someone in that limbo between being a schoolgirl and being a young lady enjoying her first season, 'when Lord Chartham pushes you to the floor.'

'That was merely a want of manners,' I chided her gently.

To my amazement, however, she responded with what some might have considered a quite unbecoming sharpness, 'But does not Mr Burke tell us that manners are more important than laws, which touch our lives only occasionally? Manners, he says, are the basis for our morality in that they barbarise or refine us.'

'He does indeed,' I smiled, wondering how such a pretty young lady should have come across the great man's writings. Before I could ask, however, we were joined by a second girl, as dark as my companion was fair.

'Pooh,' said she, 'Sophia is such a bluestocking. And to be talking about morality after a dinner party is, you know, very bad manners. Come, Mr Campion, my cousin is needed at the piano to play some country dances.'

'Her ladyship—' I began.

'Pooh, she will not object. And you know that dancing is far more important than conversation in such a situation.'

'That is what our manners tell us,' Miss Sophia conceded, with a decided twinkle.

I laughed. 'But a lady of your years, Miss Sophia, should be dancing, not concealed behind a piano,' I said, intending to sound serious, but no doubt appearing flirtatious.

'You see, Sophia, I told you you would not lack for a partner,' her pert cousin declared, 'and now you have a clergyman for the first dance.'

The violet eyes opened wide. 'I cannot dance with him, can I? We have not been introduced.'

'Parson Campion, my cousin Miss Sophia Heath. Sophia, Parson Campion. There. You may dance, but not the waltz.' She gave a roguish smile. 'It would not do,' she added, her face all seriousness again, 'for Sophia to be thought fast.'

I did not tell her that it was Sophia's conversation that was likely to set her apart. Indeed, in the other's company she was demureness personified, her eyes lowered, as if inspecting her fan for flaws, a modest row of pearls around her neck and a round-necked white gown almost identical to the ones worn by my sisters at a similar age. My mother would have approved.

Her cousin, on the other hand, displayed the town-bronze of a lady who has enjoyed her first London season, with a dress so diaphanous it revealed at least as much as it concealed. My mother would not have approved, nor of the casual way she announced that she was Charlotte Winthrop, betrothed to dear Lord Warley, to whom she gave a little wave before tripping off to join him.

Sophia was suddenly gauche, standing in social limbo. What else could I do but make my bow, and solicit her hand for the first dance?

'Are you sure?' she asked, in all seriousness. 'There are other girls properly out who lack partners.'

I smiled. 'But I have not been introduced to them.'

To my amazement, Dr Hansard, who had not, to my regret, been at the dinner table, was also dancing. In view of his advancing years, I would have expected him to be making up one of the tables of whist that Cousin Elham had set up in the book room. Nonetheless, he sought out young ladies without a partner, and led them into the dance with at least as much vigour as I.

At last, my two dances with Miss Sophia over, I was summoned to Lady Elham's side, where she sat with the other older ladies. Making my bow, I prepared to congratulate her on the delightful entertainment, but she silenced me with a gesture of her fan.

'Cousin Tobias, do not let me hear complaints of you again. I understand that you are young and idealistic, but I want no Evangelicals in this parish.'

'If your ladyship hears that I am an Evangelical, she is misled. Pray, madam, let me prove it by preaching in your own chapel here at the Priory. I understand it has fallen into disuse. I would be more than happy to become your household's chaplain.'

'You may lead us in prayers and a hymn or two, but that is all. You naughty young man,' she added, a sweet smile indicating that she would rebuke me no more, 'to set all the neighbours a-gossip like that.'

'Your ladyship, had all the neighbours been in church to hear my words in person, they would have known there was no cause for gossip.'

'No cause for gossip? With poor Widow Jenkins' husband hardly cold in his grave?'

I straightened. 'I beg your pardon, madam, but there is a serious misapprehension here. Mrs Jenkins and her family were dressed from your own poor basket and now perforce they reside in the workhouse. They come to church—'

'By your express command, I understand—'

'Because the children have not yet been baptised, and must be.'

'Mrs Jenkins too, I gather?' She eyed me archly.

'Of course. It was a deathbed promise to her husband,' I said. 'She made it as I wed them.' In my effort to scotch any foolish rumours, my voice was far too forceful for such a merry gathering, and she raised an eyebrow at its intensity.

I sought for a more neutral topic. 'Do you have news of Corby?'

'That man? What news should I have?'

'Does his new venture at the seaside prosper?'

'He betrayed my trust, Cousin. Never mention his name in this house again!'

I did not judge this as an appropriate time to mention my hope of teaching the children their letters.

As if to rescue me, Dr Hansard came to my side, bidding farewell to his hostess. I added my compliments to his, and we left together, breathing deeply the night air, chill under a sky clear enough to presage a frost.

'I see you've attracted the attentions of our little heiress,' he said, as our horses ambled side by side.

'Miss Sophia? A chit from the schoolroom who is "not quite out"?'

'You do her less than justice, Tobias. Today she is a pretty-eyed nonentity, but soon she will blossom, and if you are not careful you will be elbowed aside by all her other admirers!'

'But they may not find her bookishness to their taste,' I reflected.

'And you do?'

'Come, Dr Hansard, I am at least ten years her senior.' But that was not the reason my heart did not lift at the thought of her. I had to admit to myself that I did not mention the schoolroom sessions to her ladyship for fear that she might, despite her protestations to Mrs Beckles, oppose them, and I would have thus lost a chance of renewing my acquaintance with the delightful Lizzie. Who, I asked myself rhetorically, would make a better parson's wife, a pretty heiress or a young woman used to work? A wife prone to the vapours at the sight of naked children would not suit, and I had already seen enough of Lizzie's capability to believe she would excel in any situation.

I said none of this to Dr Hansard. I knew he would see the speciousness of my argument. Lizzie attracted me not as a cross between a nurse and a housekeeper, but because she was simply the most beautiful young woman I had ever encountered and for the first time in my life I believed myself to be deeply in love.

'I am nearly forty years her senior, but my pulses might still race at the sight of Sophia,' he laughed. But he stopped abruptly. A glance showed that his face was unwontedly serious. I conjectured that it was another lady at the sight of whom his heart beat faster, one who might welcome his advances should he make them.

'I was surprised to see you amongst the dancers,' I observed mildly.

'You expected me to be at the whist tables? These days, Tobias, I do not gamble.' He pulled his horse to a halt. 'Some might take me for a Methodist, but the truth is this. When I left India I was a veritable nabob. I was sent there to make my fortune, and make it I did. But then I lost it, almost all of it. You have seen Langley Park, and I have entertained you in some pleasant rooms. Did it ever occur to you that those were the only rooms with any furnishings in them? That is the pass to which I had come. It was the thought of losing my library that stopped me short. And to this day I have never played at so much as Speculation. Each year, I try to earn enough to hang one more set of curtains, lay one more carpet.'

'Then I admire you even more than before,' I declared, 'for your honesty and your industry. Your kindness to such folk at the Jenkinses is even more laudable in the circumstances.'

'There is a vast difference,' he observed dryly, 'between not being able to afford silk hangings and having nothing but bread to eat. Nay, what's that?' He pulled his horse to a halt and dismounted.

I followed suit.

He was bent over the path, exploring something under the starlight with his fingers. 'I thought so! Do you have a pocket knife?'

I passed it to him without a word. In a moment he was holding up a long piece of twine.

'Stretched between the bushes, my friend. Designed to trip a horse – and thus unseat a rider.'

'Another of young Chartham's little tricks,' I said lightly.

'Are you sure? Have you no other enemies? Well,' he said, coiling the twine and slipping it into his pocket, 'at least it did no harm. But keep your eyes open, young Tobias. Even a fall can harm a man.'

# CHAPTER FOUR

My efforts to become a teacher were not uniformly successful. Under duress, Mr Bulstrode, the workhouse master, approved my suggestions in principle, but he always found an excuse to cancel my classes, on the grounds he had found work more fitting for his young charges. There had been but a tepid response from the villagers, too. Jem suspected that their parents kept a weather-eye on the Priory, and if there was the merest whisper that their landlord disapproved, they would not risk sending their children to me.

Ironically Mrs Beckles had found a room and benches for my older charges, the servants at the Priory, right under the noses of the people the villagers feared most. Whether the Elhams knew or even cared, I did not enquire. But I was not a successful instructor. The more I endeavoured to help my pupils, the more I appreciated the efforts of my governess, who had contrived somehow to inculcate in me a belief that the strange symbols of the alphabet made sense – a concept that in my classes seemed to elude the youngest and the oldest alike. In desperation, I wrote to dear Addie – Miss Addison – who responded by sending me a small parcel. In it I found familiar blocks on which letters were painted in now faded colours, and some books all too clearly for children.

I also realised how very patient Addie must have been; no matter how I and the other members of the schoolroom party teased her or resisted her efforts, she was never less than smiling and calm.

'She was paid to be patient,' Hansard remarked, throwing another log on to his study fire to cheer me as I poured out my woes one evening. Even though Mrs Trent was now installed in the housekeeper's room, and her cooking was all that Mrs Beckles had promised, I still spent many evenings at Langley House, enjoying the good doctor's hospitality while Jem listened enthralled to tales of India, told with some ornamentation, perhaps, by Turner, Hansard's valet, a man not much older than he but with realms more experience of the world.

'She was not paid enough, I am sure. For though my family consider it insufferably middle class to quibble over servants' wages, she was still treated as precisely that – a servant who could be dismissed on a whim, and whose days were long and truly not well rewarded.'

'And what has become of her?' He filled my glass.

I omitted mention of a financial gift I had pressed on her when I reached my majority. 'She was left a little money, enough to achieve respectable retirement – a competence, no more, Edmund, after a lifetime's toil. The fact that her toil was with her head, not her hands, is irrelevant.'

'Did I say otherwise?' he asked, with a gesture of surrender. 'Come, there are those whom I treat who grumble that all I do is feel their pulses and give them coloured liquid. As for you, you do not even have to feel their pulses before you give them coloured liquid!'

Although he mocked the Communion service, he did so as a regular and reverent communicant, so I permitted myself to laugh at his joke.

I sipped at my wine. 'Should I ask you to feel my pulse, Edmund? After all, this too is a fine coloured liquid, very fine indeed.'

'Thank you. So do none of your pupils make progress?'

'One has had singular success,' I conceded. 'But not in my classroom. Lizzie Woodman is now *Miss* Lizzie, abigail to my cousin, Lady Elham, herself. It seems she has nimble fingers and very quiet ways. But it means her time applying herself to her letters is very much curtailed.'

'Many is the mistress who rues her maid's ability to read,' Hansard murmured, with a twinkle.

'Miss Lizzie says my cousin is kindness itself,' I said, bridling despite myself at the imputation.

'I'm sure she is.'

'She also says that she feels safer under Lady Elham's direct protection.'

'Safer? Ah, from all those young bloods desperate to get their hands on her person.'

I heard the savagery in my own voice. 'You will have heard that I had to tear one importunate admirer from her with my own bare hands! So I believe my cousin must have her best interests at heart.'

'At heart? Oh, no, Tobias. People of her rank have – in general – only their own interests at heart. If it improves the servant's lot, that is merely incidental. Look at yourself, man – you come here for your own pleasure, not for Jem's, do you not? Oh, I know he enjoys Turner's tall tales, and, for all I know, flirts abominably with that new maid of mine, but he is here because it suits you.' He poured more wine, as if to soften the home truth. 'So you have made no progress with your charges?'

'Far more since I aimed less high. But they make slow progress. I do not know whether they lack innate ability or whether they are prevented by other factors.'

He raised an eyebrow. 'What sort of factors?'

'Is it easier to learn if one is warm and well fed than if one is cold and hungry? Is it easier to learn when one is young than when one is old? Come, Edmund, these are more your fields of knowledge than mine: what say you?'

'I know my hyacinths are still blue,' he said, referring to his attempt to breed a new variety. 'Though I believe last summer's seemed to have taken on a pinker hue. Perhaps humankind is like bulbs. Perhaps we could make changes by selective breeding.'

I laughed in his face.

'Consider', he said seriously, 'your family. Are they all like you, tall and well set up?'

'Mostly. But – and this is never spoken of – I believe my mother was brought to bed of a strange, runtish child who was immediately put out to a kind family on one of our more remote estates.' I blushed. 'I swore I would never reveal my background, and that secret in particular. Edmund, pray, forget that I said that.'

He gestured acquiescence. 'My dear friend, I have always known you are from the *ton*. How else would you speak, even walk, the way you do? But your secret – such as it is – is safe with me. After all, you have spoken of nothing that would not apply to a dozen or more of the upper ten thousand. I could not possibly deduce of which family you spoke. Now,' he said, getting to his feet, 'I have rewarded myself for this past year's industry. To celebrate my new billiards table in my equally new billiards room, shall we adjourn and pot a few balls?'

My eyes had been opened to another aspect of below-stairs life by my schoolroom activities at Moreton Priory. Used as I was to life the family side of the green baize door, with some inconveniences more than outweighed by the many luxuries I took for granted, I was surprised how few of what I considered the necessities of life the servants enjoyed. Gone were the rich hangings and thick carpets, the warmth of great fires, the brilliance of candelabra; here were stone floors, green-painted walls, endless unheated corridors and the meanest spluttering working candles. All life was ruled by a row of bells hanging inside the servants' hall; at the faintest jangle, a young man or woman would set off as if his or her life depended upon it.

Of course I did not venture into the attics, where the lowest servants were accommodated, but the spartan quarters of that most charming of women, Mrs Beckles, did not augur well for her juniors. Her sitting room appeared to have been furnished with anything the family no longer valued. The carpet was Aubusson, I suspect, but was faded and had been cut to fit the room. One armchair might be Hepplewhite, but someone had had to glue an arm in place. The walls were hung with pictures by distinguished artists, but none was clean and none inspired anything other than feelings of gloom. One wall was devoted to silhouettes, the homely framing of which suggested that Mrs Beckles might have executed the portraits herself. I was sure that she had at least selected the volumes almost filling a small bookcase, where I found, alongside two or three collections of sermons, novels by Richardson and Fielding – though I was surprised to see a member of the fairer sex possessing *Tom Jones*, Smollett and a selection of Gothic tales. I was happier to see much poetry, both ancient and modern. In all, however, I was confirmed in my opinion that Mrs Beckles was an extraordinary lady – certainly my mother, who prided herself on keeping up to date with fashionable writers, did not have half so fine a personal collection.

I never had occasion to penetrate Mr Woodvine's portal, but suspected that, like that of Mr Davies, the steward, the butler's would be a slightly larger, but even drabber room. If either man left his door ajar, he could see that row of all-important bells.

Inside, there were no novels for Davies, at least, but tomes on the management of land that made me yawn to contemplate them. On the other hand, now I was supposed to be overseeing my own glebe lands, or at least making sure that Ford, my own resentful steward, did not fleece me, so I had called on Davies to ask which one he might recommend – the smallest, for preference. He had his hand outstretched to pass me one, when chaos broke out, in the form of the violent ringing of the front doorbell. Before our eyes, a succession of other bells sprang into activity, the last being that in his lordship's bedchamber. The panic crossing Davies' poor old face was catching. Like him, I took to my heels and ran whither he was summoned, pushing through knots of maids too hysterical to move aside when asked.

'It's his lordship,' gasped Mrs Beckles, clearing a way at the foot of the backstairs. 'Pray, Mr Campion, go to his room and see what you can do.'

'You have already sent for Dr Hansard?'

'Of course,' she replied simply. 'Go, sir!' She pushed me firmly between my shoulder blades.

The first thing was to clear the crowd pressing round the bed, and demand decent silence from those chattering or wailing uncontrollably.

Her ladyship alone remained icily calm. Rising from where she knelt at the bedside, she said softly, 'I fear you come too late, and that Dr Hansard's journey will also be wasted. My husband is dead. I believe that he was already dead when I managed to pull him from the stream.'

For the first time I noticed that she was indeed soaking wet. 'Fetch Miss Lizzie,' I told a huge-eyed young girl, too young in any case for such a scene.

Lizzie appeared as if by magic.

'Pray, take her ladyship to her own room and persuade her into some dry clothes. She must be chilled to the bone, and I am sure that is what Dr Hansard would advise. Hurry, Lizzie.'

Like the sensible girl she was, she acted without argument, propelling my cousin from the room with the same tactful force as I'd seen her use on the Jenkins brood.

With her example, one by one the other servants dispersed, leaving his lordship to the solemn care of his butler and his valet.

Dr Hansard, still red-faced from the exertions of a hurried journey, was closing Lord Elham's eyes and drawing a sheet over his face when her ladyship reappeared, already clad in black from head to toe. I doubt if I had ever seen her more beautiful, though I am sure that that was not her intention. She reminded me of a long-forgotten line from the Bard: 'Like Patience, in a monument, smiling at grief'. As yet, of course, she smiled not at all, and it might be many months before she allowed herself to, but her self-control and dignity were very pattern-cards of behaviour. She sank again to her knees as I led in prayer those already assembled.

When we escorted her back to her boudoir a few minutes later, in vain did Dr Hansard press laudanum drops upon her. She needed nothing, she declared, except a solitary period of quiet reflection. But her son must immediately be sent for – the new Lord Elham, she reminded us, with some emphasis.

'A bad business,' Dr Hansard observed a few minutes later, as on his orders we drank some of his new lordship's wine in the housekeeper's parlour. He had insisted on a glass for both Mrs Beckles and Mr Davies, as a restorative after shock.

'But how should it come about?' Mrs Beckles demanded. 'His lordship was no child, to go paddling when his nurse's back was turned. He was a grown man, with more sense, surely to goodness. And how came her ladyship to find him?'

Hansard favoured her with an appreciative smile. 'Those are precisely the questions I shall have to ask in my capacity of justice of the peace. Was she alone, coming by chance upon him as he lay in the water? Or were they walking together? Tell me, were they in the habit of taking afternoon strolls in each other's company?'

Her glance spoke volumes.

He got to his feet. 'Come, Campion, there is enough light left for us to see the site of the accident for ourselves. Perhaps Mr Davies will accompany us?'

Davies jumped, as if kicked. He had been silent so long in his corner that I had completely forgotten about him. 'Aye,' he said. 'And the lad who heard her ladyship's cries and came running to summon help. If we can find him.'

Mrs Beckles opened her mouth to say something, but shut it, as if suppressing an opinion she thought best not uttered. Even as she did so, it occurred to me that she would have made a better companion in our foray than old Davies, her bright eyes, in my experience, missing nothing and certainly more efficient than poor Davies' rheumy orbs. But her place, of course, was here, advising the cook on the changes that would necessarily be made to the arrangements for dinner for what was still a houseful of guests. There was also the matter of mourning for all the staff – would she have a supply of ready-made clothes set aside in some distant attic or would she be sending post haste to a warehouse supplying such garb?

I would have caught her eye to smile my sympathy, but Dr Hansard was already speaking to her in a low tone, issuing last-minute instructions about her ladyship's well-being, no doubt.

'What are you looking for?' I asked my mentor, as we stood five or six yards from the stream that had ended his lordship's existence. Davies, his job done, retired to the lee of a tree and watched our activities in silence. Of the lad there had been no sign, and Edmund wanted to waste none of the remaining light while they hunted for him.

'Anything and everything and nothing.' He drove his hands more deeply into the pockets of his riding coat.

'What could have possessed them to come a-walking on such a cold and dank day as this?' Everything was now being soaked by a thin mizzle.

'Silence, man! Your pardon, Tobias, but I must needs concentrate.'

'Of course.' Much as I would have liked to argue my point, I accepted the snub. He, after all, was the justice, I merely a clergyman. Eager to learn, I followed his eyes, trying to perceive whatever he might be noting.

A rustic bridge about ten yards away; one of the handrails hung loose. He must have fallen from there. There were footprints aplenty in the sticky mud, and the branches of many of the bushes leaning over the stream had been smashed down. From this evidence, even I could imagine the frantic activity that would have followed Elham's plunge into the stream.

I moved towards it, doing my best to avoid the area Hansard was studying. But as I did so, his head jerked up. When he saw what I was doing, he smiled broadly.

'You make an apt pupil,' he said. 'Let us look at that woodwork a little more closely, shall we? See? It is quite old, and the nail quite rusty. Let us see what the rail the other side is like. Hmm, equally old, but pretty sound.' He pointed, as Davies scuttled up.

For all that, Davies scribbled a note. I felt for him. If her ladyship so much as suspected he might have been negligent, his future would be bleak indeed. Several times, Hansard pushed the sound joint with all his might, but it would not stir.

'So why did its counterpart give way?' he wondered aloud, moving back to investigate. 'Perhaps it would repay a further look in better light. In fact, I think we should all adjourn to the Priory again. By now her ladyship may have decided she needs the services of one or both of us, Tobias, and we would not wish to fail her. Mr Davies here will find every waking moment occupied for the next week, I should imagine.'

'A well-attended funeral?'

'All the gentry from miles around, family, acquaintances.'

'Poor Mrs Beckles,' I ventured.

'I can't imagine that there is any task to which she would be unequal,' he said. 'Were I Prinny, I would seek her out when the time comes to organise the poor king's funeral and subsequently his own coronation. But before any burial can take place – and you will need to discover her ladyship's preference for the family vault at St Jude's or the mausoleum in the grounds – the coroner has to determine the cause of death.'

I stopped short. 'Are you implying that—?'

'I am implying nothing. But he will need all the evidence that you and I can provide. As a matter of fact,' he continued, 'I shall have to speak to her ladyship in my capacity as a justice; it might be – useful – if you were there.'

She was my kinswoman! 'What purpose would that serve?'

He patted me kindly on the shoulder. 'You are ever a calming influence, Tobias. Equally, you might find it beneficial, when you discuss his interment, to have me at hand. However calm she may be now, such reminders of our last end may cause spasms, palpitations and worse.'

* * *

He need not have feared. When Lady Elham admitted us to her boudoir, she had, according to a whispered aside from Lizzie, also already in mourning, been persuaded to take a mouthful of soup. Now a glass of wine was at her right hand as she reclined on her daybed.

'And how is my patient?' Dr Hansard enquired politely.

'Pray do not treat me as an invalid,' she snapped. 'You forget that my family can trace its roots to the days of the Conqueror. People of our class do not give way!'

As a student of history, I could have pointed out that William the Conqueror tended to bestow largesse on the most vicious of his henchmen; as a student of human nature, I knew better than to bite the hand that regularly provided me with my after-supper cup of tea in an exquisite china cup. Shocked by my levity at such a moment, I flushed and lowered my eyes.

'You cannot persuade me that you underwent such an ordeal with no evil consequences,' Hansard insisted gently.

She swung her legs from the daybed until she sat upright; as she did so she pressed a hand to her back and gave a quickly suppressed yelp. 'One consequence is a terrible pain in my back, Dr Hansard. I tried to drag him out, you see, and he was so very heavy.' She choked back a sob, swallowing hard and meeting our glance firmly.

We both nodded sympathetically. 'Did you see him fall?' I asked in a low voice.

'We were standing on the bridge together, for a while leaning on the rail to look for fish. At last I walked on – the weather was so very damp that I felt as if it were seeping into my bones. Elham stayed on. Then I heard a splash. I ran back and pulled and shouted and...'

'No more, if it upsets you, Lady Elham.' Hansard produced smelling salts.

She waved them away. 'I managed to get him out. I did. And I think I turned him – no, I left him lying face down, so that the water in his mouth would drain away. I have heard of sailors bringing those on the verge of death by drowning back to life, but I never thought – I had no idea how...' Her hands moved helplessly. For the first time she was losing her composure. 'I called for help, and sent a lad who came out of the woods to summon my servants. Then I tried again. Pray, forgive me—' She turned so that we could not observe her tears.

'It is quite possible that his lordship was dead before he hit the water,' Hansard said, in the tone of one exploring theories.

The quiet observation produced an extraordinary response. She was on her feet, pointing a clearly accusing finger. 'An explanation, if you please!'

'Pray, calm yourself, my lady,' I urged.

'Not until Hansard explains what he meant by that strange remark!'

'Madam, Lord Elham always ate and drank his fill. I warned him again and again that he should adopt a more abstemious habit. But he constantly disregarded my urgings. I fear that the exertion of his walk, the damp and cold of the day – perhaps, your ladyship, they brought about a seizure, a fatal seizure. If his dead weight fell on the bridge's handrail it is not unlikely that it gave way and let him plunge into the icy water. Such a shock might in itself have killed a younger, fitter man than he. If this were indeed the case, you should not repine that you were unable to revive him,' he concluded, his voice at its kindest.

As she resumed her seat, he reached for her wrist. 'I feared so. Your pulse is tumultuous, your ladyship. Pray, let me give a draught to help calm you. It should relieve the pain in your back, too.'

'If you insist, I will take the medicine, doctor. Leave it with my maid. Cousin Tobias, you will do all that is needful for the funeral, will you not?'

'Of course. I hate to ask, Lady Elham: do you want the interment to take place in the family vault in St Jude's? Or—'

She interrupted with an impulsive gesture. 'Did we not discuss, only a few weeks ago, the possibility of bringing the private chapel here at the Priory into use again? Would not that be a fitting place?'

'It would be a wonderful tribute,' I said. 'But only your immediate circle would be able to attend; there would be no room for the servants and estate workers, let alone any villagers wishing to pay their respects. If the service were at St Jude's, at least they would be able to line the route, perhaps even follow the bier.'

It was all too clear that the wishes of the villagers were far from her thoughts. She drew herself up as straight as she could. 'Lord Elham will make all the arrangements, gentlemen. My son, the eleventh Lord Elham,' she said, with the same proud emphasis as before.

# CHAPTER FIVE

Mrs Beckles was waiting for us as we left her ladyship's room, a troubled expression on her face. She did no more than curtsy, leading us in silence inexplicably down not the main staircase but the backstairs.

At the foot, she paused and turned, as if having made a decision. 'Late as it is, gentlemen, I have a favour to ask of you.'

Though he looked as weary as I'd ever seen him, Dr Hansard bowed graciously. I could do no less.

'His lordship's – his *late* lordship's – old nurse lives in the cottages at the bottom of Prior's Hill. Would you be kind enough to break the news to Nurse Abney in person? After all her years of service, she should not hear it at second hand. I would have gone myself, but as you can see, all is a-flutter here.'

She did not exaggerate. The servants' hall was buzzing with muted conversation, as every young woman in the building appeared to have a black-threaded needle in her hand and an expanse of black cloth on her lap. Young men were running backwards and forwards from Mr Davies' room and the butler's pantry. How much frantic effort was being put into maintaining the calm order above stairs.

* * *

The drizzle had cleared, leaving the night sky spangled with stars, a half-moon adding to their glimmering light. Dr Hansard let his horse follow its nose.

'He knows where he will always find an apple or a carrot,' he laughed. 'Nurse Abney is a great friend of his. She will not see seventy again, but is as spry as a woman half her age, in the summer at least. At this time of year, she suffers dreadfully in her joints. Were she a great lady, I would recommend the waters of Bath or Cheltenham. As it is, I convey from Mrs Beckles a steady supply of goose fat and worsted stockings to keep the pain at bay. Would I were more successful. But she never repines, and never accepts my offer of laudanum drops. If she cannot sleep, she reads her Bible. See – a candle still burns. It is one of her bad nights.'

The old woman, face worn by laughter or tears into a thousand creases, greeted Dr Hansard as if he were her son; I was favoured with a curtsy so deep I could scarce forbear to take her elbows to help her upright again. Dr Hansard had no such inhibition. He eased her gently into the chair by the tiny table, which indeed supported a candle and an open Bible.

'Such an honour, Mr Campion, to meet you, never having been acquainted before and you coming all the way here to my humble home, to which you are truly welcome. What a well set-up lad you are, to be sure, breaking young ladies' hearts wherever you go, I dare swear. And do you have a sweetheart yet? A parson needs a wife, and to be setting up his nursery if he can afford it. And to be sure, Dr Hansard, you look after me so well, so I can't complain about a little twinge, and goodness knows a woman of my age expects a bit of stiffness, only it stops my sewing when the days close in and the sun forgets to rise all day. Do be seated, gentlemen, pray, and take a glass of my cowslip wine. That will keep the cold out.' The words poured from her. On her feet again, not to be gainsaid, she bustled about.

Before I knew it, I was seated, though not in comfort. She insisted that Dr Hansard took her only spare chair and I sank on to the broad windowsill. Even on a night as calm as this, the window frame admitted vicious draughts, icily fingering my neck, and attempting to cancel out the heat of the bright but tiny fire. In the light of that and the extra candle she had lit in our honour, I could see that every surface was spotless, an achievement all the greater given that the floor was simply beaten earth.

The cowslip wine was excellent; I would have drunk it by the tumblerful had I not noticed the good doctor taking only the minutest of sips. He caught my eye as if to signal caution in the matter. Meanwhile, our hostess kept us amused with a steady stream of conversation.

'Nurse Abney, Parson Campion and I bring bad news from the Priory,' Hansard said at last. 'I fear his lordship will not ride this way again.'

She looked puzzled. 'But he comes every week.'

Elham had visited her here, and done nothing to ameliorate her situation! I stifled a cry of disbelief.

'I fear he will ride nowhere ever again, my dear lady.'

Hansard might have slapped her face, so hard did she recoil. 'Master Augustus! No! Not—?'

He took her hand. 'It was very swift, Nurse. And, I believe, painless.'

'But he was in his prime...' In vain did she try to quell an errant tear. Soon she was shaken with sobs.

'You were his nurse, ma'am,' I said at last, kneeling beside her and hoping to turn her mind to happier times.

She clasped my hand convulsively. 'Such a lovely little boy, with his curls so fair they looked like white floss in the morning sun. So handsome a youth, set on winning that red-haired minx. Mind you, they soon proved the old saying, *Marry in haste, repent at leisure,* didn't they? He'd hardly been wed to her ten minutes when he went galloping off on his grand tour, leaving her to cool her heels. They must have made up, of course, whatever their quarrel – and now we have the eleventh earl, young Arthur, a pretty a boy as you'd wish to see he was too, with his pretty hair just like his father's, though inclined to be gingerish. Not as sunny as his father, I dare swear, and no time for his old nurse, of course, but his mother is all goodness, all goodness. Not as kind as that dear Mrs Beckles, and were this daytime, I dare swear I would see you blush, my old friend.' She paused for breath, relinquishing my hand to pat Dr Hansard familiarly on his wrist.

How he would have answered I cannot guess, for we heard the sound of swift footsteps and a fierce knock at the door, swiftly followed by the eruption of a furious young man into the cottage, though scarcely in response to his aunt's invitation.

'Is that you, Matthew, my boy? Come in, come in, the door's never locked as you know, night or day, and here we have visitors, my love, the doctor and the parson.'

The new arrival seemed to fill the room. When I had seen him in church, I had dismissed him as a mutton-headed yokel, as he gazed like a mooncalf upon Lizzie at a time his thoughts should have been fixed on the Almighty. Now I saw him as a strapping young man who would have displayed to advantage, his eyes blazing in sudden anger, fixed for some reason on me. He extended his arm, not to shake hands, but to poke at me, though never quite making contact with my chest as he jabbed with a furious finger.

'You're the one who's spoilt my Lizzie, my pretty Lizzie! I've been walking out with her for nigh three years, Master Parson, and had hopes of her. Now she's too good for me, isn't she, Parson, with her reading and her writing and her figuring! It's Mr Campion says this, and Parson says that, and next thing I know she's her ladyship's own abigail, and well above the touch of a plain man like me. And it's all your doing!'

'Are you in your cups, man? Now,' Hansard continued, as Matthew dropped back, abashed, 'you may make your apology to Mr Campion and take yourself off.'

'Not until I know why you are here at this time of night. I had thought my aunt must be ill,' he added, with real anxiety.

Hansard explained, without so much as a hint that the death might be unnatural.

Matthew did not even feign regret. 'That penny-pinching old – I am sorry, Aunt, for I know you loved him always, as if he had been your own son, but he has left this estate in even worse heart than he found it. And as for that spendthrift son of his, and his vicious, evil ways – well, I am glad the old man is gone, but I fear his successor will be worse, far worse.'

'Come, come – enough of this,' Hansard broke in. 'You will have Mr Campion here thinking that you are of a revolutionary turn. Be on your way, man.'

'I care not this much what Mr Campion thinks,' he averred, snapping his fingers. 'The man who has stolen my intended.' All the same, he picked up his hat.

I followed Matthew through the door. 'I am sorry you think I have turned Lizzie from you, Matthew,' I said, all the time feeling deeply guilty as once that had been my precise intention. 'But she has certainly not turned to me,' I added with complete truth. 'Nay, nor to any other man, so far as I know.' Unbidden, there flashed into my mind the memory of her first encounter with Jem, when they looked as if their eyes had been fastened together. But I would admit nothing, not even to myself. 'As for your sentiments about bad landlords, you would be surprised how much I share them.'

'Share sentiments, do we? Well, let me tell you this, Parson. I intend to win my Lizzie back – and she is something we shall never share.'

I nodded as emolliently as I knew how. 'Go back inside and bid farewell to your aunt as she deserves, Matthew. If you are angry, it is not with her, and she needs the comfort of a beloved nephew tonight.'

'I do it for her, not for you. Nor for him, neither. Why, it would have been a privilege to wring the man's neck.' With that, he went back inside, and was still there when Hansard left. We could see their heads framed in the window as we mounted our horses.

'Her ladyship? Give evidence? In public?' I demanded, my voice rising with every question. 'Every feeling is offended. You cannot mean thus to expose my cousin.'

Hansard leant back in his favourite chair and took another

sip of some excellent brandy. 'Alas, it will hardly be evidence, and it will certainly not be in public – at least, not in the taproom of a public inn. Her ladyship will simply have to give an account – on oath – of what happened to her husband the day he died. In view of the circumstances, I am sure the coroner – a fellow justice, Sir Willard Comfrey – will permit her to speak in any room in the Priory large enough to hold a jury. Don't look like that, Tobias. The law should treat us all equally. It never will, of course, but we must make some effort to pretend it will.'

'No suspicion can fall on her ladyship?' In the village there were rumours enough that she had pushed Elham into the water and held him down. If pressed, even Mrs Beckles found it hard to deny she had her doubts about the complete accuracy of my cousin's account, but she took every care not to impute blame she could not substantiate.

'Do you think it should?' Hansard asked quizzically. 'I will inform the jury that I long apprehended that he would have a seizure – which he might well have done. I shall observe that the bridge was well looked after, but that Elham's dead weight might well have been enough to dislodge a rusty nail, and commend such joints to Davies' immediate attention. The jury will bring in their verdict of natural causes and the coroner will recommend that all bridges in the area should be inspected – a recommendation that everyone will promptly ignore. He will then condole with her ladyship and the new Lord Elham. You mark my words.'

'But what if—? How can you predict what a jury will do?'

'It will be a jury of her household, Tobias,' he explained, exasperated. 'You cannot imagine her being questioned by the likes of Bulmer or Miller, can you? Well, then. For God's sake, sit down and have another sip of brandy to compose you.'

For the sake of our friendship, I obeyed.

'In any case, there are aspects of the accident that are deserving of explanation, do you not think? The nearest we have to a witness to the events is the young lad who assisted her ladyship and ran for further aid. Despite Lady Elham's clear description, despite the considerable reward she has offered, he has never presented himself. I do not like to be thwarted, Tobias. I want to know that he does indeed exist – though I suppose he must have done once, for aid was indeed fetched.'

'You mean—? Will you admit your doubts to Sir Willard?'

'I can scarce tell him that I suspect her ladyship of lying and needing the lad to give credence to her tale.'

'Indeed not!'

'And then there are her ladyship's fingernails.'

Choking on my brandy, I asked, 'Did I hear you aright? Her ladyship's fingernails? What do they have to do with anything?'

He smiled expansively. 'At last I have your full attention. Tell me, Tobias, what happens when you grip something tightly to pull it along. Something covered in fabric and very heavy.'

'Her ladyship complained of pain in her back.'

'She did. And she would – in such circumstances – scarce complain that she had broken her fingernails. But I assure you that that is likely to happen – particularly if you have such long elegant nails as she, troubled by nothing more than a little delicate stitchery. Young Lizzie tells me she was not required to trim the nails in question on the day of the death.'

'You have spoken to Lizzie about this?' I asked too quickly. To cover my confusion and account for redness about my face, I placed another log on the fire.

'Only to ask about her ladyship's general health. I hope she did not notice the singularity of my question about fingernails. There were no nail parings in the waste bin, either.'

'Surely her ladyship wore gloves!' I leant back, pleased to have scored a point in such an important contest. My cousin's reputation was paramount.

'It would be easy enough to dispose of a pair of ruined gloves... No, Tobias, I will be silent. Now, let us not give this another thought.'

When the inquest finally took place, Hansard's predictions were proved right. Held in the civilised surroundings of his late lordship's library, it was the merest formality, hardly worth the effort of convening it. Even I could see that Sir Willard Comfrey was less interested in discovering the truth than in preserving the comfortable status quo. No one would have dared challenge anything, not even Hansard at his most bellicose, with her ladyship in deepest mourning standing as pale as Marie Antoinette must have looked on the tumbril. The members of the household selected as jury had no difficulty at all in agreeing that poor Lord Elham had a seizure, collapsed on to the bridge and thence into the water, and that her ladyship's efforts to save her noble husband were much to be commended. They offered their profound condolences and their deepest respects to the new Lord Elham, who had scowled his way through the proceedings. Sir

Willard had no difficulty in recording the most natural of deaths and in recommending that all bridges be inspected for weak joints.

The ladies retired to comfort her ladyship, while the men found consolation in good ale, fine wine and some of the French chef's finest delicacies. Lord Elham, even more boorish than his father, mooned around, making no effort to engage with his guests, and, though he did not dare jostle either of us, turned his back on both Dr Hansard and myself.

'I told you it would be a total waste of time,' Hansard muttered. 'Have any facts been established?'

'Not even the identity of the witness,' I agreed.

He turned to me, with an amusement out of place at such a gathering. 'And it was you who so strongly objected to the very thought of an inquest.'

'It would have been good to quash the rumours, which that cannot have done.' I straightened. 'At least there is another judge whom the guilty have to face.'

'I will see if Mr Campion is At Home,' Mrs Trent declared, with as much dignity as if she had been butler at Chatsworth fending off importunate tourists with no more claim on the duke's time than the guidebooks they clutched.

'Of course he's at home,' a male voice grumbled. 'Parsons are supposed to be at home – not like some highfalutin' lord or some such. Anyways, his horse is out at the back, with that groom of his working on it.'

'Mr Campion may be In The Building,' she conceded, still loftily, 'but that does not mean that he is At Home.'

Nor did I want to receive visitors, but my guest was in the

right. He was my churchwarden, and entitled to my attention. However, the One whom I was addressing was entitled to it too.

Asking for His blessing for my day's endeavours, I rose at last from my knees. I sensed Mrs Trent's approval, as she watched from the open door. Had I been addressing no more an illustrious personage than the meanest beggar, she would have wanted me to keep Mr Bulmer cooling his heels. One mention of his name was enough to produce an expression on her face that suggested she might be sucking a particularly sour lemon. Jem employed a much cruder analogy, concerning hens, but treated her with genuine respect, not simply on account of her years, which must have numbered sixty. She meanwhile indulged him as one might a perpetually hungry nephew, any of her light pastry and toothsome pies baked at least as much for his delectation as for mine.

I believe it was Mrs Trent's *hauteur*, not mine, that made Bulmer not merely doff his cap but twist it between his hands like a schoolboy caught raiding an orchard.

''Morning, Parson Campion,' he said cautiously, no doubt as mindful as I was of our continued hostility.

'Good morning to you, Mr Bulmer.' I tried to be cordial. 'Pray, sit down. How may I help you?'

He perched on the edge of the chair I indicated.

'May I offer you some refreshment? A glass of Madeira?'

I would have sworn he salivated at the prospect. It was rumoured in the village that though the farmer was *warm* he was also *close*.

'He's the sort of man who would rather spend someone else's money,' had been Mrs Trent's original verdict. Now she betrayed her feelings by the flicker of an eyelid when I summoned her.

'And perhaps some of your excellent biscuits, Mrs Trent?' I added.

The warm and spicy smell was wafting from the kitchen, or I am sure she would have denied their existence. The slight thud as she placed a plateful on the table at his elbow suggested that they were as pearls before swine. But the decanter was the best, and the glasses polished to an exquisite brilliance. It was clear that she had her standards to maintain.

At last, after a long sip of his wine, Bulmer got round to opening his budget. 'It's about a monument, Parson. To Lord Elham. There's still space on the chancel wall and I thought it would be – begging your pardon, Mr Miller and I thought – it would be *appropriate* for us to raise a memorial tablet, maybe with a nice bit of Latin to his late lordship. The new lord would take it kindly, I have no doubt.' With more confidence he added, 'Past generations did it, as I've no doubt you've seen. And you, being an Oxford man—'

'Cambridge, but never mind.'

He treated my interruption with fitting contempt. 'You being a scholarly man would be able to tell what they had written.'

I must treat his request seriously. 'They mostly tell the same story – of God-fearing men who were remembered by their family and tenants for their generosity in times of adversity.'

'So if we got up a subscription, like, you'd be able to tell the mason what to put on our tablet. In Latin.'

'I would indeed translate for you. What would you want to say?' Moving to my desk, I found a clean sheet of paper and dipped my pen in readiness. I envisaged much crossing out.

He cleared his throat. 'I thought you might tell me, Parson. You being lettered.'

'You knew Lord Elham better than I,' I countered. 'Did you find him kind?'

'He was always a-visiting that old nurse of his. There are them,' he confided, 'that say she's a witch, but I don't hold with such talk.'

'Indeed no. Nurse Abney is a decent, God-fearing woman.' I could have added that she was a woman with but two chairs and an earthen floor. 'How else did he show his kindness?'

'Well now, he'd make sure Mr Davies gave fair warning, if you were behind in your rent. And he spoke up for the young lad they had sentenced to transportation. They sent him to an insane asylum instead, I do recall.'

I nodded, without speaking.

'But as for kind... It all depended, didn't it? You were never sure where you were with him and that's the truth. One day he would have a conversation about your crops, as friendly as you and I, but the next he would be taking his whip to you and damning your eyes and using words I'd not utter in your company, Parson. Same as the young lord,' he reflected. 'And you wouldn't want to be crossing him.'

'Really?' I prompted.

'Him and his killings. He kills animals, so he does.'

'Do not all of us here in the country? We kill sheep and cattle for food, foxes for sport—'

'Aye, and other vermin. But when we kills them we kills them. Nay, I've said enough.' I would swear that the peal of my doorbell turned his weather-beaten skin white, as if the noble lord had overheard and was even now seeking retribution. 'But the monument, Parson – what should the words be?' he continued, apparently reassured by the gentle murmur of voices from the hallway.

Mrs Trent ushered in Mr Miller.

'What does he say about the monument?' the new arrival asked of his fellow visitor, in a stage whisper.

'We were just talking about the wording,' I said, ending the pantomime before it had begun. 'What would be your preference, Mr Miller?'

'It's not so much the wording as the paying that troubles me,' he said. 'Have you spoken to him about that yet?'

Miller shuffled, glancing at me from under his brows. He had realised that his notion of a subscription had not received my overwhelming enthusiasm.

'I believe Mr Bulmer mentioned it,' I conceded, on his behalf. 'But I confess that I did not give him enough time to explain his plans. What would be your proposals, Mr Miller?'

'Why, to collect from every household in the village, of course. Sixpence from everyone, every man, woman and child. No one can argue that that isn't fair.'

The expression on Mr Bulmer's face showed he could have thought of several arguments, but could not clearly articulate them.

Again I stepped in as his proxy. 'Are you aware of corn prices this year, Mr Miller? I am assured that in your occupation, you must know exactly how much a loaf of bread costs. If we have another harsh winter, and there is every indication that we will, then I cannot see how some families will be able to scrape together one sixpenny bit between them, let alone one for each man, woman and child.'

His face fell into meanly stubborn lines. ''Tis only right that everyone bears their share. 'Tis what his lordship would expect.'

Some deep thought process was preventing Bulmer from speaking.

'Which lordship? The dead one or the living one?' I prompted. 'If it is the former, I assure you that if he is now with the Almighty, such earthly considerations as a stone monument are no longer any concern of his.'

Bulmer produced a long, slow smile. 'And if he's in the other place,' he said, 'then he don't deserve no monument.'

Desperate not to laugh, I responded with a bow, but Miller did not. If anything, he looked even shiftier than Bulmer had done when he feared being overheard.

I continued, 'If on the other hand you fear the wrath of the young Lord Elham for your failure to honour his father, surely he can see for himself the struggle the poor have simply to survive.'

'There's the workhouse for those as can't,' Miller interjected.

I thought of the poor Jenkins family, sinking deeper into despair, despite my puny efforts to improve their lot. At least when the spring sowing came, I should be able to employ all the lads as birdscarers, but that would preclude them from ever doing more than following their poor father's occupation as the lowest of the unskilled labourers. Meanwhile, Mrs Jenkins was forced daily, whatever the weather, to clear stones from local farmers' fields.

'The workhouse is a drain on the parish,' Bulmer reflected

gloomily. 'Better they were in proper work.'

'Amen to that,' I said. 'And I am persuaded that Lord Elham will agree that keeping the families together is worth the sacrifice of a monument to his father.'

Miller shook his head doubtfully. 'You may be persuaded, Parson. But I fear his new lordship won't be.'

The question of the wording temporarily forgotten, the two men soon took their leave.

'My lord, I tell you roundly, they cannot,' I said, across my desk. This time Mrs Trent had been all too welcoming to my guest, and had shown him in with no warning, although he had declined to surrender to her care his hat, gloves and horsewhip. 'They do not have money for bread, for shoes for their feet and their children's feet. Such a demand would send many to the workhouse.' For the moment, I would let him assume that the decision had been mine, not the churchwardens'.

'It is the custom,' he said with the stubbornness of the foolish mind.

'It has always been the custom, nay, the duty, of those in the great houses to offer charity to their dependents – not simply those to whom they are related by blood or marriage, but all those on their estates. Your own mother keeps a poor basket so that your labourers' children shall not run naked; she bids Mrs Beckles send nourishing broth to those who are sick. Surely, my lord, you cannot run against the wonderful example of your mother and ask me to extort money from those who simply have none.'

'The rector says nothing but the truth,' Dr Hansard

declared, walking in unannounced. 'Have you any idea how high the corn prices have risen today?'

Elham gave the sort of extravagant shrug that I associated with Frenchmen, though carried off with so little aplomb it suggested ignorance as much as insolence.

'Have you seen the state of the cottages your workers are forced to inhabit?' I pursued. 'Even those of the most respectable have bare mud floors and are prey to damp and cold to a degree that barely separates them from your ice house in discomfort.'

'They should have been born rich, then,' he said. 'How dare you defy me in this matter? I tell you, Parson, you have crossed me once too often. And you, Hansard – your insistence on an inquest was outside of enough. You both forget yourselves.'

'Enough of these Cheltenham tragedies,' I said, with too much emphasis.

He brought his whip up, smacking it against the palm of his gloved hand. For a moment, I thought he would strike me, and braced myself for the blow. Instead, with a single sweep he removed everything from the top of my desk, at last turning on his heel and walking out. As he reached the door, he stopped. 'You will suffer for this,' he declared. 'You mark my words.'

'Well, we have made an enemy there,' Hansard said, bending to assist me in the task of recovering my possessions. The ink well had shattered, and I feared that even Mrs Trent's best efforts would be unable to rescue the carpet.

'*I*, Edmund – not you. You merely appeared at the tail end of our dispute, and cannot be held to blame.'

'Not by any rational creature, indeed. But our new lord is of limited mental capacity and an infinite capacity for spite. Good God, he actually attended the inquest. Did he not see how mild, how positively obsequious, I was? Her ladyship might have been sitting taking tea, the questions were so gentle.'

'The church and medicine must make stands for what they know to be true,' I agreed. 'In any case, how can he harm us? A man who never comes to church and is, in any case, hardly ever in residence at the Priory? He has no friends amongst the families round here. He has tried to kiss too many daughters, led too many sons over dangerous fences. And he has not,' I added as a clincher, 'settled his gaming debts.'

Hansard snorted. 'You know that there is another rumour in the village? That it was he who killed his father and his mother is protecting him?'

'No! Edmund, you jest.'

'I confess, I would like to have the power to reopen the inquest and have him questioned under oath. And by some other justice than Sir Willard. I shall keep my ear to the ground, Tobias – and so must you.'

# CHAPTER SIX

It was an interminably grey November, when it was never dry and never wet, never light but never dark, never mild but never cold. As if anticipating our desire to question him, the new Lord Elham disappeared from the scene without a word of farewell to anyone, though this offended his tenants less than the fact that he had not made the necessary round of visits to receive their congratulations. No one would have expected a formal assembly at the Priory, not with his bereaved mother still present, but there were nonetheless courtesies to observe.

Lizzie reported that her ladyship was very unsettled, talking one minute of a journey to London, another of a recuperative sojourn in Cheltenham or Bath. I suspected that Lizzie could have said a great deal more, but her loyalty to her mistress was as praiseworthy as it was absolute. In any case, our moments alone were rare, caught as they were before or after her fellow pupils had come to their lessons in reading and writing. Addie's advice and assistance had proved invaluable, and though progress was slow, for the most part it was steady.

My visits to the workhouse were less successful, as I had told Dr Hansard. Each week I took thick slabs of Mrs Trent's fruit cake to lessons. In theory it was to reward the best pupils; in reality, I could not bear to exclude any of those half-starving waifs from the best nourishment they would enjoy that week. Alas, no matter how much all might have wanted the chance if not to educate themselves, but at least be fed, the workhouse master conspired to make my activities *more honour'd in the breach than the observance*, as the Bard said. My little protégés, the Jenkins family, were no more and no less regular than any of the others, but William seemed to be cautious and watchful, whereas I remembered him to be open and sunny; perhaps he saw my befriending of all alike as some sort of betrayal of his and his siblings' hitherto special status.

The next day, I was summoned to the Priory. Her ladyship's mourning emphasised her extreme pallor, and I suspected from the redness about her eyes that she had shed tears not long since. Mrs Beckles had whispered that the new Lord Elham had unexpectedly returned and rapidly departed, after some fierce quarrel. However, Lady Elham made no reference to the cause of her current distress, and I could scarcely raise the subject, especially as Lizzie flitted in and out of the room.

Lady Elham was occupied in plain sewing for her poor basket. According to Mrs Beckles, these days this was her preferred indoor occupation. Sometimes she varied her routine by reading aloud from the Bible or Prayer Book or a book of sermons to a party of servants, who sewed or knitted as she read. Occasionally Lizzie was called on to read, so much had she improved in the lessons I had continued, despite all the upheavals, to give her fellow servants.

Her ladyship regarded me over the spectacles she affected these days for close work. 'I wish to discuss with you a project increasingly dear to my heart,' she said, without preamble. 'As you know, I acceded to your suggestion that my late husband be interred in the family mausoleum. But I still have it in mind to restore the family chapel.'

'That is excellent news, my lady. Its religious import aside, such an endeavour will bring great benefit to my parishioners,' I added with a foolish beam.

She looked at me coldly. 'How so? You are not proposing that villagers worship here?' She might have slapped my face.

'I was thinking of the skilled workers you would need to make the alterations, my lady.'

'I shall be employing the very best artists and artisans,' she said, with the clear implication that none in the village could meet her exacting standards. 'Let us proceed to the north gallery. There we will find some of the devotional paintings that the present lord's grandfather...that my late husband's father,' she corrected herself with emphasis, 'brought back from his grand tour.' She gathered her Norwich silk shawl about her, and led the way, Lizzie following in her wake.

Lady Elham paused before a number that she indicated might serve her purpose well. To my mind, those by Murillo especially, were overdramatic, but like her ladyship I enjoyed the human element of his work. I found one Virgin and Child especially moving – somehow the artist had conveyed in the young woman's eyes a terrible foreknowledge of her Son's fate.

'You feel as if you could reach out and touch that baby,' Lady Elham declared, 'and His mother so obviously adores Him.' She drifted to another picture.

'A right little imp He looks, begging your pardon, Parson,' said Lizzie, *sotto voce.*

'You don't think that looking at Him would be conducive to reverent musings?' I asked, trying not to laugh.

Lizzie shook her head. How pale she was. Like Lady Elham, she had dark shadows under her eyes, and her black gown washed all the colour from her complexion. Was she ill? I wanted to interrupt her ladyship's stream of chatter about dead overblown old masters and ask about the living. But the opportunity did not present itself. After a tantalising few minutes during which it seemed her ladyship might be about to leave us alone together, Lizzie was sent off on some errand, and I did not see her again that day.

Apart from such moments and my pedagogic interludes, I lived a life as quiet and grey as the weather. There were pleasant evenings with Dr Hansard, at his home or mine, but these were rarer than I would have liked, with an epidemic of putrid throat sweeping through the hamlet, on account, Dr Hansard said, of the weather.

But at last things changed in early December. A sharp north-easter blew away the fog and brought in sharp frosts. The bright crispness of the days inspired me to walk simply for the pleasure of God's creation, not with an eye to going anywhere. I found myself one day into the Priory woodlands. I had not, however, penetrated far when I came upon Matthew in a sunlit clearing. Even there the frost still lay.

The last time Matthew and I had met alone face to face, we had not parted on good terms, of course, and he absented himself from Sunday worship all too frequently. Should I rebuke him? Was my reluctance to do so cowardice, or a response to the displeasure so evident on his face? But it seemed his anger was not directed at me.

He kicked at something and spat. 'Did I not tell you of his lordship's vicious ways?' he demanded without preamble.

I moved closer. Living in the country, one could not be squeamish. If the Almighty provided for our sustenance the birds of the air and the animals that creep on the earth, then everyone knew that they must be killed before they could be eaten. A pig-sticking was a village event, bringing plenty in the midst of lack. Moles that destroyed crops would contribute to a warm winter waistcoat. No villager would simply kill an animal or bird – one of God's creatures – and leave it a bloody mess attracting vermin.

There at Matthew's feet was a dead mess of rabbit. Matthew's dog, an ugly, ill-favoured brute, barked once sharply and ventured a growl, but as I squatted to address him he soon greeted me as an old friend, humbling himself as I tickled the exact spot on his back that had needed attention. Perhaps I too should have a dog; it would give me company.

'That there rabbit would have filled someone's pot,' Matthew observed. 'Letting good food go to waste!'

I forbore to tell him of the food left lying untasted at the end of one the Priory dinner parties.

'But what does he have to do but peg it out to rot! It's only the frost that's kept it whole. Look here, Parson.'

The animal had been pinned by each of its paws in a horrid parody of the crucifixion, belly uppermost. From the deep tears in the flesh of the paws, it might be deduced that the animal was not dead when it was laid out and had struggled frantically to free itself.

'Killing vermin, yes. I kill crows and such and hang them on fences, but only to warn off others and protect the game. But not like this...' He swallowed. 'A good clean death. That's what they need. Even pigeons, pests though they be too.' With his gun, he gestured at a couple of wood pigeons on a nearby elm. But he made no attempt to take aim.

'I used to take a gun to wood pigeon myself,' I recalled, almost despite myself.

'And did you kill them? Not an easy target, your wood pigeon.'

I could not help boasting, 'I thought myself a failure if we did not have pigeon pie at least once a week.'

'But you don't shoot in your own woods?'

I would risk perfect frankness. 'There's far too much to be done in the way of clearing them.'

'Ah, I heard you'd taken on some men.' For the first time I fancied respect in his demeanour.

I nodded. I had employed as many men as I could afford, and more, in the hope that such employment would keep families together. In addition to the small wage, the timber would provide firewood for the workers. 'The woods are still much overgrown, and give a walker no pleasure.'

'And sport?'

'With so many men around?'

With a bark of laughter, he passed me his gun. 'Go on, Parson. Show me what you can do. It throws to the left just a mite, mind.'

So it did. But to our shared delight and my considerable relief, after a few minutes I was able to present him with a couple of brace for his aunt.

I stood in silence as he tore the rabbit free and tried to scuff a hole in the frozen earth in which to bury it. It seemed to me that he was less interested in the interment than in something else. Twice he swallowed hard. At last, coughing, he said, 'Have you seen my Lizzie recently?'

News of our occasional conversations would not bring him happiness. I compromised. 'Sometimes she sits with Lady Elham while I read her a sermon or try to distract her with a little conversation.'

'And how do you think she looks?'

'I can hardly say.'

'Nay,' he insisted. I feared for a moment he would shake me by the lapels. 'Is she in good looks, do you think?'

I reflected. 'I must admit that she looked pale last time I saw her. But I attributed that to lack of exercise and the inclement weather. Do not you?' I shot him a searching look.

'I wish I knew, Parson, and no mistake. Now her ladyship's got this idea in her head about church, and all the servants walking two by two like so many animals going into the ark, I hardly see her. It's not natural, all this religion, begging your pardon, Parson.'

Finding a convenient log, I sat down, motioning him to sit beside me. 'You refer, I collect, to the extremely deep mourning that her ladyship observes?'

'She's turning the place into a convent, so I do hear. All this Bible-reading and prayer. Can't be right, can it, Parson?'

'I confess it lacks moderation. But who would deny the good lady the solace of religion?'

'I would, and no mistake, when it denies other people their own lives!'

I nodded reflectively. Dr Hansard had said much the same,

with even more emphasis. Perhaps I had been remiss in not remonstrating with her ladyship. Such devotion was indeed almost papish in its intensity, something I certainly must not encourage in my parish.

After a few minutes' almost companionable silence, he pointed out a couple of squirrels, the sun turning their coats to burnished copper.

'I understood that they hibernated,' I objected.

He touched his lips to silence me; his own voice was no more than a murmur. 'So they do when the weather's bad. But on a day like this, why not come out? Find the nuts you've put away for just such a day? They'll go back to their dray as soon as the sun cools. And – look – there's a green woodpecker.'

The bird was working its way down the side of a tree trunk some twenty paces from us. It appeared to catch sight of us at much the same time as Matthew pointed it out. I expected it to fly off, but it merely retreated to the further side of the tree, peeping round from time to time, like a child playing hide and seek, as if to check that we could not see it. Grown men both, we threw back our heads and laughed. Bird and squirrels retreated speedily.

In something like harmony, we rose and fell into step, squinting against the low sun now casting the deepest shadows. Suddenly Matthew stopped, gripping my arm above the elbow. Narrowing his eyes, he was pointing towards a distant ride.

'Now who might that be?' he demanded, stepping forward lightly.

'A poacher?' I asked, still not certain that I had seen

anything. 'He's in danger from the mantraps whoever he is.'

'You can rest easy there, Parson. Never liked the things myself. If Mr Davies asks, they're still there, but between you and me you'll find most of them at the bottom of his lordship's lake. At the deepest part, moreover, where even the driest summer won't expose them.' He slipped the dog's chain. 'Go on, Gundy – go!'

'Gundy?' I asked.

He blushed. 'Short for Salmagundy. Mrs Beckles saw what a mixture he was and gave him the name after the salad.'

Gundy ran off purposefully, and we ran after, keeping him in sight. But the figure, real or a figment of Matthew's imagination, eluded us.

'Perhaps he's gone over the wall?' I suggested, prompted by the few sharp barks Gundy delivered at the foot of it.

Matthew swarmed up it as easily as if he'd been my nephew's monkey, but, having looked from left to right, dropped back.

'The sun's so low and with the road running due west I couldn't see anything,' he said, not even panting after the exertion. 'But I'll swear I saw someone. And any trespasser wants to be careful lest he end up like that rabbit.'

'His lordship wouldn't—' I stopped, shocked.

'There are ways and ways of killing,' he said. 'A crucifixion is one, a hanging another. Or a long slow passage to Australia. I'm not sure which I'd rather endure.'

We parted then on good terms and I set out whence I had come. He called me back, however. 'You could break a leg out here in the dusk and no one'd know. If I let you out of this here a gate you can follow the lane. It's not much better, God knows, but it should be safer.'

I had walked perhaps five hundred yards picking my way though the ruts when I was aware of a quick rush behind me. Stepping swiftly sideways, I prepared to accost whoever approached so roughly. Instead, I felt a blow to the back of my neck and knew no more.

It was pitch dark, the only light coming from the stars when I recovered my senses – I must have been lying unconscious for at least half an hour. The period seemed, in my fuddled state, a matter of importance, I know not why. I reached for my timepiece – to find it missing. Gone too were the few coins I always carried about me to bestow on any of my young parishioners prepared to open gates and give me a civil time of day. The robber had not stopped there, as I discovered when I forced myself to my feet. My boots had been taken!

It was a long and unpleasant walk back to my home – but I realised with a little lift of the heart that it was the first time I had thought of the parsonage in those terms. There would be warmth, light and comfort; there people who cared about my welfare.

I staggered on, longing only to lie down but aware that to succumb to the temptation on so cold a night might be fatal.

At last I reached the outskirts of the village. Should I stop at one of the cottages and ask for help? Or would that put them to more trouble than they could afford? Much as I feared the latter would be the case, I knew not how to persuade my legs to carry me further.

The matter was taken out of my hands. I tripped in a deep rut, and fell on my hands and knees, crying out like a vexed child at the pain.

'Who's that? Don't move! Stay where you are!'

I raised my head a little, to see the muzzle of a gun in horribly close proximity. 'It is I, Parson Campion,' I croaked. 'Do not shoot, I pray you!'

'And what would a parson be doing out here at this time of night?'

'A parson might be attending a deathbed,' I said, nettled. 'Or coming home from an afternoon with friends. Or any lawful pursuit. Pray, put that gun away and help me to my feet.'

He held his candle unpleasantly close to my face before, putting down both candle and gun, he complied. Once he had me vertical, he passed me my hat without a word, and stood back, patently expecting me to go on my way.

'I have been robbed, my good man,' I said tetchily. 'And the thief has taken my boots.'

At Eton I had roared with laughter at boys whose predicament was no less than mine now, so I suppose I should not blame my rescuer for finding my loss amusing. His bellows of mirth brought out his wife, clattering across the frozen earth in pattens.

'Joe, enough of your racket. Parson, if it would please you to step inside—' She bobbed a curtsy. She was a regular member of my congregation, even if he was not.

'Any stepping needs must be slow,' I groaned, my head by now hurting badly. 'Mrs Andrews, could you send young Henry to Jem, at the parsonage, and tell him what has befallen me? Tell Henry that tomorrow I will give reward him for his trouble, but not today. All my money has gone the way of my boots.'

'I will not bleed you, for in my opinion you have lost enough blood already,' Hansard declared, regarding me appraisingly.

Mrs Trent nodded with approval, stepping forward to adjust the bed sheets in the manner of one who has at last come into her own. 'If you will give me your instructions, Dr Hansard,' she said, 'they will be obeyed to the letter.'

'They will indeed,' agreed Jem, who was clearly not to be ousted by a comparative newcomer to my little household.

I closed my eyes, too weary to be fought over. Dr Hansard, amusement in his voice, asked, 'Which of you will take the first watch? Because the other must sleep while he or she can. I anticipate a high fever in the morning, and possibly an inflammation of the lung. At very least,' he added, 'Parson Campion will have a ringing headache, and must be fed a lowering diet for two or three days. I'm sure I can rely on you to provide some of your excellent broth, Mrs Trent, and on Jem to fend off unwelcome visitors.'

'I always did tell Mr Campion he should employ a butler,' Mrs Trent fussed.

'I fancy Dr Hansard means visitors who may not come to the front door,' Jem said. 'I'll guard him with my life, as you well know, sir.'

'Why should I need guarding?' I asked, sounding pettish even to my own ears.

'Because someone did not expect you to survive this afternoon's attack,' Hansard said grimly. 'By taking your boots, he made it less likely that, should you regain consciousness before the cold – which is deeper than ever tonight – took you, you would be able to reach help.'

I clapped a hand to my head. 'My good friend – you must pay young Henry for his services.'

'I've already done that,' Jem said quickly.

I cursed inwardly. Jem could be so high in the instep that recompensing him was nigh on impossible. I meant to say something incisive. Instead, the words came out almost of their own volition: 'I feel devilish sick.' And I promptly cast up my accounts.

'Aye, he's done to a cow's thumb,' Jem opined. 'Do you show the good doctor out, Mrs Trent. I'll take the first watch.'

If there was any argument, I neither knew nor cared any more.

# CHAPTER SEVEN

For several days I was as weak as a kitten, but at last I rebelled against all the kindness threatening to smother me and insisted that I was well enough to come downstairs, albeit in a frogged brocade dressing gown that clearly overawed the girl dusting the hall.

'Beg pardon, sir,' she said, dropping a low curtsy, and scrambling back out of sight.

Search my memory as I might, I could come to only one conclusion – I was certainly not acquainted with her. No doubt I would learn more of her when Mrs Trent came to report the day's affairs, one of which, I was determined, should be the preparation of something other than chicken or mutton broth. It was not, however, Mrs Trent who presented herself in my study, in which a middling fire aspired to take the chill off the room, but Mrs Beckles, who immediately cajoled the logs into life.

'Mrs Trent is an admirable woman,' she declared, with no preamble, 'but your illness was enough to tax her powers to the limit, and I took it upon myself to send her a little assistant. No, don't fly into the boughs.'

Humbly, I said, 'I would not dare. But does the new maid meet with Mrs Trent's approval?'

'Mrs Trent was more exhausted than she cares to admit by her share of the nursing.'

'But Jem bore his part. And more.'

'Indeed. And do you not think that having to permit Jem to do that was more exhausting than doing it all herself? Come, Mr Campion, you must know how decent loyal servants must fight to serve their master when they fear he is dying!'

'I was never dying.'

'That is something you may discuss with Dr Hansard – whose idea it was to introduce Susan into the household. And mine,' she conceded, her eyes twinkling as she allowed her dimples to show.

'But who would want me to die?'

'Who indeed? The menfolk have their theories, Mr Campion, and I was never one to spoil a good argument. So I will report that Lady Elham, who before she left for a week or so in Bath, sent her best love and a huge basket of fruit from her – from *his lordship's* – succession houses.'

What I wanted to do was demand whether Lizzie had gone too. Instead, I asked mildly, 'How was her ladyship?'

'She kept her room much of the time. And, until it became so very cold, wandered about the grounds a great deal, as if seeking out places where she and her late husband enjoyed happy moments.' Mrs Beckles spoke without emphasis, but still I sensed a great deal of irony. 'She saw no visitors and of course paid no calls. I trust this visit to Bath will return her to health,' she added punctiliously.

'I wonder she does not move to the Dower House, if she wishes a retired life,' I said, trying to keep my chagrin at losing Lizzie from my voice.

Whatever her intentions had been, Mrs Beckles pulled up a chair and sat opposite me. 'Lady Elham still rules the roast at the Priory, that is why. The new Lord Elham, who you may remember about the time of your accident left us for the Lord knows where, has never shown an inclination to take a wife, despite the efforts of some of the mothers in the district, who perceive him as a very eligible *parti*. And the Priory must have a mistress.'

'What of the daughters of these mothers?'

'You must have seen, Mr Campion, better, than I.' She raised her eyebrows to prompt me.

'He is a regular guest at all the neighbouring houses,' I said supinely.

'And does that make him a welcome suitor?'

'The young ladies appear loath to engage in more than the mildest flirtation.'

'And with you, Mr Campion? Surely they would do more than flirt!'

'I would never step beyond the line,' I said, adding, 'I do not see how I can, circumstanced as I am.'

She spread her hands, encompassing in a gesture the whole of the rectory and possibly the glebe lands too. 'My dear sir, a parson needs a wife. But you look fagged to death – I tire you with my gabble-mongering. Let me ring for Susan to make up your fire and then I may make you known to each other.'

Susan was short and slightly built, with mouse-brown hair. Her complexion was brown, too, as were her eyes. She was not ill-favoured, but was as yet a mere dab of a girl who might blossom or not.

Mrs Beckles laid a kind hand on her shoulder. 'Make your

curtsy to Mr Campion, Susan. Mr Campion, you will know Susan's sister, Lizzie.'

Lizzie's sister. But there was no resemblance at all. I forced myself to say evenly, 'Indeed I do, Susan. She is Lady Elham's abigail.' I stretched out my hand. 'Welcome to the rectory, Susan – may I hope to teach you your letters, as I have taught Lizzie?'

When Dr Hansard visited me at about five o'clock on the day of Mrs Beckles' call, I urged him to support my plea for a more varied diet.

'A little boiled chicken would do you no harm, Tobias. Or some calves' foot jelly would be very nourishing.'

'As you are my friend, Hansard, enough. Unless you wish to share them with me? I am persuaded that Mrs Trent might easily lay covers for two.'

'Touché! Now, let me feel your pulse. Excellent. It is no longer tumultuous. And your broken head mends well,' he conceded, replacing the bandage with a new one. 'You must have a sound constitution. I feared, as you must know, that you might suffer an inflammation of the lung, but I can detect nothing amiss.'

'Of course you cannot. Just tell me when I may discard these confounded slippers.'

He inspected my feet. 'Parson Campion, I declare you sound in mind, wind and limb. And I prescribe—'

'Not more pap, I beg you!'

'A glass of the burgundy Mrs Trent is even now decanting. Can you not detect the odours emanating from her kitchen? She is cooking you a fine dinner – on my orders,' he chuckled.

'And you will stay to sup with me?' I fear I sounded over-anxious. I was surprised that he had been so sparing of his visits while I was unwell, and felt quite ill-used to have been left so lonely.

'With all my heart, since you clearly have a fit of the blue-devils. In fact,' he added with a smile, 'I intended to anyway. A man who has successfully delivered twins deserves no less.'

'Twins!' I thanked goodness that I had not openly carped.

'A son and a daughter to Farmer Bulmer's eldest son and his wife. The poor lady had to endure a very long labour.' His smile slipped and I realised how knocked-up he looked. Face bleak, he continued, 'At one point I feared the worst, that I should have to cut the babes out of her in the hope of saving her life, if not theirs. And even that might not have done the trick. But – just as I despaired – she managed to deliver the first, a lusty girl.'

'Thank God!'

'Amen. The boy is punier than I like, but with luck he may survive.'

'Is there any doubt?' My time here – indeed, my recent illness – had made me much more aware of human frailty.

'I can hope – and you can pray.' He made an obvious effort to sound more cheerful. 'Now, childbed apart, I have not been idle. I have also endeavoured to discover what I could about your assailant.' He sat down, in the manner of a man prepared to talk his talk.

'You know who attacked me?'

'I fear your auditory faculties must have been affected by that blow. No, I have failed signally to discover him. Matthew declares that he saw a shadowy figure escape from the woods of the Priory parkland, and that you both gave chase. His description was worth this much.' Hansard snapped his fingers. 'So what is your recollection of the event?'

I snapped my fingers in return. 'And to my shame,' I added, 'I saw even less of the trespasser than Matthew did. In fact, had not the wretch hit my skull, I would have considered him to be a mere figment of Matthew's imagination.'

'Your injuries were real enough,' Hansard observed mildly. 'And your property stolen.'

'What folly,' I said, 'to steal something like my timepiece, engraved with my name!'

Hansard's eyes opened wide. 'You had rather he had stolen something anonymous?'

'If he was driven to such straits as to need to steal, and to go to such lengths to do it, then I would he had profited from it, not put a noose around his neck if he tried to sell the watch.'

Hansard shook his head firmly. 'Come, my young friend, what a bag of moonshine that is! And you a parson, supposed to preach morality. *Thou shalt not steal*. You made it a text for your sermon only the other day.'

'I am grateful that Dr Hansard was not asleep.'

'I might have been resting my eyes, Parson Campion, but my ears were ever open.'

When our laughter died down, I leant forward seriously. 'Edmund, had he asked, I would have given him the watch – or its monetary equivalent. You know that.'

'I do. I wish he had done so. You would have been spared near death by drowning in broth. But to return to my point. I have found simply an invisible man. No one in the village or on any of the surrounding estates – Matthew and possibly yourself excepted – saw hide or hair of him. But I have sent out messages to my fellow justices in Warwick and Leamington, asking them to tell me should it come to their notice that someone is trying to pawn or sell your watch. The boots and the money you must bid farewell to, I fear—'

I gestured impatiently. 'They do not matter. The coins were meant to be given away, and boots can be replaced. The timepiece, alas, cannot. It was a gift from my grandfather when I came of age, and is engraved accordingly. So we have no reports of vagrants, tramps, deserters or soldiers invalided out of the army? I pray God it was no local man.'

'Amen, for it would be a hanging offence, as you said.' He spoke with the solemn voice of a man bound to carry out the demands of the law.

I thought of Matthew's reflections on punishment, but said nothing. What if Matthew's affability had been assumed, the better to lure me into a trap? What if the assailant was none other than Matthew himself, disposing of one he saw as a rival in love? Unwilling to share my fear with even such a good and discreet man as Edmund, I asked if it were permitted me to join him in a glass of sherry or Madeira before we supped.

'Indeed. I will pour it myself, with your permission.' As he passed me a mere half-glass, he asked, 'Are there any of your acquaintance who might wish to harm – perhaps kill – you?'

'Call me mutton-headed, but I cannot. I know – and regret – that my churchwardens do not hold me in high regard, but they are decent respectable men who would not sink to murder. I would consider the workhouse master neither decent nor respectable, but cannot think he would do me active harm, thwart me how he may in the matter of the children's schooling.'

We sipped in silence for a few moments. Before he said, with a degree of hesitation unusual in one so blunt, 'Has anyone threatened you? Anyone, Tobias? Come, don't try to bamboozle me.'

'There was that attempt to trip us...We never found the culprit.' I made a greater effort. 'You know that Lord Elham does not care for me. Nor for you,' I hastened to add.

'But he did not attack my property with a horsewhip. I fear he is not at all times a rational creature.'

'I cannot believe – even had he been in the vicinity at the time, which I am sure he was not...No, that is not the act of a gentleman.'

Sensing my discomfort, Dr Hansard turned the subject and we did not return to it that evening.

The very next day I began Susan's reading lessons. She was clearly a diligent child, eager to please and very swift to learn, so much so I promised her her own pencils and paper to that she might practise forming the letters when Mrs Trent could spare her from other duties. I also introduced her to Jem, who treated her with the same avuncular briskness as he had treated the Jenkins children, popping her on horseback and leading her round the yard.

Mrs Trent looked on, smiling sardonically. 'I thought the girl was here to learn to dust and clean,' she observed, 'but it seems she's here to learn to read and ride.'

I laughed at her quip. 'First and foremost she is here to assist you,' I said, serious once more. 'My illness imposed on you intolerably, Mrs Trent.'

She bridled, but half-heartedly.

'Indeed, I became aware of how very much falls to your capable hands. As yet Susan is too young and too ill-fed to be of much assistance, but if we are both patient with her, and both teach her all we can, I'm sure she will be a credit to you.'

Did she notice the change of pronoun? I think not. Certainly when Mrs Trent summoned her to learn to raise a pie, she did so in kind and encouraging tones.

Jem winked at me over their departing heads. 'You parsons can always twist hatchet-faced old ladies round your little fingers,' he observed, returning to the stables, but humming as he went.

'The last parson, he didn't hold with such stuff,' Dusty Miller reflected, looking round the bare church. 'Holly. Mistletoe. He said they were heathenish, and we should be ashamed of ourselves for thinking of it.'

'And did you feel ashamed?' I countered, a twinkle in my eye.

It was the first time I had been permitted to return to St Jude's since my accident. I had been giving thanks for my survival and praying for the miscreant. I was adding an urgent prayer for Mrs Bulmer, still very weak after her confinement, and for her new babes when Mr Miller pushed open the great oak door, and had stood, waiting for me to rise, his hat clutched respectfully between his hands. Only when I rose did he open his budget.

'Ashamed? Nay, we'd been putting Christmas swags and garlands in the church as long as I can remember – and my father, and his father before him,' he said, puffing his chest in pride at the length of the tradition.

I smiled. 'And probably his father before him. By all means let us deck the church with the Almighty's winter gifts to us. Do we have mummers in the village?'

His eyes rounded. 'We did. And a little choir going from house to house.'

'Could the mummers be persuaded to recall their parts? And the choir their carols?'

'Won't her ladyship mind, her still being in deepest black?'

'You know she is not at the Priory at the moment?' I leant back against a pew. Even though all the cuts were now healed, there was a lingering tenderness in my feet that did not like to be probed. Perhaps that was how in time her ladyship would feel about her bereavement; the outward signs might have gone, but little inward pangs of pain were inevitable. 'But I will approach his lordship – or at least his steward.' If Elham thought the petition was from me, he would veto the plans forthwith.

According to Mrs Trent his lordship had but three days ago arrived back in the neighbourhood, and would no doubt engage in the local round of parties and impromptu balls, though his mourning naturally precluded his dancing. His elevation to his father's title had clearly had very little beneficial effect on him, and tales of his extravagance circulated round the village. His new independence, indeed, made it easier for him to support what some said was a life of debauchery. So long as this was confined to London and his other estates elsewhere in the country, the villagers were inclined to view such activity with an indulgent eye – he was scarcely into his majority, and young men would be young men.

'I cannot imagine anyone objecting,' I continued, 'provided, of course, that you do not allow any entertainments to go beyond the line of what is pleasing. The family might not want carol-singers in the main hall of the Priory, but surely they would not mind them in the servants' hall.

Mr Miller gave one of his rare, gap-toothed smiles. 'It'll be like old times, Parson.' To my amazement, he took my hand and pumped it vigorously. 'The church will look a picture, and the carol-singers and mummers will do you proud.' He bustled off, presumably to tell his cronies. As soon as he left the building, I could hear him whistling the familiar tune of 'The Holly and the Ivy.'

His simple pleasure was infectious. I too could have whistled; instead, I bowed my head in thanks to the Almighty for the coming of the holy season and all the innocent joys it brought.

Then, despite the cold, as bitter I had ever known it at home in Derbyshire, I set out for a walk, only to be overtaken by Dr Hansard, tooling along in his gig.

'There is a footman down with earache at the Priory,' he said, pulling his horses to a standstill. 'Mrs Beckles has done her best by placing a roasted onion in the offending orifice and even dosing the lad with laudanum drops, but she is not satisfied with his progress. Do you care to hop up and come along? Make up your mind, man – I daren't keep the horses standing.'

Of course I got up beside him, but dreaded visiting the Priory knowing that Lizzie was elsewhere.

The moment she laid eyes on me, Mrs Beckles almost dragged me into the warmth, and pressed on me what she described as Cook's special hot punch. Goodness knew what it contained, but I felt a wonderful warmth spread through my body. She settled me beside the fire, assuring herself of my comfort with covert glances.

'Tell me about her ladyship's plans,' I said.

'I know more of her departure than of her return,' she said, sitting too. 'All I can tell you is that, without warning, at six o'clock one evening she summoned her travelling chaise, gave me my last instructions and set off. Just like that.'

'With no warning? In the dark of a winter's evening? Do you have any idea why she should get such a maggot in her brain?'

'None at all, Mr Campion. Had it been his lordship, no one would have remarked on it, of course. Ah, Dr Hansard.' It was as if someone had lit a whole branch of candles to light her face.

Shutting the door behind him, Hansard came in and helped them both to punch, though she was inclined to resist. Then he asked, 'And is she still away?'

She nodded.

'Perhaps,' I reflected slowly, 'she found unbearable the prospect of spending Christmas alone in a place that must have rung with laughter in earlier years. The death of her husband must weigh heavily at such a happy season.'

Mrs Beckles accorded me a glance so expressive that she could not have said more clearly in words that I was attributing to her ladyship feelings she did not have.

'But the chapel...all her plans for a funerary monument for the late lord...her deep mourning... Were they all sham?'

She poured me another cup of punch. 'All is not what it seems in many families,' she said. 'As housekeeper, I get to know who is discovered by an early housemaid in whose bed. And who is never found in his wife's.'

I nodded; how many years had I spent in such households myself, when rumours of infidelities regularly ebbed and flowed on the tide of gossip and on dits?

'She is a lady of some taste and discernment. Not to wrap it up in clean linen, Doctor Hansard, was not his late lordship a bullying oaf?'

I had never imagined that such observations, such judgements, were made behind the green baize door. My family had often had the most intimate conversations in front of the servants, as if behind their wooden countenances the footmen had wooden ears.

'Almost as bad as his son,' Hansard agreed.

She took another sip from her cup and leant forward confidingly. 'We understand that there has been a falling-out between her and his young lordship, Mr Campion. According to his valet, his lordship proposed to bring – forgive me – his *chère amie*, and install her here.'

'Good God! And what did her ladyship have to say?' Hansard demanded.

'A very great deal, all of it to the point,' Mrs Beckles declared with satisfaction. 'But the young man – I still cannot think of him as a noble lord – left the Priory in a great temper, they say.'

'I suspected he was loose in the haft,' I confessed. 'But to sink to this... It is beyond anything – to bring a Paphian under your mother's roof!'

'And to suggest it was time she removed to the Dower House, moreover,' she added.

Feeling that she had been too indiscreet – I could only presume that it was the punch that had loosened her tongue – I decided to turn the subject and repeated Mr Miller's request and my response.

'So the village will enjoy a good old-fashioned Christmas,' she said, clapping her hands, as I concluded. 'God bless you for your part in it. There's little enough cheer in people's lives, and a beautiful church and the old customs will do us all good.'

'I hoped for her ladyship's blessing on the activities,' I admitted. 'But now—?'

'Oh, his lordship has left us again – and in any case, I cannot think he would agree, so contrary he is. Next time I write to her ladyship for further instructions, I will ask her. Who knows, she may well be back before I can pick up my pen, her return as precipitate as her departure!'

The weather still being viciously cold, and neither of Bulmer's grandchildren flourishing as they ought, I offered to baptise them in their home.

'It will be just as good, won't it, Parson? Just as good as if it was in the font?' Bulmer asked anxiously, warming his legs before a roaring fire in the farmhouse kitchen.

As a churchwarden, he should not have needed to ask. But a man's anxiety for his family may make him forgetful of theology, so I simply assured him that that was the case.

'It's the lad. Edmund, she fancies calling him, after the good doctor. Poor little mite, his limbs flop and his head rolls.' The big man was uncomfortably close to tears.

I averted my face so that he could recover himself. 'And your granddaughter?'

'Got a fine pair of lungs, that I will say,' he admitted grudgingly. 'She's to be Fanny, it seems.'

'And your daughter-in-law?'

He turned and spat into the fire. 'That Dr Hansard says there must be no more babies yet a while. What's he mean by that, Parson? A man needs an heir.'

'Your son is young yet,' I said, desperate to find a few words of comfort. 'And your daughter-in-law will get her strength back in due course, pray God.'

He stared out of the window at the darkening sky. 'Maybe. They say heathens can put away their wives if they don't produce a boy-child.'

'My friend, don't let your mind turn that way,' I urged. 'Your son is a credit to you. Your grandson may well prove the same.'

'I've seen runts in litters before,' he said. 'And you get fond of them, and still they die.'

'But they do not have Dr Hansard to care for them.'

He managed half a smile. 'Nor do they. Now, when do you think he and that prime article down at the Priory will be troubling you for the banns…?'

# CHAPTER EIGHT

The approach to Christmas and the continued crisp weather set in train the neighbourhood's social round. There were some eighteen families who considered each other socially acceptable to both dine and dance with. Other, less favoured, families and individuals would be invited to arrive after dinner had ended. My family would have considered such a limited acquaintance wearisome in the extreme, but I was grateful for the opportunity to meet my fellow men. My head insisted that it was appropriate for a clergyman to meet all his parishioners, even those whose church-going hardly earned them the name. My heart admitted that the periods of solitude uninterrupted by my good friend Edmund were inclined to lower my spirits.

Lord Elham was again absent from the Priory, and, as before, the number of young men being sadly deficient, I was much in demand as a dancing partner, either in private houses or at public balls in Leamington or Warwick. Amidst all the practised insipidities of the young ladies, I found most entertainment in the company of Miss Sophia Heath, whose violet eyes met mine with a decided air of encouragement whenever the country dance was made up, even though officially she was still not out. I supposed that practice was needed in all things, even flirtation, and was happy to indulge her with mild repartee and occasional references to the writings of Burke. Despite my inclination, I was careful not to pay her particular attention, however, lest her chances on the marriage mart be tarnished.

'In the spring,' she confided as we applauded the musicians one evening at the Leamington Assembly Rooms, 'Mama and Papa are to take a house in town for my presentation. Mr Campion, it is most important that I "take", as you may understand that with three other younger sisters, I have a duty to marry well to launch them.'

'Duty is very important,' I agreed, 'but liking must enter into it. You parents would not press you to marry even a marquis if you did not respect him.'

'Respect! Mr Campion, I desire nothing less than an earl prostrate at my feet!' she laughed.

'That would mean that he respected you,' I countered.

'But I would not permit such prostration if I did not like him,' she responded, eyes wide open. 'And unless he had at least ten thousand a year,' she added with a delightful grin.

At last I returned her to her seat, in the hope of more conversation. But her hand was soon claimed by Lord Warley's younger brother. She looked into his face with the same teasing amusement that had so engaged me.

Lady Heath caught my eye. I bowed. 'You have a most charming, indeed, an original daughter,' I said, smiling.

She tapped me firmly on the arm with her fan. 'Not charming enough, and too original,' she declared. 'Won't take if they think she's bookish. Pray don't encourage her, Parson.'

In another life I would have depressed such pretension by the considered use of my quizzing glass. But a country parson did not snub a parishioner who contributed generously to the poor, especially one administering a well-placed warning.

I bowed again, not coldly. 'Were I on the look-out for a wife,' I said, 'I should look no further than a young woman both bookish and original. But I fear I do not enjoy the ten thousand a year she considers a prerequisite for a suitor.'

She looked at me searchingly, and nodded. We had made our positions clear with no loss of face on either side. With luck, Miss Sophia's heart was as untroubled by me, as mine was by her.

Alas, it was not the case that my heart was whole. It was other eyes than Miss Sophia's that troubled my sleep and blurred my thoughts when I should have been preparing my sermons. It was still those lovelier eyes of Lizzie.

I had not seen her for some weeks now, of course, and was constantly tormented by news that her ladyship planned to return, and then that she did not. Of course, not being an acknowledged lover, I could not write to her. A polite note to her ladyship including an enquiry about her health had gone unanswered.

No doubt Matthew was suffering equally, and his unlettered state meant he would neither write nor expect a letter. If their betrothal was unofficial, there was no doubt that he considered it binding. I felt for him. Christmas was a bittersweet time for all lovers in service, especially when one was the personal maid of a lady, and at her mistress's beck and call just as much as at any other time, so perhaps he would not even have seen her then. As it was, although the celebrations would be much curtailed at the Priory, there was no suggestion that any of the servants would be given extra days' holiday with their families.

'But think, Mr Campion,' Mrs Beckles sighed, when I pointed this out, 'where would they all go? There's no room at home for most of the youngsters, not with the cot being filled with a new baby every year, regular as clockwork, in many households where there are nine and ten in a two-bedroom cottage. Having a son or daughter who's a servant living in a great house is many families' saving grace.'

'Of course. And it would be a long journey home for some of them.'

'And at least they eat well here. Very well. They do say,' she added, with something like anger, 'that some labourers are so hungry this year they're dipping toast into stewed tea to make it look like meat. And that's all they get, day in, day out.'

'Thank God for your generosity,' I said.

I knew she would turn the compliment. 'Mr Campion, I have been meaning to ask you if Susan continues to give satisfaction. Is Mrs Trent happy with her work?'

'Indeed she is. Susan is a real asset to our little household.' I added, 'When she is not working at her chores, she enjoys the company of Jem and the horses.'

'Jem.' She bit her lip and turned from me. 'Mr Campion, might I ask you something else?'

'Of course! What is your question? Is something worrying you?'

'No. It is probably my imagination.' She shook her head firmly. 'I will not speak of it now. Well, as you've probably heard from Dr Hansard, Mr Davies has succumbed to a bout of lumbago.' When she spoke Edmund's name, a tiny smile played about her lips. 'So although I hear none of the family will grace us with their presence – though this has not stopped them relegating the mummers and carol-singers to the servants' hall – I have more than enough to do, and must not stand gossiping.'

Poor Hansard's time was taken up with an outbreak of what we feared was scarlet fever. Mercifully he was soon able to confirm it as a simple measles epidemic. Even that, no more than a nursery ailment in the big houses, claimed lives in the cottages, and I had a steady, sad stream of burials to deal with. Some families dealt with their bereavements phlegmatically; others grieved so painfully I had had to pull more than one woman back from her infant's coffin. Many belatedly asked me to baptise the surviving children.

'Do you not object,' Dr Hansard demanded, 'that they treat christening as some sort of celestial insurance policy? Mind you, it seems to have worked for Farmer Bulmer's grandson.'

'He still does not thrive,' I said.

'He is not dead, either. Though,' he added soberly, 'I cannot imagine that he can survive beyond infancy.'

I shook my head sadly. I visited the farmhouse regularly, reading quietly to the young mother, who, thank God, at last showed signs of physical recovery but remained very low in spirits.

'And it also seems to have been remarkably efficacious for the whole of Mrs Jenkins' brood,' Hansard said, as if determined not to end the conversation on a sad note. 'They are all flourishing despite the rigours of the workhouse.'

'Flourishing physically. But that rogue of a workhouse master still thwarts all my plans for regular schooling.'

'Did you truly expect him to endorse them?'

'Can he not understand that regular periods of study are necessary for the boys and girls if they are to profess beyond simple repetition? One or two can put letters together to make a simple word, but for the majority I might be trying to teach them Chinese!'

'He fears they will end up aping their betters,' Edmund suggested. 'In other words, better than himself.'

It occurred to me that since he wanted the children to submit to physical toil, the workhouse master could scarcely object to my finding employment for some of them. Clearing my woodland was still a priority. Not only would it benefit me in the long run, as Ford agreed with some reluctance, it would also assist the families of the men I had taken on. But there were some jobs that workhouse boys could do equally well, such as gathering up twigs and bundling them, like gleaners in a cornfield. I could make sure they were well fed, and hope that the extra pennies I distributed would not find their way into the master's pockets. Certainly I paid him handsomely enough for the privilege. If he confiscated their cash, I would have to find a way of paying in kind.

Encouraged by a hearty breakfast, an idea which I owed to Jem, the team started work at first light. At intervals came more food and drink, with a few pence to jingle in their pockets as they swaggered back to the workhouse at the end of the day, for all the world like their adult counterparts. They returned the next day, and the next. Soon I would have woodland to be proud of.

'Pigs,' Farmer Bulmer declared, spitting copiously as he leant on the fence already supporting Ford and me as we watched the activity.

'I beg your pardon?'

'Pigs. That's what you need. Pigs. Any undergrowth your lads have left, the pigs'll finish. And they'll root around and leave good manure behind, won't they, Mr Ford? And good bacon, too, though that'll take a little longer.'

Ford sucked his teeth, a sure prelude to pessimism.

'Until we have provided ourselves with some,' I said, before he could actually voice his objections, 'could not you supply the swine, Mr Bulmer?'

'Why, that I could, with all my heart, Parson.' With a glance at Ford, he added, 'And then we would share the profits.'

Ford brightened; I did not demur.

'And your grandson?' I asked, as we shook hands on the deal. 'How is he?'

He shook his head. 'Still weakly. Dr Hansard, he says, give him time. And my daughter-in-law too. But I don't like the look of him, Parson, and that's a fact. He's dwindling. Well, you've seen him yourself.'

I nodded, unable to disagree.

When a frantic knocking disturbed my supper that night, I feared it was Bulmer, sending for me with bad news. But the voice I heard in conversation with Mrs Trent was female, and vaguely familiar.

'A Person is wishful to see you,' Mrs Trent announced. 'I have informed her that you are dining, but she insists that she must see you, and that she will not stir until she has.'

A Person? Whom would Mrs Trent dismiss so cavalierly? Could it be that Lizzie?

'Where is she?' I demanded, dabbing my lips and preparing to rise.

'In the hallway, sir.'

'Is she respectable?'

Her slight bow suggested that the woman would not have penetrated beyond the door had she not been.

'Pray show her into my study. I will speak to her immediately.'

To my amazement – and, I admit, my profound disappointment – my late visitor was none other that Mrs Jenkins. She had been tricked out in some gown far too large for her, and looked more waiflike than a child. Neither was she perfectly clean. No wonder Mrs Trent had been apprehensive.

'Pray take a seat, Mrs Jenkins,' I said, bowing over her hand.

To my horror, she fell instead at my feet. 'Please forgive him! I don't know what came into his head! William didn't mean it, your honour, and I can't bear to think of him hanged!'

'Enough! Enough! Pray, Mrs Jenkins, rise.'

She clutched at my knees. 'For God's sake!'

'Please! I must insist you stop this.' Extricating myself with some difficulty I rang the bell. 'Some wine, please,' I told a startled Susan, 'for Mrs Jenkins and myself. Now, please, be seated, and tell me what young William has done.'

She at last understood that I wished her to compose herself, which she did with difficulty. Knowing that Susan would re-appear at any moment, I did not press her to embark on what I suspected would be a difficult narrative.

At last – I noticed that Mrs Trent had sent in the third-best glasses – I persuaded her to take some wine.

'I deduce that William is in some sort of trouble?'

'The worst! The very worst! And only you can save him from the noose!'

She was too distressed for me to discuss the finer points of the law. 'I will do everything in my power,' I said quietly. 'You have my word. Mrs Jenkins – Maggie! Tell me what troubles you.'

'They've taken him – he'll be up before the Assizes and be hanged!' she sobbed.

'Whatever he has done, of course I will speak up for him. Dr Hansard will no doubt add his voice to mine. But pray, Mrs Jenkins – what crime has he committed?'

'A watch, sir. He had stolen a watch. The master found it on him tonight, when he came back from working on your land. He searches all the lads, and takes what you have given them.'

'He steals from them! My God, the justices shall hear of this!' But such indignation was academic as far as Mrs Jenkins was concerned.

'My boy – you know he's a good lad, sir. And they say there's blood on the watch, and he must have hurt the owner when he took it from him. Pray, Mr Campion, what am I to do?'

I knew of only one answer. 'We must send for Dr Hansard.'

# CHAPTER NINE

I reeled from the stench, pressing my handkerchief to my mouth. Even Dr Hansard took a step back. To think that any human being should be kept in such conditions, let alone a child!

We had set out for Warwick at first light to see what could be done for William Jenkins, his mother having perforce returned to the workhouse. To our horror we had found him confined in semi-darkness with adults, many of them hardened criminals, I feared, awaiting their trial.

The gaoler shook his keys. 'Was you wishing to speak to the lad or not, gents?'

'Emphatically yes,' I said. 'But equally emphatically not here in the common cell! You must have a room where—'

'There's my office. But—' The offer hung tantalisingly in the air.

Hansard spoke before I could fumble coins into the man's hands. 'A justice of the peace does not need to give bribes, man. We will adjourn to your office. Now, man.'

Within seconds, William was plucked from the unspeakable mire, which still clung to his clothes and bare feet, and dragged into the comparative comfort of the gaoler's office. At least there was a fire burning sluggishly in a once handsome fireplace, but that merely served to accentuate the odour he brought with him. He would need another session under a pump to return him to a civilised state.

He fell at my feet, much as his mother had done, his tear-streaked face upraised to mine. It was hard to make out exactly what he said, his voice hoarse with tears and his thin body racked with sobs. 'I didn't mean, I didn't – I – I—!'

I bent to pull him to his feet. 'I'm sure you didn't, William.' Over my shoulder I said, 'Gaoler, some bread and milk if you please. Well, man, what are you waiting for?'

'Can't leave the prisoner,' he said stolidly.

'And are you imagining a justice of the peace and a man of the cloth will spirit him away?' Hansard demanded. 'Go – before I report you! Now, William,' he asked in his kindest tone, 'what do you want to say? Slowly!'

This time William took a deep breath and straightened his shoulders. 'I didn't do it!'

'What didn't you do?' I asked.

'Steal a watch.'

Hansard's eyes met mine over the boy's head. How on earth could we save him from the gallows if the jury thought otherwise?

'I *found* it. I found it in your woods, Parson. Only Old Bully Bulstrode, he searched me for the pennies you pay us and found it in my pocket. The watch. I would have given it over, Parson, honest!'

To my shame, I suspended judgement on that assertion.

William sensed the need for some corroboration. 'I'd have shown it to you when you taught us our letters!'

'Why did you not show it to Mr Ford, the steward? He can

read and would have understood the importance of the find.' I said.

The child shifted from foot to foot. What was he trying to hide, when for a moment he had been winning me round?

'And where is the watch now?' Hansard asked.

'Locked up as evidence,' said the gaoler, returning with a chipped mug and hunk of bread, which he deposited on a corner of his filthy desk.

'May I see it?' Hansard asked. It was a question expecting a positive response. 'Do I have to ask again?' he thundered.

William, clearly desperate to reach for the sustenance, quailed under the anger, despite the fact that it was not directed at him, and withdrew his hand. The gaoler moved with what he no doubt regarded as fitting and injured dignity. Taking from his pocket a heavy bunch of keys on a chain attached to his leather belt, he ponderously made his way to a floor-to-ceiling cupboard. I had seen the Kemble brothers on the London stage, and neither had a better sense of timing than this brute of a man. In a terror of suspense, we all watched as he fitted a key to the lock, discarding it as the wrong one.

At last realising that to protract his moment of glory might result in trouble, he selected another key and opened the door, ferreting within for a strong box.

Forestalling another histrionic display, I said, in my father's voice and tone, 'I do not intend to wait all day, my man.' Three pairs of eyes shot to my face. Was it shame or even – disgraceful in the circumstances – amusement that I felt at the impersonation?

At last the watch was placed ceremoniously on Hansard's

outstretched palm. It was gold, shining unabated in the dimness of the vile room, despite the mud still adhering to it.

'Is there an inscription inside?' I asked, a resumption of my bored drawl masking my excitement.

'I told you, there's letters what you taught us!' William put in eagerly. 'But the writing's all fancy.'

'And in Latin,' Hansard added, looking at me over his spectacles.

'And what might it say? In the King's English, if you don't mind!' said the gaoler.

'I do mind,' I snapped. 'Dr Hansard, a translation might embarrass me and would make our friend none the wiser. The gist is,' I added more graciously, 'that my grandfather presented the watch to me, on the occasion of my twenty-first birthday.' I gave the date.

Hansard opened it, carefully removing a scrap of leaf-mould. At last he nodded, amusement chasing interest around his craggy features. 'The very same.' He pointed it out for the gaoler's benefit.

The gaoler responded by clipping William's ear. 'Steal from a man of the cloth, would you, you varmint! Well, I hope they hangs you good and high, that's all I can say.'

'On the contrary,' I said, drawing William closer to me, whence he could reach for the bread, which, notwithstanding his filthy hands, he tore and crammed into his mouth. Mastication was inhibited by gaps where his milk teeth had not yet been replaced by an adult set. 'In fact, far from being punished, William shall receive a reward. A footpad stole the watch from me some weeks ago. Clearly he realised that the inscription made it a liability rather than an asset, and threw it into what was then impenetrable undergrowth on my glebe land. William was one of a party from the workhouse clearing scrub. He tells the simple truth when he said he found it.'

'So why didn't he hand it over to the workhouse master of his own free will?'

'Clearly you did not hear him telling you that he wanted to show it to me so that I could decipher the inscription. Very well, I think we have completed our business here.' William grasped my hand in terror. 'Dr Hansard, you will know the procedure for securing William's instant release. Gaoler, pray return the lad's belongings.'

'Belongings! Him! Came in just like this, didn't he?'

'He was wearing boots last time I saw him,' I said. Then I thought better of arguing. The lad would have grown since he had first been equipped. 'Find him some pattens, if you please. William, part of your reward will be a new pair of boots.'

Jem, who had been walking my gig's horses during our visit to the gaol, greeted William as an old friend, rolling him up in a horse blanket and hauling him up to sit beside him. 'Pshaw, lad, you stink,' he said.

The child shivered violently, either reacting to the ordeal he had undergone or fearing cold water.

Jem rubbed his filthy head affectionately. 'We'll have to see if Mrs Trent or Mrs Beckles can't find something warmer than pump water to wash you with. And then, with luck, more breeches from Lady Elham's clothes basket for you.'

Dr Hansard caught my eye. 'Perhaps not a bad suggestion,' he said very casually. 'Mrs Beckles has a way with children, no doubt about that.'

'And she will have some nourishing broth at hand,' I

agreed, with a serene smile, as if Mrs Trent had never produced such a comestible. 'But first, I see a bootmaker's over there...'

'Not returning, Mr Campion! Not until the spring at the earliest!' Mrs Beckles declared, busying herself with clothing from the poor basket that might fit William. We were all in the Priory scullery, where Jem was sluicing William with water heated in the washing boiler.

I stared at her, unable to believe my ears. 'Such a long absence,' I managed.

She nodded as if she herself did not believe what she was saying. 'Only two days ago Lady Elham notified me that she had changed her mind and that she would after all spend the festive season here! The carol-singers, the mummers – thanks to you, all are prepared!' she continued. 'The chef, the kitchen staff – everyone is at sixes and sevens. First there was to be nothing to do, then we were to hold the usual feast. Now we are to put Holland covers over all the furniture and mothball the hangings.' She spoke with a mixture of exasperation and disappointment. 'So goodness knows when we shall see her or Lizzie again.'

'Indeed!' I managed to say.

Hansard declared, 'I am sure that young William is clean enough now, Jem. Can you help him into his new clothes?'

Jem obliged.

A silence deepened around us. Hansard, his voice over-bright, said, 'Good fellow. Now let us go forthwith. His mother must be in agonies waiting for our return.'

She must be indeed. So why had three grown men neglected

to give the poor woman a thought until now?

We had a curious, three-cornered conversation on the way home. William was wise enough to remain silent, and was in any case too occupied with the cold pie Mrs Beckles had pressed on him as a parting gift. But it was only right to involve Jem, who might have ideas of his own about the best form of reward for the boy.

'You mustn't spoil the lad, or raise false expectations,' he said. I wondered if he spoke from bitter experience. 'What I would do is this...'

'A place of my own!' I believe that had not Dr Hansard been at hand, Mrs Jenkins must have not only staggered but actually fallen. He guided her carefully to one of the few chairs in the workhouse master's office, and wafted a vinaigrette under her nose.

I nodded. Jem had reminded us of a tiny cottage which my predecessor had once used as a byre. 'It is not a fine palace, Mrs Jenkins, and I fear it will need a great deal of work before you and your family can move in,' I told her. 'I will waive the rent for a year and a day, after which, should you have the means, I shall expect a regular, if small, sum. There is enough land for an industrious family to grow sufficient food for themselves, and I will provide seeds and some hens.' That was what Jem had suggested, in lieu of a financial reward, which, he averred, Mrs Jenkins would have no idea of managing. He had some doubts about her ability to run her tiny smallholding, but agreed that some of the men my steward employed on my behalf might be expected to do the heavier digging until William were able.

'For the slops they've had to live on, it's surprising young William can lift his hand to pick his nose,' he had observed.

'Please, your honour, can we not move in now, as it is?' she pleaded.

I spread my hands. 'The roof leaks, there is no door, there is no glass in the windows. The whole place is caked with cow dung. How could you possibly move in?'

She shook her head dumbly. After a moment, she whispered, 'We'd be together, sir.'

'How could she dream of living in what is little more than a hut?' I demanded in something like irritation, as we tooled back from the workhouse, myself handling the ribbons. It was as if Mrs Jenkins' disappointment had crept into my veins.

'Impossible – in this cold!' Hansard snapped.

'Hard but not impossible, begging your pardons,' Jem cut in. 'If you pulled the men out of your woodland today and set them all to work on the byre, they could make it weatherproof at least.'

'But a mud floor!'

Hansard stroked his chin. 'Consider in what condition you first met them, Tobias. One might have said that animals would have disdained such a place. But she contrived to raise her little brood there.'

'I cannot let it be said that I let anyone quit the shelter of the workhouse for such a place!'

'It won't be such a place if you accept Jem's advice. Talk to Ford today, and they could be rehoused by Friday. I warrant Mrs Beckles could lay her hands on a few sticks of furniture and a pan or two. In fact, I'll ride back myself to ask her.'

Jem pulled the gig to a halt by the stables. Dr Hansard suited the deed to his words, mounting his horse the moment Jem had saddled it and riding forth like a lover half his age. Jem and I exchanged a dour grin.

While he was rubbing down the horses, I brought him a tankard of ale. 'A strange business, up at the Priory,' I suggested.

'They say her ladyship's ever been prone to such fancies,' he said, paying particular attention to the hind leg furthest from me. 'And it isn't as if she's only the one place to live, is it, now?'

'No, indeed.' What we both hoped, but neither said, was that Dr Hansard might elicit more information from Mrs Beckles and indeed the other servants if he was on his own. 'I must make arrangements about that cottage,' I said, as another silence grew between us.

'Aye,' he said, as if he were as glad to be rid of me as I to be free of his – indeed, of anyone's – company. What in my heart I wanted was a period of quiet reflection, or at least a physical vent for my feelings, like rubbing down a whole team of horses. What I must have was a colloquy with my steward, whom I eventually ran to earth in the Silent Woman, a smoke-filled den no larger than Mrs Trent's kitchen.

'So this is how you manage my lands, Mr Ford! This is how you supervise gangs of men and boys put to clear it. This is how a child finds a valuable item and knows no one to show it to – with the direst of consequences!'

He staggered to his feet. 'Mr Campion – I—'

'Outside, now! Unless you prefer I should drag you out myself? And then have the pleasure of horsewhipping you?'

I stood with my back to the sun, so he had the added disadvantage of having to squint at me. I could also see the deep creases and growth of stubble. He looked less like my man of business than one of the labourers he was supposed to be supervising. He shook constantly, and though he tried to cover his mouth with one trembling hand, I caught sickening waves of gin fumes.

My father, had he ever seen his vastly superior steward in such a state, would undoubtedly have dismissed him on the spot. My anger was such that I was ready to do the same. But obscurely I recognised that Ford was not the entire cause of my anger, perhaps not even the major part. My father's steward too would have had a deputy who was more than capable of taking over the estate and maintaining its superlative standards. He had, after all, been a disciple of Mr Coke of Holkham. But – having been remiss in failing to act after our first falling-out – to whom would I turn if I dismissed this poor specimen? Was he better than the nothing I would be left with if, as I was perfectly entitled to do, I despatched him from post and home alike this very day? More to the point, Christmas was almost upon us, and how could a man of God make a family homeless at such a season?

I looked him up and down. 'Go home and put your head under the pump. I will see you at four o'clock.'

By then I might have made a decision. If only this were a matter on which I might consult Jem or Hansard. Only then did I recall that there was something more pressing to do. 'The moment you're sober, take the men from the West Copse down to the old byre. I want it habitable – by humans – by Friday noon. You – and all the men – will work by lamplight if necessary. And the boys from the workhouse can help too. It is to be a palace. In fact,' I smiled, but grimly, 'we will postpone our talk until Friday at four. Be off with you.'

My continuing anger could only be assuaged by a fierce walk, so I set off I knew not in which direction. But soon I realised that I was heading towards the woodland where I had last met Matthew. If I had hated hearing of Lizzie's continued absence in so bald a way, how would he feel if the news came without warning – in the inn, or in the servants' hall? I turned my footsteps into the woods, calling from time to time.

I found him in the same walk as I, apparently heading for home, his gun under one arm and a brace of pigeons in his right hand.

He greeted me with the politeness of one not particularly wanting his solitude disturbed.

So I came quickly to the point. 'Matthew, I have two pieces of news for you. The first is good, the second profoundly disappointing for you, I fear.'

'And what might that one be?' he asked truculently.

'It concerns Lizzie. Mrs Beckles tells me that she and Lady Elham will not after all be home for Christmas.'

He paled under his tan, but asked casually, 'I thought her ladyship planned to return?'

'Exactly so. But apparently Lady Elham took a sudden fancy to spend the festive season at another of her houses. I am very sorry.'

'Just like that?'

'Just like that. I had asked her, since the celebrations would be much curtailed, if her servants could be given longer holidays, but it seems she left no instructions for that. Matthew, I believe Lizzie had no choice in the matter.'

He spat. 'Which of us does? Not John Coachman. You know he had to turn out at six at night when with his rheumatics he should have been at home with his wife by the fire, not driving God knows how far with only the moon for light? She's not heard from him since, not a word.'

How could I defend Lady Elham? But how many times had my family and I demanded on a whim the services of coachman, valet or abigail? How many times had dinner had to be held back because one of us could not make the effort to be on time, or brought forward because of a whim to visit the theatre? And how many times had I given peremptory orders like those I had given to Ford, but with far less justification?

I said humbly, 'But there is good news too. The footpad to whom you gave chase thought better of stealing my watch.'

He turned incredulously. 'It has been found?'

'It has indeed. And by none other than young William Jenkins. He was one of the work party clearing my woods,' I added, when Matthew did not speak. To fill the continuing silence I told him of William's arrest, and the conditions in the gaol from which we had rescued him.

'At least he's got a new pair of boots and some of Lady Elham's clothing for his pains,' I concluded.

'Why the poor basket?'

If I had answered him truly, my answer would not have pleased him. He did not need to know I went in the hopes of hearing news of his betrothed.

'I knew there would be something there to fit him. At some

point in the gaol he'd been stripped almost naked. And though I could have shopped for new attire in Warwick, I thought of his mother waiting for news of him.' May God forgive me my lie.

Matthew nodded absently. As if he had forgotten my presence he started to walk back towards the road.

I fell into step with him. 'And soon,' I added, 'he will have a new home.'

That stopped him in his tracks. 'How so?'

'The family cannot live as they are, separated from each other, ill-fed, unhappy. You will recall an old cottage on my glebe lands—'

'That's scarce fit for animals, let alone humans!'

'I know it. But by the end of the week it will have a new roof and everything in my power to make it habitable. So some good has come of it all.' Why did I need this man's approval? Even as I spoke, I heard a note of pleading in my voice.

'So it has,' he said quietly. 'I'll bid you good afternoon, then, Parson.'

# CHAPTER TEN

When a peace-making letter arrived from my mother, begging me to return to Derbyshire for Christmas, I was sorely tempted to accept her invitation. But how could a shepherd abandon his flock at such a season? Wolves might not prowl the environs of Moreton St Jude, but poverty and sickness did. Furthermore, even if I had had time to recruit a temporary replacement – and I knew from my days at Cambridge that there were many poor Fellows who would have been delighted to earn a little money – I did not wish to fail the mummers and the carol-singers who were sadly disappointed by my cousin's continued absence.

Most important, this was the first Christmas I could worship in my own church, leading what I knew was a growing congregation and hoped would be larger yet. There would be midnight Communion for those minded to present themselves at the Lord's Table. I had also arranged a service in the early afternoon of Christmas Day itself, asking all to attend so that they might give thanks for the events of the forthcoming evening.

In Lady Elham's absence, on Mrs Beckles' instructions, Gaston and Cook had prepared a feast for all the estate workers to be held, despite her ladyship's original instructions to the contrary, in the great hall. We all agreed that what the head did not know, the heart could not worry about. When I realised that a few of the villagers would be excluded from the treat, I prevailed on my good friend, who in truth needed no persuasion, to extend the invitation to all. Farmer Bulmer contributed two sides of beef, and Mr Miller enough flour for all to have fine white bread for a change. Other families contributed what food and drink they could. Dr Hansard and I had undertaken to provide small gifts for all the children.

'I only wish,' Edmund said, 'that such benevolence might be continued throughout the year and extend beyond enough food and drink to render an army bilious to decent roofs and fair wages. Look at them all, tugging their forelocks and curtsying as if the King himself were here.'

'To my mind Mrs Beckles is worth ten of the proper hostess,' I declared, pot valiant, 'and even Mr Davies is a better host than our new lord.'

Hansard regarded me over the rim of his glass. 'Indeed. I wonder where Elham spends his Christmas.'

I could do no more than shrug; I could hardly tell him that when I wrote to decline my parents' invitation, I had asked if his whereabouts might be known. There was, after all, a tenuous family connection, and in any case, doings in one quarter of the *ton* usually became common knowledge to the rest.

Grateful for their generosity in proffering the olive branch, I had responded with a communication full of my news, which must have cost my mother two or three florins to receive. To my enormous surprise, she responded with vigour, and we embarked on a correspondence that gave me, at least, every satisfaction.

'And her ladyship?' he pursued.

'I believe Mrs Beckles may know her whereabouts,' I replied, happy to give him a further excuse to talk to her.

With a smile on my face, I turned to others in the room, determined that none, especially Jem or Matthew, should suspect the sadness, even despair, in my heart. I had no right to blight their seasonal good cheer with my own sorrow, despite a suspicion I could not deny that I would never see my beloved Lizzie again. I could understand why she had not written if to me – that was beyond the bounds of my hopes – but she should have communicated with Mrs Beckles, to whom she owed so much. Lady Elham, deciding for some inexplicable reason to rent a house in Bath, insisted in a letter to Mrs Beckles that both were enjoying the sights of that city, and would think of me when they worshipped in the cathedral. Bath! When a lady of her rank might stay anywhere! It might once have been fashionable, but now had a sadly *passé* air, the beau monde turning their backs on it as too provincial and too damp, whatever the healing reputation of its waters.

If Mrs Beckles was concerned, she gave no sign of it now. The mummers had acted, the carol-singers had given of their lusty best, and now a couple of fiddlers had taken themselves up on to an impromptu stage. She smiled as one knowing that she had done her very best and accomplished it without anyone realising the effort it must have cost. In the absence of her ladyship and her son, I insisted it was she who with Dr Hansard should open the dance. I sought the hand of Mrs

Jenkins, as wide-eyed with wonder as her children, all of whom, despite what I would have considered the still primitive conditions of what they now proudly called their cottage, were visibly happier, and, to my eyes, slightly less thin. Mrs Jenkins had no notion of dancing, but I grasped her firmly and whirled her around, just as many men were whirling their partners. It was not elegant, it was not decorous, but it was great fun.

In the midst of it all, I saw Dr Hansard slip away, his face no longer convivial. Indeed, such was his solemnity that I returned Mrs Jenkins to her bench with a courtly bow and followed.

A temporary nursery had been established in the room I used as my schoolroom, so that those mothers with babes in arms and children too young to enjoy all the jollity could take it in turns to care for the whole group. The woman on duty now, one of Farmer Gates' brood, had been more conscientious than most, walking up and down between the pallets on which her and her friends' children lay to see that they were settled. But one was too peaceful.

Edmund Hansard had him in his arms now, his puny namesake, and tears were running down his old cheeks onto the young ones. But there was no complaint from the babe. The Almighty had chosen this of all the nights in the year to call little Edmund home.

The babe's was not the only death to cast a pall over the village. Soon there came news from Lady Elham that John Coachman had taken a chill, which had gone to his lungs, with fatal consequences. Mrs Sanderson – some were surprised to know that John had a more conventional surname – reeled when I visited her with Mrs Beckles to break the news.

'But he was so well! He had his rheumatics, but you'd expect that in a man of near sixty out in all weathers. A chill!' she repeated, between sobs.

In any extraordinary act of kindness, her ladyship offered to send her travelling carriage to take the widow – to Bath for the funeral.

'How could I go that far?' Mrs Sanderson demanded. 'And in her ladyship's coach, dressed like this? And to leave now! A hundred miles!'

In vain did we try to persuade her. All too predictably, she could not comprehend the possibility of travelling so far, even in a luxurious coach.

At least she had some consolation. Her ladyship had also promised that she would not be thrown out of her home of thirty years, although it was a tied cottage. Mrs Sanderson was unable to read the letter herself, but pressed it into my hand for confirmation of what Mrs Beckles had read. What neither of us cared to add at this stage was that the arrangement could only be provisional. It depended, of course, on the agreement of Lord Elham, who was currently travelling abroad.

Mrs Beckles' eyes met mine: we both hoped devoutly that his lordship might be delayed indefinitely. In the meantime, Mrs Sanderson need not hear of the proviso until she was over the shock.

* * *

And so the winter limped on, the roads still frozen in iron-hard ruts. It was impossible to till the earth, or to extract any root crops from it. There must have been death from hunger, had it not been for the charity and hard work of the more fortunate of my parishioners, whom I exhorted each week from the pulpit to share what little they had. Yeoman farmers, landed gentry and even members of the minor aristocracy volunteered or were morally coerced into giving bread and soup. Mrs Beckles contrived daily to feed what Lady Elham, still sojourning in Bath, insisted must be only the deserving poor. Mr Woodvine, the new butler, abetted her, sending good port wine into households where yet another invalid was struggling to recover. When either turned to me for a decision whether such and such were deserving, my reply was always the same: 'Tell me which of my parishioners deserves to starve to death.'

Soon they did not bother to ask. Nor did they ask where the extra supplies of warm clothing sprang from. I would have told them that a great lady of my acquaintance had heard of the villagers' plight; I would not have told them that the lady in question was my mother, who, alas, had so far failed to obtain hard news of the Elhams, mother or son. Even with all this charity, no villager exactly prospered, but at least few were forced into the workhouse and no one starved.

Elsewhere in the country, we heard with a shudder, there were more Corn Riots.

'Did you ever hear the like?' Dr Hansard demanded, removing his spectacles and using them to tap the offending headline. 'They're bringing out the militia and telling them to fire upon their fellow men!'

I turned away, unable to speak.

'Why can they not see that if the people did not starve, they would be peaceable? It may be good for the souls of the rich to dispense largesse, but is it good for the souls of the poor receiving it? And what of those villages with no wealthy patron? How are they to survive? Workhouses must be overflowing!' he continued, rumbling on in similar vein until I had composed myself again. 'And do not tell me that people would rather work hard for a living wage than be pauperised! Look at your Mrs Jenkins. She toils from dawn to dusk – never were there chickens more cosseted, I dare swear, but she is happy to do it because their eggs are feeding her children and bringing in a steady – if pitifully small – income.'

'If only I could have done more with her cottage,' I fretted. 'I once condemned my father for his wickedness in uprooting a whole village so that he might build a fashionable folly. But at least he replaced the apologies for dwellings – they were nearly as bad as those at Marsh Bottom – with good, sound cottages. Each had its own pump, there were proper ashpits, and every family had enough land to grow a year-long supply of vegetables and keep a pig. Aye, and he provided a church, a school and an inn.'

'A model village, in other words?'

I nodded. 'I thought it stiff and ugly at first. But now I know what the picturesque conceals. The folly of our artists to hail tumbledown, higgledy-piggledy slums as romantic!'

Glancing at me from under his eyebrows, he got up to pour me another glass of wine. 'Come, Tobias, it is many weeks since I let you beat me at billiards. I have had a fire burning in the billiards room all day in hopes that you will do so this time without my assistance.'

But I could not be comforted with a game of billiards every day, not when news came from Lady Elham in a letter with neither address nor date that shocked us all to the core. Lizzie was never coming back!

'The wench has taken it into her head to leave my service for that of a lady living a less retired life,' she wrote indignantly to Mrs Beckles. 'And to London she must go, to my cousin, Lady Templemead. In vain have I remonstrated her, reminded her of what she owes me and my family, and not least my dear cousin Campion, who taught her her letters. No doubt she will write to you when she has time. But I should warn you that she is not the Lizzie Woodman whom we once held in the highest regard.'

'And you, poor Mr Campion,' Mrs Beckles said, 'will no doubt take upon yourself the unhappy task of breaking the news to the other pretenders to her hand, Matthew and Jem.'

'Jem?' I repeated, sitting down sharply.

'My dear Tobias,' she said gently, removing the letter from my nerveless fingers and substituting a glass of wine, 'you and Matthew are not the only ones who carried a torch for her. Can you not think of the times Jem insisted you come here by gig, as befitting a gentleman, so that you did not have to present yourself at dinner in your riding boots? Why do you think he should want to spend an evening in the servants' hall, when he might have been snug in his own quarters? Oh, you gentlemen – you're so blind!'

I blushed deeply. I had thought his concern was as always for me, and once or twice had absolutely forbidden him to turn out with me. And on other occasions, thinking he enjoyed Dr Hansard's valet Turner's company as much as I enjoyed the master's, I had veritably prised him out. Then I recalled the day of Jenkins' death. 'I did see a look exchanged between them… But Matthew! Was she not pledged to Matthew?'

'In his mind at least. But I believe that as soon as she and Jem set eyes upon each other they fell in love.' She sighed at the thought of their romance.

'But he is even older than I!'

'When did love ever look at a calendar?' she asked. But she looked away quickly.

I felt unequal to broaching the matter of her and Dr Hansard. Gathering my hat and my riding cloak – this was a journey on which Jem had not pressed to accompany me – I pressed her hand in farewell.

'I have no need to ask you to be gentle with the lads,' she said, returning the pressure. 'And in any case, they will have ways to dealing with their emotions. I see a whole forest of trees succumbing to Matthew's axe – his aunt will not need any more logs for weeks. Jem will make sure your horses glow, so make sure Titus is muddy enough to justify his exertions. And you – you, Tobias – what will you do?' To my surprise, she enfolded me in her arms as my nurse was used to do. At last pushing me on my way, with a little squeeze of the shoulders, she said, 'You will behave as the Stoic Dr Hansard says you are. You will be all sympathy and compassion and ask nothing for yourself.'

'There is one other person who deserves to know the news,'

I remembered. 'Mrs Woodman. I hardly know the lady. She is a Methodist, I believe, and does not hold with me.'

'But you still made sure she received extra fuel when the frost set in.'

I gave a shamefaced smile. 'Perhaps that was not in the interests of Christian forgiveness, but more because she was Lizzie's mother.'

'Would you prefer that I broke the news to her?'

'I would indeed.'

Matthew flung his axe down so hard it quivered inches deep into the tree stump. Then he turned on me. 'I knew as how all that learning would turn out, making her dissatisfied with her lot. I knew it! And 'tis all your meddlesome teaching, Parson!'

'You do not think that having seen life in a city, she has become dissatisfied with a country existence? She may also feel that if she earns more, she can send more home to her mother and be able to find Susan a better place than in a country parsonage. But if it is my doing, Matthew, I ask your pardon. And beg you to believe it was never my intention.' Never did I speak more sincerely.

By way of reply, he turned and punched the nearest tree.

'I do not have the address of her new employer,' I said. 'But I could write to Lady Elham on your behalf, and ask her to forward a letter asking her to write to you.'

'Much good it would do, seeing as I can't read,' he spat.

'You deserve to hear in her own words why she made the decision,' I urged.

'And who would read it to me? You, you, with your fine letters!'

'I would have thought Mrs Beckles would be the one best fitted to deliver her sentiments, not the man you see – quite wrongly – as the cause of your distress.'

His face still averted, he said, his voice thick with tears, 'In that case, Parson, I would be indebted if you would write to her.'

Without wishing to intrude further on his grief, I walked off in silence.

Breaking the news to Jem was a different matter. Matthew was an accredited suitor, but Jem and she had had but an illicit romance, if such indeed it was. Jem and I had been friends as boys, when there was no social chasm to divide, and cricket bats and fishing rods to unite us. We had rescued each other from many scrapes. Our friendship had even survived my time at Eton. But our ways had diverged when I went up to Cambridge and his becoming my groom set us irretrievably apart. Could I for a moment recapture our previous innocence?

At this time of day he would be mucking out the stables, so I changed from my clerical garb and donned boots to join him.

He raised an eyebrow, and grinned, but threw me a shovel without comment. I filled the wheelbarrow; he trundled it away and emptied it. Together we completed the task in no time, a fact I celebrated by fetching a couple of tankards of Mrs Trent's homebrew from the kitchen.

We moved into the lea of the stables, warmed by a feeble sun.

'Got yourself in a scrape, have you?' he asked, touching his tankard against mine. It was an expression he had often used when we were lads together.

'Not me. I'm worried, that's all. About Lizzie Woodman.'

'What's wrong with her?' he asked swiftly.

'Nothing yet, as far as I know. But I always worry when a country-raised girl decides to seek her fortune in London, and according to Lady Elham that is what Lizzie proposes.'

'Is she out of her mind?'

Did he mean Lizzie or her ladyship? I waited in silence.

'Has she simply quit her ladyship's service or has she found other employment to go to?'

'Lady Elham tells me she has gone to her cousin, Lady Templemead. Even so…'

'Even so indeed.' He spat. ''Tis a bad business, but it could be worse. She did not write directly to you, Toby?'

'No, indeed. She has not written even to Mrs Beckles. It was Lady Elham who told her.'

'What is she thinking of?' he asked harshly. 'Her friends deserve better than that. I had not thought it of her.'

I had not expected him to sound so censorious, though he had always been the first to speak plainly if my conduct was ever found lacking. But as I took the tankards to return them to the kitchen, I caught sight of his face. His gruffness had been an attempt to conceal his tears.

If I could not write directly to Lizzie, I had every right to ask my cousin for further details, a plan which met with Mrs Beckles' instant approval. We hoped that Lady Elham would write back by return. She did not. Days merged into weeks, and weeks into a month. Still there was no news.

'No doubt she's gone up to London for the start of the season,' I said, as Mrs Beckles commiserated with me.

'But surely she's left directions with her Bath household for her correspondence to be forwarded to her.'

'You would have thought so.' I grew restless, thinking I might go down to the capital myself.

But I did not, because my parish duties increased. In the icy weather, even the most reluctant family conceded that it was worth sending their children to my school if only to get them from under their feet. They also knew there would be warmth and a solid meal for the little scholars. I divided the lessons between letters and numbers, ending each morning with a lesson from the Bible.

'And do you charge them?' Mrs Beckles demanded, arriving as I was waving the last child off.

'A halfpenny a month,' I conceded. 'And another halfpenny when the child can read and write his name. Mrs Beckles, there is so much more I could do! If there were space, Mrs Trent could teach the girls to sew, or to cook.'

She smiled. 'I think your master must be proud of you,' she said affectionately.

'The bishop?' I asked, suppressing a sharp reply that as far as I could see he cared nothing for any of those he had ordained, especially some of the curates whose pitiful stipends were on a level with farm labourers'.

'No, your Master! The One who told His disciples to suffer little children to come unto Him. Now, Tobias, I want you to look over my shoulder. What do you see?'

I blinked. 'The sky?'

'Exactly. And what colour is it?'

'Blue.'

By now she was laughing. 'So what should you do? You should go out and enjoy what nature has to offer. Wrap up warm, for the wind is still chill, and enjoy yourself.'

'But—'

'Go and do as you're told, for once, my lad.'

It was the first of many solitary walks. As the weather grew insensibly more benign, and the frost began to lift, I ranged further and further afield, taking an interest in the changes about me. How different was this Warwickshire spring from the much later ones I had been used to in Derbyshire. Despite the cold, the trees were coming much earlier into bud, and the fields were greening before – I should imagine – the snow had left the Peaks. I was especially charmed by the birds, increasingly frantic in their courtship and nesting, though my own heart remained empty, hollow.

'You should make a study of them, Tobias,' Edmund said one night as I enthused about the structure of a robin's nest I had come across.

'It would be a gentlemanly occupation, would it not?'

'It would be better than that. It would be a scientific one, and add to the sum of human knowledge.'

I nodded. If both Dr Hansard and Mrs Beckles thought I needed fresh air and a new interest, who was I to argue?

And so began one of the most fascinating episodes of my life. And then, though I was as yet in blissful ignorance, by far the worst.

* * *

At last I received a letter from Lady Elham, also undated and without an address. She was sorry to tell me, she said, that Lizzie had not taken advantage of her place in Lady Templemead's establishment for long. She had told her new employer that she was homesick, and had left by stagecoach for Warwick, from where she hoped to obtain a lift to Moreton St Jude from a farmer or a carrier. However, she added, Lady Templemead knew not whether to believe this, as a footman had disappeared from her service the day Lizzie left. She believed that far from being in Warwickshire, Lizzie was in an illicit embrace.

Lady Elham still clung, she declared, to the belief that Lizzie missed her family and friends. She hoped I would remind Lizzie of her good fortune in being taken up as an abigail to a lady of fashion, and not live to repent the folly in giving up such a situation.

Lizzie on her way home! My heart rejoiced, even if my head insisted it was a most unlikely possibility.

'But this time I would leave it to you, my dear Mrs Beckles, to tell my rivals in love,' I declared. 'For I could not wish them well with an honest heart.'

For several moments I did not notice the disquiet in her eyes. At last she said, 'I wonder when she set out. And I wonder why she has not safely arrived.'

'She's a country girl, born and bred. She will not mind a long walk if she finds no cart coming this way.'

'Of course she won't.' But the look of foreboding did not leave her face.

'What is it you fear?'

She turned from me, pacing her parlour in her agitation.

'Her ladyship does not tell us when she set out, but it was clearly an accomplished fact when she wrote. So why is there no sign of the poor child?'

I rode to Leamington and then with increasing desperation to Warwick, just in case her ladyship had made a mistake as to the destination. But there was no sign of Lizzie ever having travelled by stage or even post to either town. She had simply disappeared.

Lady Elham, to whom I wrote in haste, replied at leisure that Lady Templemead had retired to one of her West Country estates, she knew not which one, but she would write to her at once. But did I not realise, she asked, why girls usually left good places? Reliable as Lizzie had once been, she suspected that Lady Templemead's fears were fulfilled, that Lizzie's head had indeed been turned by one of her fellow servants and – to put the matter crudely – the girl had probably found herself in a promising way. Perhaps she had persuaded the man to marry her; perhaps not. It was likely that in either case she had been too ashamed to confess the matter to Lady Templemead. If that turned out to be the case, she would wash her hands of the girl, and so should we.

'Any other girl and I might have believed it,' Mrs Beckles sighed. 'But not Lizzie. She had too many scruples, too much loyalty, to embark on such a flirtation.'

'But it might not have been a flirtation,' I said, reminding her of the then Lord Chartham's assault upon her. 'It might have been far worse.'

'It might indeed. She wouldn't be the first young woman to

be forcibly deflowered and then discarded.' She turned to me and took my hands. 'My poor Tobias, what are you going to tell the others?'

'God help me, I don't know,' I confessed, and fell sobbing into her arms.

# CHAPTER ELEVEN

More and more I turned to the study of ornithology to comfort my aching heart, the innocence of my new feathered friends compensating in part for the woes of my human ones. How Matthew and Jem dealt with their grief, I respected them too much to ask, Mrs Beckles having kindly broken the news to them.

But by some paradox, speaking to Mrs Woodman, a woman whom I suspected of cordially despising me, had fallen to my lot. It was not, I am sure, what Mrs Beckles would have wished, but, without a word of warning, the new Lord Elham had announced a plan to return, and Mrs Beckles was manoeuvring the great house over the shoals of chaos, all too aware that by the time everything was ready he might have changed his mind.

Mrs Woodman greeted me with caution, perhaps even suspicion, not warmth. Trying to keep my voice steady, I read aloud to her Lady Elham's letter.

I expected tears, railing against an unkind world, or even cursing the Will of God, and had provided myself with a vinaigrette.

She looked slowly at the letter and then at me. Then, her whole frame shaking, she cursed Lizzie. However I had tried to dress the matter up, Mrs Woodman thought Lizzie to blame. Terrible words penetrated the inarticulate sobs. 'No daughter of mine,' I distinguished.

I tried to remonstrate. She pointed with a gnarled finger at the door. 'Leave me!'

And I did as I was bidden, fearful that I would say something I later repented.

Hardly had Lord Elham called off than his mother did indeed return. One of her first acts was to summon me. Never had her ladyship, who could, as Lizzie had once observed, charm the ducks off the water, looked more regal, so intimidating, staring down her aquiline nose.

'You should know that the wench has been found and been taken care of,' she declared, the rouge standing out on her otherwise ashen cheeks. How had her new maid allowed her to appear like this?

'Some workhouse?'

'Indeed no. And,' she added, with a smile that showed neither humour nor affection, 'I can guarantee that the babe will not be abandoned in some foundling hospital. Lady Templemead knows her duty better than that. There is one proviso, Mr Campion, to her generosity. Neither you nor any others of her suitors will attempt to find her. Or her protection will be at an end.'

'But—'

'Did I not make myself clear? Now, if you will excuse me, I have much to do.'

I managed to restrain a bark of ironic laughter. Once I might have agreed that ladies in her position had much to occupy their hands and their minds. Now I knew otherwise. It appalled me that what I would once unthinkingly have spent on a suit of not extravagant clothes would have fed a family – nay, two or three families – for a year.

On impulse I went down to see what I had come to regard as *my* little family, to see how they did in what was now less of a hovel and far more recognisable as a cottage. The thatch was waterproof, and a curl of smoke issued from the newly built chimney. There was a solid front door. From somewhere Mrs Beckles had conjured curtains, which hung cheerily at the clean glass of the windows.

Usually I crammed my pockets with sweetmeats or, on Dr Hansard's express instruction, fruit for the children; sometimes I took the luxury of some fresh new tea for Mrs Jenkins as a gift from Mrs Beckles. Occasionally they had the pleasure I found I could not deny them of giving me something in return, an egg that they could ill afford but that their dignity insisted I accept. In return I would soon offer them another gift. Mr Ford had at last found some pigs he deemed suitable, and they, not Farmer Bulmer's, would roam my glebe lands. I had resolved that the Jenkinses would have some of their first litter.

I found William chopping logs, every bit the man of the family at ten – my earlier estimate of his age had been quite inaccurate. Unlike his sisters, he still treated me with some reserve, as if embarrassed that once he had clung to me like the frightened child he was. Something had certainly happened to him, perhaps in that hell-hole of a gaol, to take the shine out of his eyes.

His mother was gathering clothes from the washing line. One day I had discovered that all she could do was spread them on bushes to dry, and had made her a gift of proper rope, which, I had had to claim, had come wrapped round a parcel. She would not have accepted it otherwise, seemingly thinking that to accept anything from me in some way compromised her. I respected her reticence, hoping one day that she would tell me shyly that she was walking out with another man. She was, after all, still in her twenties, a fact I had never grasped until I had seen her washed, with tidy hair and a gown befitting a young widow. The weight she had gained since leaving the starvation regime of the workhouse made her quite comely. Might Jem or more likely Matthew one day turn his eyes in this direction? Pray God it was only one of them, however!

'William works very hard,' I said, knowing that this would please her. 'Thank goodness we have so many trees here, Mrs Jenkins. Where I come from, the poor things are permanently bent and twisted, the wind blows so fiercely. Instead of hedges, we have dry-stone walls.'

She looked at me in disbelief, incapable it seemed of imagining anything other than this village.

'Are all the children well?'

'Pretty well, thank you, Parson. I see young Mrs Bulmer is out and about again.' She pushed a lock of hair, torn from its cap by the wind, out of her eyes.

'Yes, God be praised. And Fanny, her little daughter, is thriving.'

'Maybe it was a blessing, losing the other,' she said.

I was so taken aback, I must have stared. 'You can call a death a blessing?'

'The poor mite was bound to die, they say. And it's best it should sooner rather than later, isn't it? And if Jenkins had lived, we'd still have been back down there.' She gestured with a thick thumb towards Marsh Bottom as I tried to follow her shocking, pragmatic reasoning. 'Or more likely in the workhouse,' she conceded. 'But now we're here.' She smiled. 'And the children are thriving.' As she often did she repeated the word I had used, as if she wished to establish it was the correct one. I do not think that even if she had had the chance she would ever have found book learning easy, but she would have been a rewarding pupil.

'Are you sure William is well?' I risked. 'He seems very quiet, almost unhappy, some days.'

She attended to another errant lock of hair. 'Sometimes he shouts out at night.'

'A nightmare? A bad dream?'

'Maybe. And he cries. But he won't tell me why in the morning. He's too grown up.'

I nodded. I would ask Dr Hansard to call in next time he passed by, in the hopes that he could help with a mild sleeping draught, perhaps – though families like this did not have the luxury of physicking themselves.

Any fears I had of rivalry between Lizzie's lovers might be put to rest, as I discovered to my infinite embarrassment. Taking a walk along the river one evening, I heard a low but urgent scream. Thinking in my innocence someone was in pain, I hastened on, but even as I did so I registered that it was not that sort of scream. There it came again, and again, with a low grunting as a sort of ground-bass. Two pairs of feet in close juxtaposition told me that I must turn immediately and hasten away. My instincts bade me give no hint of what I had seen;

my conscience made me consider making such lewd behaviour a subject for my next sermon. Having at last put what I considered was sufficient distance between myself and the lovers, I paused to recover my breath. I leant on a bridge just like the one on which the late Lord Elham had met his end, and even had enough sense to test that it would take my weight. I forced myself to examine my feelings. Were they truly of disgust, or of envy? Did I not in my heart wish I could bury my longing for Lizzie between the thighs of another?

If only there were some maiden to whom I could turn my affections. My thoughts turned briefly to the charming Miss Sophie Heath, she with the violet eyes and the extraordinary interest in Burke. Had she found her belted earl, with his ten thousand a year? And had he prostrated himself before her? Did she ever think kindly of the country parson who had stood up with her at her first impromptu dance?

Behind me I could hear carefree laughter. I did not know the woman, but I knew her swain. It was Matthew. To avoid embarrassment, though I do not know which would have been the greater, mine or his, I strode off, hoping that they were so engrossed with each other they did not see me.

When I preached the following Sunday, it was not to condemn furtive couplings in a riverside bush, but to urge my listeners to ponder the meaning of true charity. It was as much for my benefit as for my parishioners'.

Try how I might, I could detect no resemblance between Susan and her lost sister. There was nothing in her voice, her face or her bearing to show the relationship. She would never be anything but short and sturdy, with a determined walk far removed from Lizzie's ladylike glide. Her voice, now under Mrs Trent's tutelage losing the strong local burr, was light, where Lizzie's had been deep. Susan's eyes were so dark a brown they were almost black, in her brown complexion. My Lizzie – but it was foolish even to think of her more, except to remember her in my prayers.

One day Hansard caught me looking at Susan. 'Think of my blue hyacinths turning pink,' he said, following me into my study and making himself at home in his favourite chair.

'I can only think of a more obvious explanation,' I said prosaically, sitting in mine. 'That Mrs Woodman has had two husbands – or at least,' I added, thinking of the riverbank lovers, 'two different men to her bed.'

'So worldly-wise, Tobias! You impress me. But the wench is too young to mend your heart anyway. Aye, and Jem's.'

'He treats her like the sister he would have had her become,' I said. 'I ought to send him on his way, Edmund. How in this village can he find another to love?'

'How can you? But I don't notice your packing your bags. Which reminds me, I hope to have a drawing room soon. How shall I celebrate its arrival?'

'By introducing a mistress to your house? Come, Edmund, all this talk of love, and you and Mrs Beckles have been smelling of April and May ever since I arrived! Nothing would give me more happiness than for me to join you in matrimony.'

Had I presumed too much on our friendship?

'You are right. I am honoured that Maria and I have an understanding,' he said repressively.

'Why not wed her? A more respectable widow I never met.

Nor a greater lady,' I added, in perfect truth.

For reply, he rose from his chair, pacing towards the window and looking out. 'And you are no bad catch! You still have your teeth; you stride about like a man half your age. True, you cannot expect to set up your nursery, but—' As he spun on his heel, I saw his face, and stopped abruptly.

'My friend, you presume too far!'

'I am sorry for it. Pray, Edmund, forgive me.' I stood in contrition, head bent.

After a silence lasting minutes, it seemed, he clapped me on the arm and pushed me gently back into my chair. He, however, did not sit, but returned to the window and his inspection of the gathering dusk.

He might have spoken to the glass itself, so little expression was there in his voice. 'Nothing in the whole world would give me more pleasure than to pledge myself to her in holy matrimony. But I am not at all a good catch, Tobias. How could I confess to her why half my rooms have no hangings? Why I can afford only the bare minimum of servants – and do not think I would let any wife of mine toil over the stove.'

'Some see pride as deadly sin,' I remarked. 'Whether it is or not, my friend, do not let it ruin your life and another's.' Knowing I had said enough, perhaps more than enough, I turned the conversation. 'Now, did I tell you that blue tits are already exploring the hole in the tree at the bottom of my garden…?'

# CHAPTER TWELVE

It was March, and the most beautiful early spring morning. All of my young pupils had been drafted, without so much as a by-your-leave, into the fields, and my lesson was *ipso facto* cancelled. So, with the delightful feeling that I too was wagging, I donned my hat and boots and set forth on one of the walks I had come to love. My path took me through fields and meadows, all coming to life, under the clear blue skies that had allowed an overnight frost and promised another. Becoming over-warm, I strayed into the woodlands of the Priory estate, for no other reason than that was where my feet took me. Perhaps at the back of my mind was the knowledge that Mrs Beckles would assuredly offer me a welcoming nuncheon whatever time I presented myself, while at home Mrs Trent and Susan had decided that every mote of dust should be driven from my study.

Sitting on a fallen branch at the edge of the woods, my eye was caught by a bird, flitting to and fro through the woodland to her unseen nesting place. It was as one of the *genus Sylviidae*, the warblers. I could not tell in the dim light that was all the noble trees permitted whether she was a sedge-warbler or a whitethroat. I resolved to tread softly in the hope of seeing her more closely – perhaps even finding her nest.

There! I was almost upon her! A whitethroat, surely, with the building material of her nest in her beak – soft, delicate threads, blowing in the breeze as she darted with purpose into a rowan tree. The thread was red.

Dared I tiptoe closer?

A rank, sweetish smell permeated the otherwise perfect sylvan scene – no doubt one of the briefly returned Lord Elham's illicit kills, left to rot and poison the pure air. If I saw it, I would ask Matthew to bury it. I pressed on.

Now, while the bird was on another foray, I reached my target, her nest. A miracle of workmanship, it was even lined to protect the eggs and then the young. That much I had expected. Now I saw what I feared, that the lining was not grey-green dried grass, but that it was all a soft red. I reached to touch. Alas, yes – it was as soft and fine as hair. It was hair.

Whence had it come? I reached and plucked a single fibre. Surely I could not fail to recognise that glow, that lustre? Did that mean—?

It could not, must not be Lizzie's hair.

Cursing my morbid imaginings for such a foolish fancy, I stumbled blindly away, only to disturb a vile fevered cloud of flies, buzzing about a sinister mound, the source of the evil, pungent sickly smell. A wash of hair tumbling from it confirmed what in my heart I knew—

I fell in what I hoped would be eternal oblivion.

'It is indeed she, my poor friend,' Dr Hansard whispered, pressing a draught of something bitter between my lips. I had swooned again when I had returned with him to this terrible place. Dr Hansard knelt solemnly beside me. I must have run to fetch him, but I could recall nothing of my journey to Langley House, or our return together, on horseback. I must have borrowed his spare mount. Yes, the animals were tethered over there, quietly eating the fresh grass.

Kneeling, he and I regarded the poor rotting mortal remains, from which with infinite gentleness he dusted the earth that had covered them in the shallowest of graves.

Intellectually, spiritually, indeed, I apprehended the facts of our last end. Since we had no need of our earthly body, why should it not return, ashes to ashes, dust to dust? I recalled a bishop's tomb cover, I knew not in which cathedral, with the good man depicted in a state of advanced decay. I had even laughed at Hamlet's savage quips about Polonius being at supper, where a convocation of worms ate him.

But nothing had prepared me, even remotely, for the sight of my Lizzie's half decayed, eyeless face, for the stench of her dear body. I turned again to vomit once more. Dr Hansard took the opportunity to cover her with a sheet he must have brought for the purpose.

'The poor child. I will see that she is prepared for a decent burial. Will you wish to see her again before you read the service? To see how she died?' He regarded me from beneath his thick brows, and resumed his gentle brushing of the earth away from the shallow grave.

'Of course,' I whispered, steeling myself for the ordeal. 'And what better place than in this vernal setting?'

Waves and waves of nausea again induced me to the weakness of a child, but I forced myself to observe what the good doctor indicated – the long slice that had almost severed poor Lizzie's head. There was another gash.

'The killer plucked out her womb,' Hansard breathed, as ashen as myself.

As justice of the peace, Hansard had another function – to determine the identity of the killer. To this end, he insisted that no one but ourselves should know the details of Lizzie's fate. He sent me back for his curricle and a device he had used before for conveying sad corpses, which he kept, he said, in his stables. George would know where he kept it, but George was not to be allowed to accompany me. I knew that he wished to keep me occupied, suspected that he wished to keep me away from Lizzie while he made further, unspeakable investigations. Before, when I had helped him look at the place where his late lordship had died, I had blundered about, irritating him. This time I resolved to be as calm and efficient as any man.

'As you can see,' Hansard said, without preamble, 'that is an old table top, flat and thin.' As he spoke, he slid it deftly under the pitiful remains. 'And these leather straps to fasten the poor child in place.' He had done all this without removing her temporary shroud. 'Now, let us lift together, as pall-bearers do. And now, softly, softly, on to the back of the gig: there. You are doing very well, Tobias. I am proud of you.'

Eyes awash, I essayed a smile. 'I understand you are doing this to assist in discovering her killer, though I know not how it will.'

He gave a bark of grim laughter. 'To be frank, neither do I, as yet. But I promise you most solemnly, my dear young friend, that I will find whoever did this and that justice will be done.' I think he spoke to Lizzie, rather than to me.

So solemn was his promise, I found myself adding a stern 'Amen'.

The poor body decently stowed in the cool of his cellar, he pressed me to join him for dinner to assist him, as he kindly put it, in his cogitations. Before he would admit us to the house, however, he insisted that we strip and douse ourselves under the pump, lending me clothes some ten years out of fashion to replace those of mine he solemnly burnt.

As we watched the bonfire from the window of his dressing room, he said, 'One day we will know how disease comes about and how to prevent it. I know there are far better doctors than I who will insist that such measures are unnecessary, men who will not wash their hands even after handling the dead. But it always seems to me a matter of manners, to oneself and to others. If I crush a stem of lavender between my fingers as I walk down the garden path, I enjoy pressing my fingertips to my nose to remind myself of it later during the day. If I do not enjoy touching and smelling something, why should I inflict the memory of that experience on my senses? And we should extend that courtesy to other people, too – in my case, to my patients. Why touch something pure, like a newborn babe, with hands that last handled an old man's leg covered with running sores?' He looked at me sagely. 'Aye, I know you think me a gabble-monger, but what else should we speak of? And, let me tell you, it is not often I lose a mother to puerperal fever, so perhaps I have right on my side. Now, I think we deserve the warmth of a fire, and a glass of my finest sherry. Come this way. Ah, now, employ that sense of smell again. Is not Cook doing us proud?'

We drank deeply first of sherry, then, with the two courses set before us, of claret, or I swear no morsel of the excellent rib of beef, with a fricassee of turnips and mutton pie, and an even better cheese could have passed my lips. But when he offered port and brandy, I waved the decanters away. We needed our wits, I said, to be unfuddled.

'We do indeed. Let us go into my study, so I can record any useful ideas either of us may have.' All the same, as he gestured me before him, he picked up the decanters and carried them through.

He took his place behind his desk, suddenly removing his wig and hanging it, in a gesture I found endearing, on the back of his chair, and scratching his scalp with vigour.

'Who might have wanted Lizzie dead?' he demanded, with brutal directness. He donned his spectacles, trimmed a pen and reached for a clean sheet of paper, as if to make note of our ideas. To my knowledge, however, he did not put pen to paper. 'Her death was no accident,' he added dryly.

I tried to match his manner with a short laugh. 'I would have thought any rivals to her hand would rather the others were dead, rather than the object of their affections.'

'So if you or Jem or Matthew had been found thus you would have pointed the finger at the surviving lover.'

'Assuming I was alive to point the finger,' I said. I stopped short – how much wine had I drunk? Lying only feet from me was the desecrated corpse of the most beautiful woman it had ever been my privilege to meet, and here I was making jokes.

As if he read my mind, Edmund said, 'In my experience, laughter – especially angry, sardonic laughter – is one way of acknowledging that while we grieve, we still have to go on living. Consider Dean Swift's impotent rage at the plight of the starving Irish peasantry and his response, *A Modest Proposal*.' He might have ruminated thus for longer, but visibly straightened his shoulders. 'Very well, you wish to exonerate both Matthew and Jem.'

'I do. Surely I do. Jem is more than my friend, Edmund, he is my mentor. He taught me everything an elder brother would teach – the decencies of life in practical affairs. To my governess, my school and my university I owe my intellectual education, but it was from him I had my moral one. And yet he is now my servant, dependent on me for his food and clothes. I often think that he should be the clergyman, I the groom.'

'Your generosity—'

'My honesty!'

'—does you credit, Tobias. But – as I believe my friend Mrs Beckles pointed out to you – you did not even realise that there was a *tendresse* between Jem and poor Lizzie. How well does any man know another, when the passions are involved?'

'As soon say that I killed her!' I declared.

'Very well. Did you? You had motive and possibly opportunity.'

'Motive? I?'

'You loved a woman promised to another. You could not have her – perhaps you pressed your suit and she rejected you – and so you decided that no one else should have her.'

I buried my head in my hands. I had not felt such fury, but that did not mean that another – perhaps someone I knew – had not. 'I tell you truly, that I would have conducted her marriage ceremony and baptised her children with so much spiritual love that no one would have suspected me of carnality.'

He came to lay his hands on my shoulders. 'I believe you, my young friend. Or,' he added, straightening, 'we would not be having this conversation.' He returned to his desk. 'Now, you do not wish Jem to be a suspect, though I think we must at least question him, and I believe that you are innocent. What about the third young man, Matthew?'

I stared into the fire. Matthew certainly felt animosity towards me, holding me responsible for depriving him of Lizzie's affections. He missed her when she went away with Lady Elham. But he had now found another love. Did that have a bearing on the case?

'Does your silence imply that you think him guilty?'

I shook my head. 'I came across him...in the most compromising of circumstances. I think you might say he has found solace with another.'

'Yes, young Annie Barton. I wondered if you had heard.'

'Oh, I heard! And I fear I also saw. I did not know that that was the young lady in the case, however.'

'You decently averted your gaze.'

'Let us say that I did not recognise her footwear. Lady! She is—'

He shook his head, lest I damn her without ever having met her. 'She is a young woman with strong appetites. I am glad she is not my daughter, and I would not employ her as a servant, but I would not judge her any more than I would judge a young animal.'

I swallowed hard. 'She does not come to church, and I have never had a conversation with her.'

'Certainly not a criminal conversation!' he laughed. 'Though in fact it would be fornication, I suppose, not adultery. Very well, I think we must question Matthew. It may be he had turned to Annie Barton without apprising Lizzie of the matter. Let us say, for sake of argument, that she found out and remonstrated with him. He, irritated, lost his temper and strangled her to silence her. How do you like that theory?'

'You omit one fact,' I said. 'Poor Lizzie had her throat slit. And whoever did that hated her enough to tear out her womb. Matthew abhors physical cruelty – many a time I have heard him rail against the new Lord Elham's proclivities.' I fell silent, trying to suppress a fearsome accusation.

Edmund looked me straight in the eye. 'I wonder if his lordship's proclivities extend to torturing innocent serving maids.'

# CHAPTER THIRTEEN

'We must question him!' I said, ready to seize my hat and dash off instanter.

'We must indeed. But we must also question the other young men. Unless there is very good cause to suspect Elham, even I would hesitate thus to enrage the family. And we have to think of a reason why he should want her dead.'

I pointed an accusing finger in the direction of the Priory. 'He saw her as a plaything! He and his friends!' I recounted the story of my first evening in the village.

'You want to preserve a plaything for future use,' he said.

'His own mother's abigail! Surely Lady Elham would not permit – no, she took Lizzie under her wing that she might the better protect her. In any case,' I said, trying to be rational, 'if it were he, why wait for her to make her way back to the Priory before killing her? It would be much easier to dispose of your unwanted inamorata in London, in those hideous anonymous stews of poverty. God knows how many bodies end up in the Thames.'

'But in London they have the Bow Street Runners to detect such crimes. Here in Moreton St Jude we have not so much as a village constable to turn to – which is a matter I propose to raise at the inquest.'

'But what can we do? We cannot let such a vicious death go uninvestigated and unpunished. So let us speak to Jem and to Matthew now. Then we may make similar demands of Elham,' I added, challenging him to argue.

'Of course. Though I would suggest we wait till tomorrow. There is in any case an impediment. Only the murderer knows that Lizzie has died. We need to break the news.'

I quailed at the thought. 'Would it...would it be possible...for us to do the task together? Matthew... Jem...'

'I never thought of anything else, my dear friend. As parson the lot must inevitably fall to you, but I will be at hand not merely to support you but also to observe. I trust we will see nothing but grief, but if there is guilt to be detected, I will be there to record it.'

'And if – as I hope and pray – we find nothing to raise our suspicions?'

'Then we have to speak to Lord Elham. In any case, we should admit Mrs Beckles to our counsels. As housekeeper, she has a pretty good idea of her underlings' welfare. In any case, can you imagine, once we have spoken to the young men, that the news will not be all round the village?'

'*All* the news?' I demanded.

'As much as we care to reveal of it. If anyone knows anything it will be round the parish the instant I reveal what has happened. Possibly all we have to do is sit here and wait for the information to come to us.'

I struck one fist in the palm of the other in my frustration.

'It may be quicker in the end,' he cautioned me. 'There is nothing like a home question to silence gossipers. Now, although I usually rely on old Mrs Smith's help with lyings in and layings out, I will prepare Lizzie for burial myself, with that terrible throat injury as an excuse. I cannot imagine that even her own mother will wish to do more than kiss a square inch of her forehead in farewell.'

I shuddered at the thought of those empty eye sockets. 'If that.' I swallowed hard, forcing back bile. 'Why, when I last spoke, Mrs Woodman was ready to disown her for her folly in leaving Lady Templemead's protection. I expected anger, indeed, resentment, for I am sure that Lizzie sent home as much as she could afford, but not *such* bitterness.'

'And that is the first call we have to make tomorrow,' he reflected. 'In my care for the young men, I had forgotten the other sister and even the mother.' He looked at the clock. 'Will you be riding home tonight or would you care to accept my hospitality?'

I gave a rueful smile. 'If I did what I wished, and accepted, I should have to send your groom out into the cold with a message for my household, lest Jem or Mrs Trent worry that I am fallen into some mantrap. Ten to one Jem would speed to the Priory and disturb everyone there by demanding a search party.'

'You underrate Jem. Assuredly he would look for you here. But you are right. And at least under cover of darkness you may make your way home with no one questioning your borrowed finery!'

We agreed that I would join him at first light the following morning to call upon Mrs Woodman. He and I often set off on such errands together, and this one would excite no comment.

'You are to play a parson grieving for a parishioner he found in quite normal circumstances,' Dr Hansard declared. 'As if the poor child was caught on her journey by inclement weather and simply collapsed with exhaustion seeking the shelter of a hedgerow.'

'A stout countrywoman? Never!' In any case, all feelings would be offended by such an untruth, especially when the facts became generally known.

'In my experience, a criminal can best be unmasked if he believes that he has not been found out. Trust me, Tobias. We both have our parts to play.'

Mrs Woodman was plucking a chicken when we arrived. No doubt the sight of our grim, unsmiling faces hinted at what we had to tell her, but even her anxiety did not stop her polishing with her apron the seats she offered. The cottage was somewhat larger than the average, although it had never had to house more than Mr and Mrs Woodman and their two daughters. Mr Woodman had died soon after Susan was born – at least the child presumed so, not having a single memory of him. The little family had been left a tiny amount by a very distant relative, according to Farmer Bulmer, which kept them out of the workhouse. Perhaps it had been enough to buy a better quality of furniture than I was accustomed to see in cottages; some would not have been out of place in a yeoman farmer's house.

'I am so very sorry, Mrs Woodman,' I began, 'but I come with the very worst of news. Lizzie is dead.'

'She was dead to me, as soon as I heard what she had done,' the woman said obdurately.

'I think she was coming back here to see you,' I pursued,

that being the theory Dr Hansard and I had agreed to propound.

'And now she is dead? How should that be?'

Dr Hansard gave a vague and evidently unsatisfactory response.

Mrs Woodman fixed him with a cold stare. 'What should she expect, leaving her post and traipsing round the countryside like a hoyden?'

Dr Hansard stood up. 'Madam, I think you fail to understand. Your daughter is dead.'

And then she repeated what she had once said to me. 'She is no daughter of mine.'

Before either of us could remonstrate, there was a frantic banging at the door.

I stepped forward to answer it.

A child stood before me, white to the lips. 'They said in the village that you and Dr Hansard were here. Parson, my father's had a fall! '

'Tom, is it not? Tom Broom? Wait, I will summon the doctor.'

He got to his feet at once, begging Mrs Woodman's pardon, and promising to call later. 'Let the dead bury the dead,' he growled, as we set off after an already speeding Tom. 'And though Mrs Woodman herself is alive, her feelings seem long dead.'

When it transpired that Thomas Broom senior had broken a leg, and had no immediate need of my services, I set off for home.

* * *

I found Matthew waiting for me, taller and broader than ever, in the bright spring sunshine.

'They say in the village that you've found her, Rector.'

I had expected the news to travel fast. This had positively flown. What did his demeanour suggest? Guilt? Or simple pain?

'Might I be permitted to say one last goodbye?' he asked.

Without speaking, and desperately wishing I could postpone what I suspected would be a very unpleasant conversation until Dr Hansard might be present, I led him round to the back garden, out of Jem's line of vision, to my favourite bench. Although he withdrew his tobacco pouch, he made no effort to fill a pipe.

'Why do you want to bid her farewell, Matthew?'

His face worked, but at last he straightened and spoke like a man. 'Because I am walking out with another young maid, Mr Campion. And I want to do the decent thing by everyone.'

What better philosophy could that be? I was torn between two desires – either to show him the poor corpse and revolt him into a confession, or to let him think of the girl as she once was, so that he might take his new sweetheart without care. Patting him gently on the shoulder, I left him there while I repaired for a moment's silent prayer.

I returned with my smaller Bible in my hand.

'I want you to swear on this, with as much solemnity as if you were in a court of law, that you had nothing to do with her death.'

Without hesitation he laid his rough hand on the Book. 'I take God as my witness that I loved sweet Lizzie Woodman and harmed not a hair on her head. Nor did her any other harm neither,' he added, as if wishing to cover all points. 'And I swear that had I had her by my side now, my thoughts would never have strayed to any other maiden, be she never so beautiful.' His voice shook.

It seemed to me a good oath. Would it satisfy Doctor Hansard?

'I believe you, Matthew. But as for saying your farewells to Lizzie, let me think on it a little longer.'

He reflected for a few moments, swallowing hard from time to time. 'Why do you hesitate, Parson? Is she…how long…she is…?'

'I do no know how long she lay there, Matthew. Her face is...damaged.' I thought of the decomposing rabbit I had watched him bury, the day I myself was assaulted.

So perhaps did he. 'It's a crying shame! Why can't God take us to Him as we are?'

'I think, my friend, He does exactly that,' I said, laying a hand on his shoulder. 'He takes our lovely souls and dresses them in brighter raiment that we can imagine.'

'If anyone deserves to be in heaven, it is my Lizzie,' he agreed, breaking from me and running from the garden.

# CHAPTER FOURTEEN

It was inevitable that those in the house should hear some of the commotion of Matthew's departure, and I braced myself for the swift arrival of either Susan or Jem. In the event, it was Mrs Trent who emerged, raising an eyebrow and mouthing, 'Lizzie?'

Deducing from my solemn inclination of the head that this must be the case, she disappeared, returning in an instant with Susan, whose eyes were round with terror.

I walked to meet her, and returned to the bench Matthew had vacated, my arm about her shoulders.

'My poor child,' I said, with all the tenderness at my command, as I seated her beside me, 'I have to tell you that your sweet sister is no more. I found her yesterday afternoon, in the Priory woods. At present her body lies at Dr Hansard's.'

Susan nodded, having regained her composure commendably quickly. She took me aback with her next question. 'Has she been dead long?'

'Why do you ask?' And why had I never put that question myself to Dr Hansard?

'I don't like to think of her falling and getting covered by snow. And it's been such a very hard winter.'

'I think she died very quickly,' I temporised, not judging her ready for all the facts yet. The rate that the rumour was speeding about the village, however, I was not optimistic.

'Does my mother know yet?'

'Dr Hansard and I broke the news to her this morning, before we told anyone else.'

'And Matthew knows. And Jem?'

'Not yet. Nor Mrs Beckles. And I would rather you spoke of it to no one,' I added. 'I am sure you will wish to spend a few days with your mother so that you may comfort each other.'

'Must I go?' she asked, with strong reluctance.

'Your mother has lost her elder daughter. It is your duty – as you love your mother – to support her at this difficult time,' I had said firmly, unprepared for the reply that so shocked me.

'It is your duty to love your family,' Susan said carefully, 'but I do not see how you have to like them. Mother never liked Lizzie.' She lifted her chin with what seemed defiance.

Nonplussed, I said, 'I'm sure she loved her, as a mother should. And I'm sure you loved her as a sister.'

She nodded. 'But Mama never did like Lizzie, you see, Mr Campion. At least, that was how it seemed to me.'

'Not like a daughter who was beautiful and kind and good!'

'I think she'd have liked her better if she'd been squat and brown like me,' Susan said, with a tone of voice I could not identify.

'Why should you think such a thing?'

'I don't know. It was the way she looked at her. Everyone made such a fuss of Lizzie, you see. Strangers would toss her a penny just to see her smile.'

'But would not that make your mother love her more?'

She shook her head.

'Did you love her, but not like her?'

She shrugged. 'At least I always had her hand-me-downs,' she said, implicitly accepting the accusation. 'Until she went into service, at least. Sometimes she used to smuggle me an apple or some cake in church.'

'So she was kind?'

'Someone would always see her doing it and smile. And then they would look from her to me, as if they could not believe their eyes. Do you have a big brother, Mr Campion?'

I was disconcerted by the question, but answered directly, 'I do. And two sisters older than me, and one younger.'

'Is your big brother very handsome?'

His portrait by Lawrence certainly suggested so. 'Yes.'

'And very rich?'

'Richer than me.'

'And did you never want to be your big brother?'

And inherit three titles, more acres that this child could imagine – and more money than even I could comprehend, especially after my sojourn here at Moreton St Jude? Smiling, I shook my head. 'Did you want to be your big sister?'

'I would have liked to be as beautiful. But if I had been her, I would be dead now, would I not?'

A hand clenched about my heart. It had nothing to do with Lizzie's death, but her living sister's pain, only some of which, I was sure, was caused by her loss. 'Susan, you are not grown yet. You will become as lovely to look at as Lizzie. And meantime you are just as kind and good.' Turning her face to me, I smoothed her hair where it struggled from its little cap.

She shook her head resolutely. 'Lizzie was beautiful from a

baby, they say. Tell me, Mr Campion, sir, did you ever see eyes the colour of hers? Except on angels in church windows? And look at my eyes, and tell me whether men will ever look at me like they looked at her!'

I was astounded. Half of me wished to rebuke her for want of maidenly modesty, the other wished to be able to tell her truthfully that better men would look at her in better ways. If only Hansard had been here – he would have advised me. No, he would have said spontaneously exactly what was right.

'And it's no good your telling me that God loves me as I am!' She gave a violent sob.

'You know that He does.' I took her hand, and then pulled her towards me so that she could cry on my shoulder. A casual observer would have seen me comforting a bereaved child. Perhaps I was. But I was also pondering what she was had said about Lizzie's relationship with the rest of her little family. Moreover, who was it that poor Susan would have liked to be loved by? She was coming to an age when it was usual for young ladies to fancy themselves in love. My sister Harriet, for instance, was once so besotted with the pastry chef that he had to be sent to the London house until she got over him.

She was speaking again. 'I really do not have to go back to Mama's cottage, do I? Pray say I don't, Mr Campion.' I could see her grasping for a reason. 'Mrs Trent needs me too much here. You know that she is spring-cleaning, and I do not see how she can get on without me,' she added with a note of triumph.

'If your mama needs you, then I fear that the spring-cleaning must be done without you – or perhaps when you come back. I will speak to your mother, and to Mrs Trent.'

Defeated, she rose to her feet. Then she turned those big brown eyes to mine. 'You said that she died quickly. Did she fall and break her neck or did someone kill her?'

'I can't imagine why you should think that!'

'Because you speak as if you are concealing a secret.'

I believe I blushed. 'I have told you nothing but the truth.' Not, of course, I conceded under my breath, the whole truth. Perhaps to expiate, I said, 'Now, Susan, I have a mind to go across to the church to say Matins. It would be an honour if you would accompany me there. Fetch your cloak and bonnet and we will go directly.'

To my sad amusement, Susan was more preoccupied with the state of the church woodwork than with the timeless words I uttered.

'All that lovely carving, Mr Campion, on those funny chairs in the chancel,' she said, as she bustled back to the rectory by my side.

'The choir stalls?'

'That's it – it's sinful that everything's all clogged up with dust. I don't know how Mrs Clark let them get like that.'

There was no need to tell her that Mrs Clark was so unwell it was hard for her to lift her hand, let alone a duster, and that none of Hansard's remedies could arrest her disease.

'Can't I take a damp duster to them, and then a nice bit of beeswax?'

'Of course you can,' I said, touched that of all those who worshipped regularly it should be she who wanted to take responsibility for the lovely old fabric. On the other hand, it might have been a subtle attempt to persuade me that she was too valuable to part with. 'But first we must pay a visit to your mama. Go and ask Mrs Trent to pack a basket of things she may find useful.'

Her walk indoors was far less purposeful.

So, indeed, was my own. I had the unenviable task of telling Jem what had befallen a woman of whom he was not the acknowledged lover but whom everyone told me he adored. My secret but despicable hope was that he had already heard, and would have prepared himself for what he must have known would be an uncomfortable interview.

With a heart heavy at my cowardice and inadequacy, I dawdled into the stable yard.

Hands in pockets, Jem was waiting for me. 'They say you found her.'

'And you were the next to be told,' I said.

'I'd like to see her.'

'She's—' I glanced to see that Susan could not overhear '—she's not…her body has been—'

'I shall see worse when I join up, I daresay.'

'"Join up"?'

Uncharacteristically, he spat. 'You're settled here; she's gone – what's to keep me?'

Where the words issuing out of my mouth came from, I have no idea, but I thanked the Almighty for them. 'Because I need you to help me find her murderer!'

Mrs Trent packed a basket of comforting food and drink for Mrs Woodman; it lay behind the seat with the rush-basket containing a few items of clothing I had insisted Susan bring in preparation for a short stay. After much pleading, I had agreed that it need not be mentioned unless Mrs Woodman particularly expressed her desire for her remaining daughter's company.

Off we headed in my gig, Jem teaching her how to drive, he said, to an inch. We went via the Priory, in order to break the news to Mrs Beckles ourselves. I, however, would have staked the National Debt that Dr Hansard had been there before us, and indeed, when she heard us arrive, Mrs Beckles ran from the house.

'It's a bad business,' she said, speaking equally to us all. 'And I am truly sorry for your loss.' It would have been impossible to say to whom she addressed the words – all of us, no doubt. 'Susan, I hear that there are some new-hatched chickens in the kitchen garden. Do you think your mother might find them useful? Off you go and get some. Good girl.' Turning to us, she said, 'I hear it was an unnatural death.'

'It was. I am taking Jem to pay his respects to her.'

'With Susan?'

'We are taking her to spend a few days with her mother – as a comfort.'

'Of course. But do not let it be too long a stay, Tobias. Mrs Woodman is not the most sociable of women, and while I dare swear that having Susan's company might do the mother good, I cannot believe that the mother's will assist the daughter. Now, I do believe that I could lay my hands on some mourning garments for the pair of them – do you care to come into the house for a glass of wine while I search? No? I will be back in an instant.'

She rightly judged that neither was fit for company. We did not speak until Susan came running, still, however much she wanted to be a grown woman, an energetic child. She had three chickens in an old trug, covered with what looked like a scarecrow's hat. Even as we settled our new passengers, Mrs Beckles returned, nodding with pleasure as she watched Susan lift a corner of the hat to stroke a fluffy head.

'Always balance a death with a new birth,' Mrs Beckles whispered, as she passed up a bundle of clothing.

Susan was separated from her new charges only by a further driving lesson, Jem as infinitely patient as his father had been when he had taught me.

'There,' he said, lifting her down, 'soon you'll be a first-rate fiddler. If only the Four Horse Club would admit ladies, I swear you'd be the first to be elected.'

She turned away almost pettishly at his well-meant jest. But soon she was in charity with him again, as he kept her outside Mrs Woodman's cottage to help repair a primitive henhouse, long since fallen into desuetude.

'I have brought Susan to keep you company,' I told Mrs Woodman, who had opened her door sharply at the sound of sudden laughter.

'So I see. And how am I supposed to feed her?'

I produced the basket of food. The clothing was more warmly received, and, without prompting, she asked me to convey her thanks to Mrs Beckles. At this point Susan, mindful of her duty, or, more probably, reminded of it by Jem, presented herself. With her hands full of yellow fluff, smiling at her benefactor, she conveyed all the excitement of life, not death. At least the child would have something to love while she stayed until just after the funeral, an arrangement we had swiftly agreed on.

* * *

As Jem and I regarded the sheet covering the corpse, Dr Hansard called me.

I left the cellar, carefully closing the door behind me, guessing the summons was spurious. Jem should have his moment alone with her.

'I cannot believe that either young man was responsible for the poor girl's death. Nevertheless, I discouraged Matthew from doing more than lay a hand on her shroud in farewell.'

'On what grounds?'

'What has filled your nose, your eyes, your mind since your sad discovery?' Hansard asked, holding my gaze. 'Can you, with such knowledge, imagine continuing your courtship of another young maid? Let the young man be a pall-bearer. Let him – if he can – read a lesson at her obsequies, much though that will offend Jem. But let us preserve him from the present sight of a woman he loved in the flesh…'

'And Jem?'

'As you heard, I asked him not to disturb her shroud. If he disregards my request, then—' Hansard shrugged expressively.

At this moment Jem appeared. He was as white as the sheet with which Hansard had covered Lizzie. He looked straight at me, almost repeating my earlier words. 'When do we begin our hunt for her killer?'

# CHAPTER FIFTEEN

We adjourned to Dr Hansard's study to review the situation; this time, he retained his wig. He poured us all wine, including Jem, who was as controlled as he was white.

'The coroner – Sir Willard Comfrey once more, Tobias – will hold the inquest tomorrow,' Hansard said baldly. 'There is no doubt that Sir Willard will direct the jury to bring in a verdict of unlawful killing. Matthew will almost certainly be questioned, and Tobias will be called upon to give evidence about how he found her, but I do not see any need you to be called, Jem, since your admiration for Lizzie was not common knowledge.'

'I would trust – I *do* trust – Jem with my life,' I declared. 'With anyone's life.'

Jem nodded, but said nothing. He took a sip of wine. 'Where will the inquest take place?' he asked with apparent calm.

Hansard replied, 'There will no doubt be considerable interest. I have left a note asking for Lord Elham's permission to hold it in one of his rooms.'

'And you expect Lord Elham to admit hoi polloi to his premises?' I snorted. 'When he himself might be the murderer?'

Jem gasped.

'We can discount no young man in the area,' Hansard said smoothly, casting a warning look in my direction. 'The due process of law must be observed, when there are outward and visible signs that poor Lizzie's death could not possibly have been the result of natural causes.'

'Who will comprise the jury?' I asked. 'And will the questions be any more searching than at the inquest into the late Lord Elham's death?'

'They can scarce be otherwise,' Hansard replied. 'In any case, I have taken the precaution of asking a fellow doctor to examine the body. He will be arriving shortly. And then we must arrange the funeral.'

'Another doctor?' Jem repeated, with anger rather than doubt. 'It's obvious how she died! You've just said so yourself. Begging your pardon,' he added as an afterthought.

'All too obvious. But not how soon after her journey back from London she died. If we are trying to find a killer, we need to know this, do we not? Tobias? Are you unwell?'

I blinked hard. 'This morning, when I broke the news to Susan, she asked when Lizzie had been killed. She hated to think of her dying of cold.'

'I take it you did not reveal the true cause of death?'

'How could I? Or...the other injury...'

We were interrupted by the sound of a carriage arriving. Within seconds, Mrs Page was ushering in a man no older than Jem, with a familiar handsome face topped by a haircut as fashionable as his coat.

'Dr Toone. Thank you for coming at such short notice. May I introduce two good friends of mine, Parson Campion and

Jem—' He stopped short: he'd never heard Jem granted the courtesy of a surname.

'Turbeville,' I supplied, as seamlesslessly as I could. It was clear that Toone had still not recognised me in my clerical bands. I would not remind him yet of our acquaintance, however, the circumstances having been not altogether auspicious.

Dr Toone beamed delightedly me, seizing a glass of wine as if he had spent a month in a desert and plunging into talk about the European situation before he was even seated. In fact, when offered a chair, he declined it, out of the blue declaring that he was there to do a job, and do a job he must.

Jem and I did not expect an invitation to join the medical men, and would, I dare swear, have declined it had it been forthcoming.

'You were not serious about joining the army?' I asked to fill the sudden awkward silence.

'I cannot see my way forward, Toby, and that's a fact. Not in any direction.'

'I understand. By now you should have been in charge of the stables of a great house, with all the responsibility and rewards that such a position entails. Instead, your loyalty to me has made you settle for a backwater like this where you are kicking your heels for hours upon end. I can see that you have transformed the stables that Hetherington left, and that the horses are in tiptop condition, but you must hate the periods of idleness I inflict upon you.' I would not remark on the difference between our stations in life, even with my much diminished income. Any attempt I had made to be generous had always been rebuffed, with a gentle admonition that what I offered was not seemly.

'That's what a servant does, wait for his master's call,' he said, without a note of criticism. 'And I have you to thank for my being able to read to fill my time. When we come to the Park here, I don't bother with books, because there's no denying the stories of India and such Turner tells in the kitchen while away the time nicely. And there's good companionship too at the Priory, even when Lizzie is – when Lizzie *was* – called away to mend her ladyship's flounce or some such. But losing Lizzie – even though she and I hardly – has cast me adrift. If only it were harvest time, you'd never see a scythe used so swiftly,' he gestured, as if extreme physical activity would numb his pain.

I nodded my understanding. 'At least I have my work about the parish,' I said, tacitly acknowledging that I understood his grief because I shared it.

'But I doubt if you'll want to stay here for much longer.'

'I cannot quit my place until we have laid Lizzie to rest and seen justice done.'

He clapped me on the shoulder, as he'd done when we were boys, and I'd mastered a cricket stroke he'd been trying to teach me. 'Yes, Toby, we'll worry about all this when we've done our duty.' He said no more, withdrawing to stare at the garden, or at something in his imagination.

Rather than disturb the mood by ringing for a servant, I made up the fire myself, and tried to settle beside it. At last I said, 'I saw you and Lizzie exchange a glance the first day you met. Certainly her feelings for Matthew diminished from that day forth. And – just before her ladyship left – Lizzie wished to speak to me "as a parson". I think she wanted to talk about you.'

'Not about you?'

'She never regarded me as more than a pious schoolmaster. I confess that her new learning would have made her an apter parson's wife than had she remained unlettered, but she never once looked at me as she looked at you.'

Still staring into the distance, he nodded two or three times. Then he straightened. 'Thank you, Toby.'

The clock ticked by many heavy minutes before the two doctors reappeared, laughing heartily about something. I could see Jem tighten his jaw in resentment; indeed, it was hard to comprehend how anyone could be mirthful in such circumstances. They both smelt strongly of lavender water, something it transpired that Dr Toone liked to wipe over his hands after washing them.

'Well?' Jem asked at last, more master than man.

No doubt Hansard had explained to Toone how someone clearly dressed as a groom should be on equal terms with us, and it was the younger doctor who responded, 'We have a slight difficulty.'

Jem opened his mouth, a derisive expression on his face.

Hansard hurried to explain. 'It concerns what Tobias mentioned earlier, the time, not the manner, of death.'

'But that was only Susan's fancy!' I objected.

He shook his head. 'Sometimes fancies lead to great discoveries. In this case, my distinguished colleague here noticed some damage to the tissues – to Lizzie's body – that he cannot explain. We are both wondering... But that need not concern us now. I believe we will find a nuncheon in the breakfast parlour, so I suggest that we adjourn there, gentlemen.'

Jem hung back. 'It would only cause awkwardness, Tobias. So let me be. I shall keep my ears open backstairs, as I'm sure you will do with the medical men.'

There was no doubt that the doctors were more relaxed without him. Whereas Edmund no longer touched cards, it seemed that Toone was still a gambler. Now apparently rusticating, he had a passion for horse-racing that kept him perpetually poor, which was why he had turned his hand – and, I suspect, his considerable intelligence – to medicine. They resolutely kept their conversation general till I had finished my repast, and prepared to leave them. Since there was no doubt that the coroner would release the poor corpse for burial, it was now my task to arrange Lizzie's obsequies.

Scarcely to my surprise, through his steward, Mr Davies, Lord Elham denied permission to use any part of the Priory for the inquest. Mr Davies added that his lordship was no longer in residence, and that his absence this time promised to be protracted. During this period, a great deal of redecoration had to be undertaken in the larger rooms, an excuse which did not seem even to have convinced poor Davies. So, lacking any other large enough building, the coroner sat in the solemn surroundings of St Jude's, the lectern doing duty for the witness stand. Despite the continued warm spring sunshine, which positively summoned workers to the fields and to their gardens, many of the villagers presented themselves, with a jury being swiftly selected.

I gave evidence of having found poor Lizzie's body, and explained my subsequent actions. Edmund described her injuries, beginning with the slit throat and concluding with the information that brought the temporary courtroom into uproar, that Lizzie had been further violated. One woman fainted. Two men looked as if they were ready to.

Then, very solemnly, Edmund asked the coroner for permission to introduce Dr Toone. 'I am a lowly country physician,' he explained, with a self-deprecating smile. 'My colleague here is an expert in what happens after death.'

'I take it that you mean what happens to the body, not to the soul?' Comfrey asked with a smirk.

Edmund bowed. 'May he have permission to speak?'

Toone hardly waited for permission. In an instant, he was on his feet, clutching the Bible and swearing his oath as the jury and onlookers gave an audible gasp.

Sir Willard viewed him without notable enthusiasm, obviously preferring his medical information to come from older and possibly wiser lips. 'I cannot see any need for another opinion, Dr Hansard,' he said, 'but clearly my objections have been pre-empted.'

Assuredly they had. Dr Hansard had once told me that everything about me declared me to have been born into the *ton*; looking at Toone through the eyes of the villagers, I could see exactly what he meant. His bearing, his demeanour were those of a gentleman, an impression hardly denied by the London elegance of his coat. His cravat was snow-white, tied as exquisitely as if he were bound for Boodle's or White's. As for his boots, you would almost believe the claim made by most valets that the only polish to use involved champagne in the recipe. Could anyone believe the word of such a fine buck?

'Tell me, Dr Toone, do your conclusions differ in some way from Dr Hansard's?'

'They do not differ, rather they augment his findings. Dr Hansard has testified that Miss Woodman's throat was cut and that damage was inflicted on her lower abdomen. What he did not tell you was that her womb was removed.' Overriding the murmurs of horror, he continued, 'We found it buried a little apart from the body. Although it had endured the same ravages of decomposition as the rest of the cadaver, it was possible to determine with close examination what I believe to be a salient fact. At the time of her death, Miss Woodman was with child.'

I know not what I said or did. At last, the hubbub erupting around us, I came to my senses sufficiently to catch Edmund's eye. Surely this could not be true! A slight but solemn inclination of the head confirmed the awful words.

Toone barely waited for a lull before continuing, 'I fear I cannot give an opinion about the time the poor young lady died. The decomposition is such that in normal circumstances I should have suggested that it was about two or three weeks ago. But there is something about the tissue – something – no, I cannot give my oath as to when she might have met her end. But I would speculate—'

'We will deal in facts, not speculation,' Sir Willard said. 'You may stand down. Mrs Woodman, please take the stand.'

Peering over his spectacles at the poor woman, so blue about the lips I feared for her health, he asked severely, 'Was your daughter married?'

The mother might not have liked her daughter but the shock of hearing such a question in such a public place was too much for her. She tottered, and would have fallen had it not been for Dr Toone's swift response. Sweeping her up, he carried her bodily from the church.

'I think I can record that as a negative,' the coroner said.

'Indeed you may not,' I objected, rising to my feet. 'Miss Woodman did not find it easy to write; her mother is almost certainly completely unlettered. Miss Woodman might not have been able to obtain a frank; she would not have wished a poor widow to bear the cost of receiving a letter that would have been useless. Lady Elham,' I continued, rather more calmly, 'has informed me that Miss Woodman left her service for Lady Templemead, but soon left that place too. The clear implication was that a young man was involved. For a young lady of Lizzie's good character that would mean only one thing, marriage.'

'I fear that that is pure conjecture, Parson. Your idealism does you credit, young man, but let me assure you that in the lower orders, a test of the woman's fertility before marriage is almost the norm. Common-law marriage—'

'—which is no marriage at all, not in the eyes of the Church!'

'—is the nearest many couples get to the legal state. It is enough for them and for their neighbours.'

My head swam. Could I really believe that Lizzie...?

Assured of his audience, Comfrey steepled his hands with a self-satisfaction I would have liked to smash. 'Miss Woodman would not be the first young woman to give way to the urgings of a man she loved and who promised her love in return.'

I could not argue. It had been true of my predecessor's serving maid. As soon as Mr Hetherington had discovered the young lady in the case to be with child, he had married her forthwith and they were now – quite respectably – man and wife. Why, even in more exalted circles like my own family's, once the heir had been provided, with possibly a second son as insurance, married couples could go much their own ways, provided that discretion – and thus the decencies – were preserved.

I nonetheless stood my ground. 'I believe Miss Woodman to have been a modest and decent young woman, and that somewhere in Cheltenham or London there may be even now a bereft young husband wondering why his wife has not returned.' My voice sounded as confident as it ought. It was supported by my better-hearted parishioners, one of whom, Farmer Gates, rose to his feet.

'Begging your pardon, your honour, shouldn't someone be searching for this poor lad?'

'I will undertake to set the matter in train,' Dr Hansard said, perhaps to spare me further speech, or even to take such an impossible task from my hands.

'In that case we can return at last to the business of this inquest. Now, in such cases there is usually a jealous ex-lover,' Sir Willard declared so complacently that I swear that it was only the House in which we sat that prevented me from wreaking violence upon him. 'With whom was Miss Woodman – in the absence of any proof to the contrary I shall continue to refer to her thus – walking out at the time of her death?'

Matthew rose to his feet, manly in his declaration. 'That was I, your honour. I am proud to say so, begging the pardon of my present sweetheart.'

'And were you responsible for Miss Woodman's – er – condition?'

He winced, but said, 'I wanted to wed the maid, not just bed her. And maid she was, as far as I was concerned.' He made no attempt to meet his current inamorata's eyes. 'I have not seen her since before Christmas. She quit the village without even leaving me word, sir, and my affections have since turned elsewhere.'

The coroner stared at him, as if trying to cow him into a confession, but Matthew held his gaze, head proudly raised.

Mrs Beckles gave evidence as to the day of her departure. She looked as if she might have said more, and rarely had I seen her face so troubled.

'I repeat, you may stand down. You have given all the information I need.'

She opened her mouth once more, but closed it with a snap, and retired to her pew.

'Very well, jury members, it is time to bring in your verdict. And I beg leave to inform you that death by misadventure is not appropriate.'

It took the jury less than a minute to record a verdict of murder by person or persons unknown.

As soon as the yeomen farmers and other neighbours departed, one kindly taking up poor Mrs Woodman in his cart, Toone approached me, urging me away from any stragglers. 'Yesterday you said that the dead girl's sister—'

'Susan—'

'—that Susan was afraid her sister might have frozen to death. Did she say why?'

I shook my head. 'We have had one of the coldest winters

the villagers can recall – almost as cold as those I was used to in Derbyshire,' I added with a smile.

Still he did not place me. 'Did the frost lie long?'

'As far as I recall from two or three weeks before Christmas till about two weeks ago.'

'Indeed!' Looking over his shoulder for Edmund, deep in conversation with a still anxious-looking Mrs Beckles, he summoned him with a jerk of his head. 'Parson Campion has the same recollection of the hard weather's duration as yourself. So our theory might be correct.'

Lest Edmund take offence at having to have his word corroborated, I intervened quickly. 'It would be more fitting to have any further conversation in the privacy of my study. Mrs Beckles, would you do us the honour of accompanying us?' As I introduced her to Toone, I offered her my arm, receiving an ambiguous smile from Hansard for my pains. What Toone might make of a society where grooms and housekeepers were accorded such courtesy I no longer cared.

Possibly Mrs Beckles' sense of rightness coincided with his and Jem's. Once in the rectory, she withdrew immediately to Mrs Trent's room, there, no doubt, to regale her with the day's doings. As for Jem, I had seen him withdraw to the stables, where he would almost certainly be giving Titus the brushing of his life.

Rightly assuming that Mrs Trent would have laid out a cold collation of abundance and excellence in the dining room, I led the doctors there.

Once more, Dr Toone seized on the wine I poured with more haste than manners. He looked about him, at the plainly furnished but well-proportioned room, frowning and occasionally shooting glances at me as if he were searching the recesses of his memory.

I waited until their plates were laden and their glasses once again full before broaching the matter that had so intrigued me and which Mrs Woodman's collapse had prevented our hearing.

'Yesterday and again today you referred to matters which caused you to be unsure of the time of Lizzie's death. Would you now care to enlighten me?'

Hansard said, 'To be blunt, Tobias, it is not impossible that Lizzie was killed just at the start the cold weather. The frost came so swiftly, you will recall, and was so intense, that her corpse might have been frozen in a near-perfect state. It was only when the warmer weather arrived that decomposition began.'

'So while she might well have died only two weeks or so ago,' Toone concluded, emptying his glass yet again, 'she might equally have died before Christmas.'

'That is surely impossible,' I said. 'She left with her ladyship, took employment with Lady Templemead and took up with a suitor. Lady Elham documents all that in her letters.'

Toone nodded, with surprising humility. 'It was a mere supposition. I once saw a man who had fallen in the Alps at the beginning of winter. When his body was retrieved it was in almost exactly the same state of decomposition as Lizzie's. A sad business, whenever it happened.'

'Indeed,' Hansard said slowly. He stared into his glass of Burgundy as if it would provide him with the information he clearly sought. 'Have you yet apprised her ladyship of these sad events, Tobias?'

'No, but I will write immediately. And if there is a poor relict, then he must be sought out too.'

'I wonder,' he said slowly, 'if such news might not better be delivered face to face, than by means of a cold letter, both to her ladyship and Lizzie's supposed husband or paramour.'

'Is this because you think it would be kinder, or because you may glean something from their reactions?' I asked.

The answer was a gleam in Hansard's eye and a throaty chuckle.

It was not until our repast was completed that we all took a stroll in the wilderness at the south end of my garden. Hansard dawdled behind as something caught his eye.

Toone took my arm and drew me to a halt. He inspected my face. 'By God, I do know you, don't I?'

'Indeed, I thought you were far too exalted a personage at Eton to notice, let alone recall, someone as junior as myself.' I was reasonably sure that neither of us would forget the beatings he had administered, but I would not be so rag-mannered as to remind him of those.

Perhaps I did not need to. I would have sworn that he blushed slightly. Perhaps he had taken up the healing arts not to pay his racing debts, but to assuage the guilt that his cruel violence had caused. After all, I had not been the only lad who had had to sleep on his belly for days after the punishment – and I had had the protection of my older brothers.

'But I'd have thought with your family you would not need a career to support you, youngest son though you might be. Why the Church, for God's sake?'

I smiled. 'It was precisely for that reason. I had the honour of taking Holy Orders not to embark upon a career, but for the sake of God, or,' I added, 'more accurately for the love of God.'

As if it was bad manners to speak of one's religion, Toone flushed, and changed the subject. 'And when do you and Dr Hansard propose to carry forward your inquiries?'

'I must conduct the funeral before I leave my flock,' I said. 'And I must find a curate to take divine service while I am away.'

Toone snorted with laughter. 'What a queer cove you've turned out to be, Campion! Everyone knows that country clergy are the greatest idlers known to man, sitting in their sinecures and making as much money from God as most make from Mammon!'

'I fear I cannot contradict you,' I said. 'But I have had two good examples in good works. The first is Dr Hansard.' Overhearing, he came over and bowed in acknowledgement. 'The second is my groom, Jem Turbeville, whose instinct for what a man ought to do is the strongest I have ever known. Neither would let me sit twiddling my thumbs when I could be doing God's work.'

'Are you also turned Methodist, Edmund?' Toone asked my friend.

'Not I! I work to lay down treasure in this life, not the hereafter, as Tobias will tell you.'

'Tobias will tell you,' I corrected my friend with an affectionate smile, 'that often the good doctor works for precisely the same rewards as the pastor. But I hear the voices of some of my flock, gentlemen. Edmund, may I call on you this evening to discuss our way forward?'

With that they could scarce do other than take their leave, and so it was arranged.

# CHAPTER SIXTEEN

'Do I hear you aright?' I thundered, gripping the top of my desk as if to overturn it and throw it at my visitors. 'Not bury Lizzie in hallowed ground? How dare you make such a suggestion!'

Miller glanced briefly at Bulmer. 'After all, her mother's a Methody. Don't hold with the proper church.'

'That is completely irrelevant.' Perhaps some of my fury was as a result of Toone's earlier needling, but I was truly enraged by their lack of charity. 'Lizzie Woodman was baptised as an infant and later confirmed into the Church of England. She attended every service her mistress permitted her to and took Holy Communion whenever she could. And yet you are telling me that I must deny her a Christian burial.' I took a turn around my study. 'An innocent girl, victim of the most horrible crime,' I said, pointing an accusing finger at both in turn.

Bulmer coughed, not deferentially. 'It's on account of that crime, Parson, that we knows she's not innocent. Out of the bonds of wedlock that child was conceived, and that no one can deny.' He had gathered confidence as he spoke, and now stood straight, his chin jutting.

As calmly as I could, I said, 'As you heard at the inquest, it may well be that Lizzie was married. Her employer in London—'

'None of the doctors mentioned her wearing a wedding ring,' Miller put in slyly.

Nor had I seen one. Hoping to disguise my dismay, I said sharply, 'Her fingers were much decayed. I doubt if one would have stayed in place.' I had the satisfaction of seeing both men change colour.

'I don't see why the parish should have to pay for her burial, not if she were married to a Londoner,' Bulmer said, recovering.

Miller's hand was still to his mouth.

'Are you proposing to journey there – or perhaps to Bath – to seek out this poor bereft man and dun him for a few shillings? Pah! Gentlemen, I will pay for her burial myself. And now, may I have the honour of bidding you good day?' I rang the bell.

As her grim smile showed, Mrs Trent would be pleased to show them out.

It was of course only men gathered around the graveside to hear the mighty words of the funeral service. As the acknowledged sweetheart, it fell to Matthew to scatter the first earth on the coffin. At least Annie Barton was not there to see him do it.

Jem and I exchanged a sad half-smile. We knew better than to enter the sort of competition that Laertes and Hamlet engaged in over Ophelia's corpse. How many years was it since we had enacted the play with the rest of my brothers and sisters one wet day in the hayloft? Jem had taken a part with manly confidence – the first gravedigger, by some twist of irony. But though the memory was vivid, our present pain bleached all the pleasure from it.

The final prayer said, we went our separate ways. I saw Jem drawing Matthew in the direction of the Silent Woman, while I sought consolation with Edmund in the privacy of my study. Toone had departed the previous evening, the better to prepare for his sojourn here. Hansard could no more leave the villagers without a medical man than I could leave them without a curate. I doubted if either of us was satisfied that our deputy could fulfil the role to our satisfaction.

'When do we start?' I asked the moment I had poured Madeira for us both. 'And for where? Have you ascertained where Lady Elham might be?'

'Mrs Beckles understands that she is in Bath,' Edmund replied formally. He added, 'Tobias, something is troubling...my friend...and I know not what it might be.'

'Mrs Beckles looked anxious at the inquest,' I agreed. 'Would you prefer me to ask her? I have promised to collect young Susan later today – I could take her to see the Priory fowl and raise the matter then.'

'I am sure that Mrs Trent would also be delighted to rear some chickens,' I assured Susan, 'especially if you were to make them your especial care. And Jem would make them a coop, I have no doubt of that. Go and choose your chicks now.' I waited until she was out of earshot before I turned to Mrs Beckles. 'You are worried about something, are you not? I saw your face when you tried to give evidence.'

She nodded, biting her lip.

'I know you told the truth and nothing but the truth, Mrs Beckles. But I think the coroner himself prevented you from telling the whole truth.'

She met my eye. 'Indeed, I sometimes believe that Catholics are fortunate to have to go to confession!'

'The Church of England has always taught that you *may* confess. Does what you have to say require the secrecy of the confessional?'

She shook her head. 'I know you will need to tell Dr Hansard, but that neither of you will spread it further. Mr Campion,' she said, very stiff and resolute, 'one of my unwelcome...duties as housekeeper is to ensure that female servants do not...are not...' She blushed painfully, but continued, 'I had a terrible fear that Lizzie might have been with child before her ladyship left the Priory. To be completely frank, I was relieved not to have to say that in public.'

In my mind's eye I saw the wan face of poor Lizzie the morning she asked if she could speak to me in my capacity as a clergyman. I had assured Jem that I thought she wanted to speak about breaking off her betrothal to Matthew; now it occurred to me that she might have had an altogether more formidable problem to discuss. Nonetheless I prevaricated. 'Surely not! Not Lizzie! Why, Matthew took his oath that they had not...not anticipated marriage.'

'There are other young men than Matthew.'

'And Lizzie need not necessarily have wanted their attentions,' I agreed with feeling, recalling the day that we first met.

To my surprise, she took both my hands in hers, as if to comfort me. I returned the firm pressure before releasing them.

'Had Dr Toone no idea how advanced her pregnancy might have been?' she asked, businesslike again.

'I did not ask. I confess to finding myself squeamish, Mrs Beckles. But Dr Hansard would surely enlighten you – if it was possible to determine such a thing. I know nothing of natural science.'

'Nor want to, I dare swear,' she said, with a warm and understanding smile.

No wonder Dr Hansard was enamoured of her. Why was he so stiff-necked about his financial situation? Mrs Beckles would care not a whit that the house was not completely furnished – indeed, I suspected that she would have enjoyed putting the remaining rooms in order. Certainly nothing in this world could have given me more happiness than to marry them in St Jude's. Never would two better or kinder people have been united in matrimony.

'You know Dr Hansard and I are to leave for Bath to break the news to Lady Elham?'

I thought she blushed. 'I do indeed. What if you do not find her at home?'

'Then we shall have all the longer to execute any commissions with which you care to entrust us. Come, Mrs Beckles, surely you cannot let us venture into such a fashionable city without demanding we purchase lace or ribbons or gloves? I know my sisters would never have let me stray to within ten miles of it without producing a list.'

I thought her laugh was forced. Leaning closer, I asked, 'Are you still troubled by your evidence?'

'No. But I am worried about what I hear of young Lord Elham. They say he is wild to dissipation.'

'Indeed. I am surprised his mother does not try to influence him.'

'And how would he react if she did? He always had a temper, Mr Campion, so strong that it was hard to impose one's will on him. You saw how he behaved to you simply for interfering with his friend's pleasure.'

'And I have seen the remains of animals he has tortured,' I agreed. We looked straight into each other's eyes. It was clear that she too suspected he might have had a part in Lizzie's demise. I shivered; it was one thing to utter such a thought in anger, another to find such a sensible and loyal family retainer sharing it.

She referred obliquely to our fear. 'I have furnished Dr Hansard with details of his lordship's comings and goings. You realise how very little time he has spent here? I hope and pray... Ah, are those the ones you have chosen, Susan?' she asked, interrupting herself as the girl returned with another trug seething with pretty chicks. 'Mind you ask Jem to build them a strong coop – the foxes are always hungry at this time of year.'

As we made our farewells, I uttered a silent prayer that he might be sober enough to hit a nail straight.

Susan was so pleased to have birds of her own to care for that she hardly registered my announcement that I must go on a journey to break the news of her sister's death to Lady Elham. I made no mention of a possible widower. She skipped off to watch Jem assemble her new chicken run and coop; after his visit to the inn his usual deft touch was quite missing and he fumbled with the nails she insisted on handing him.

Mrs Trent came out to watch the proceedings, looking at them with troubled affection. 'That's how it is with young girls – they must lose their heart to the first handsome man they see, however unsuitable he might be,' she said. 'At least he's a good reliable man who will let her down gently,' she added, as we watched the two brown heads together. 'Or will make her a good husband if he's that way inclined.'

'But—' I nearly exclaimed that it was the other sister that Jem had loved. 'But he is more than twice her age.' I corrected myself.

'And how many marriages do you know that are perfectly happy despite such a difference of years?'

I smiled my acquiescence, but went to my bedchamber, vaguely troubled. And it was not the thought of packing for myself for the very first time that was the problem, though that soon proved almost an impossibility.

A discreet knock on my door announced a surprising but more than welcome visitor. It was Turner, Dr Hansard's valet. He declared that he was on loan for the rest of the day, his master being downstairs in my drawing room. Without using so many words he implied what I knew all too well to be true – that my endeavours had already made his task as valet more difficult and that I should recruit myself with a glass of sherry with Edmund before dinner. It was clear that he assumed he would be accompanying his master.

'I think we should travel in comfort and in style,' Edmund announced. He was warming his back at the fire Mrs Trent had had lit to take the chill off the evening air. 'After all, I have a perfectly good travelling-chaise that needs no more than fettling up. We'd need a groom, but I promised Toone I'd leave my George here – he knows the lanes and by-roads like the back of his hand. Do you think Jem would care to come? I cannot think he would prefer to cool his heels here.'

Neither could I. 'Nothing would do him more good than quitting the place.' Would it ease Susan's alleged *tendresse* for him? I knew not.

Knowing it would offend him if we went down the kitchen in search of him, I rang the bell, bidding Susan send him up to us. He came with a pale weariness I'd never seen in him, and with the most perfunctory of smiles. Hansard pressed a glass of claret into his hand, observing him closely.

'Jem, Dr Hansard has thoughts of using his own equipage to get us to Bath. Would you have any objection to taking charge of it?'

Jem's eyes lit up, but the clouds soon returned. 'That's George Deakins' job.'

'Dr Toone needs George to guide him round the district,' Hansard said. 'Imagine trying to find a patient without a local man to help. Would you come in George's stead?'

He was clearly torn, but looked at me shrewdly. As if we were lads, he said gruffly, 'Don't get any maggots in your head about – well, being kind to me.'

Hansard stepped in. 'For goodness' sake, Jem, how can we manage without you?'

'You could travel post.'

I was sure his apparent reluctance was an attempt to conceal a great desire to quit, even for a short time, the site of so much distress.

'We prefer not to,' I said, with, I hoped, just the right amount of chill. In fact he smothered a grin. 'And though we could hire a man to do your work,' I added more conciliatingly, 'he could not do it as well as you. Moreover, he could not help us in other ways as you certainly could.'

Had he been a dog, his ears would have pricked. 'In what way help?'

'You could obtain backstairs information where we could not. In her hurried journeys, her ladyship will have left disgruntled servants behind, and irritated grooms. Would you use your eyes and ears where we cannot?' And – if of course he indeed existed – poor Lizzie's husband was likely to be a fellow servant, so it might well fall to Jem to find him. 'And, I should warn you, we may all have to proceed to London.'

Grudgingly he said, 'As it happens, I've got cousins in both Bath and London I wouldn't mind seeing again. How much work does your chaise need before it's ready? Not that I can imagine that George would neglect it in any way,' he added quickly. 'We'll have it ready by ten.' And, downing his wine in one gulp, he replaced the glass on its tray and left the room without further ceremony.

Hansard and I drank a great deal more though at a leisurely pace.

'It seems to me,' I grumbled, though with a twinkle in my eye, 'that we are ruled by our servants. Why not give them the slip and travel post?'

'And have them pursuing us on the stage coach, as if we were lovers eloping for Gretna Green? I think not! And, to be honest with you, Tobias, there are few things more needful to a man's comfort than a valet like Turner watching over one's clothing.'

He was right, of course – I was never more aware of my

recent sartorial inadequacies than now. But I responded with a jest. 'And necessary for giving one status at an inn, of course. You or I would not bruit ourselves abroad, but rely upon it, our two men between them will convince any landlords that we should be given the best bedrooms, the best private parlours.'

'And properly aired sheets – do not forget those... A toast, Tobias, to our journey!'

# CHAPTER SEVENTEEN

We took nearly three days to reach Bath, preferring to make the journey in easy stages, despite Jem's obvious impatience. While Turner plainly thought we should take rooms in the York House Hotel, we preferred the less expensive but still eminently respectable Pelican, in Walcot Street, which had the reputation of having a particularly good ordinary and was also very convenient for Lady Elham's house in Camden Place. Needless to say, we bespoke a private parlour, which Turner submitted to a contemptuous stare that immediately elicited the services of a maid and a feather duster.

Leaving Jem and Turner to their various duties, Dr Hansard and I set out on foot, despite a thin, mizzling rain, to leave our cards for her ladyship. We did not move briskly, or even purposefully. Rather, we feasted our eyes on the elegance of the architecture and on the attire of those similarly promenading. We soon saw that the latter, though it was not of course of the first stare of fashion, Bath no longer being the haunt of the beau monde, was far more stylish than our own.

After my sojourn in the country, I had forgotten the sheer noise of a bustling town – the street-vendors, the chair-men, the carriages. There was a ceaseless clink of pattens protecting even the most elegant feet from the muddy streets. But however sensible their footwear, the ladies eschewed practical outdoors clothes for delicate muslin dresses, of necessity sheltering beneath umbrellas carried by their equally elegant beaux.

Our feet carried us insensibly to the abbey, at the bottom of the town. As we came towards it, fitful sun gleamed through the rain, highlighting the warm golden stone and making it a house fit for God indeed. Inside we found trysting serving men and girls, middle-aged ladies weighed down with shopping simply sitting and staring about them and provincials like us armed with guides to the city. We also found a quiet corner, where, as one, we knelt in silent prayer, our souls uplifted by the light and grace of the building.

Try how we might, once we had quitted the abbey, we could not maintain the solemnity due to our endeavour. On Bond Street, Milsom Street and Bath Street, we dawdled before the rich variety of shops.

I ventured to point at the ware in one window. 'Tell me, Dr Hansard, do you not think that that bonnet would suit Mrs Beckles? The gold silk one, cut exactly like a jockey's cap?' It had a most charming little tassel at the back

'Indeed it would. But I fear it would offend her sense of delicacy were I to buy it for her.'

'Surely she would not be offended by an addition to her library?' I pointed at Duffield's. 'A volume of Scott's poetry, perhaps?'

Despite himself, knowing her absolute weakness for books, Hansard drifted into the shop. I hesitated outside, and then darted into what was clearly an expensive *modiste*'s. The ambiguity of Hansard's relationship to Mrs Beckles might prevent him from buying personal gifts. But from one who stood almost as a son in her affections, surely a shawl would not be unacceptable, even if I could not afford the very best Norfolk silk – at fifty guineas! – that Lady Elham always wore. How many mouths would such a sum feed for a year? Then I too stepped into Duffield's, to wallow in the glorious and inimitable perfume of new books, far more beautiful to me than any floral concoction from Paris. Eschewing the temptation of other men's sermons no matter how much better they might be than my own poor offerings, I contented myself with buying a leather-bound prayer book for Susan.

'Come, Tobias, a girl of her age would thank you more for ribbons and lace!' Hansard declared as I explained my purchase.

'Then she shall have both,' I declared. 'And Mrs Trent must have finery too!'

'And Jem and Turner must not be forgotten.'

For the next hour we were like two schoolboys suddenly released in a fairground with a year's pocket money. The best that could be said of us was that in this temple to Mammon, neither of us wasted our money on ourselves, a modish suit of clothes each apart. True, Dr Hansard found a new bag for his medical needs, and I well-made gloves, but these were necessities rather than luxuries, as were the boots we discovered we both required. All were despatched back to the Pelican, for our later inspection. Only then did we recall the serious reason for our presence in the city, and we crept guiltily back up to Camden Place.

As we expected, the houses in such a fashionable area were elegant in the extreme, and in the first stare of fashion. After looking about us, gaping like veritable hayseeds, at last we sought the address that Mrs Beckles had assured us was her ladyship's.

To our horror we found the knocker had been removed, and the shutters and blinds firmly closed. No one was at home! A few pence elicited the information of a crossing sweeper that the house had not been occupied for many a day. He spat copiously. He clearly could not understand why anyone in possession of such a property should not be in want of a tenant. Every other householder, he averred, was keen to rent out their properties, often for huge sums.

'How many days has it been vacant?' I asked.

'Hard to tell, there's been so much coming and going.'

'But you would know Lady Elham's carriage, black and gold with a crest on the door?'

He spat again. 'So be they all – some flasher than others. But I know her ladyship's carriage all right. But there have been others too, a-coming and a-going.'

I pressed another coin into his filthy palm, and he knuckled his forehead. But he clearly saw it as payment for information already given than an encouragement to dredge his memory further. 'When did you last see her ladyship's coach?' I prompted him.

'It must be soon after Christmas.'

'So Mrs Beckles was mistaken,' I said sadly, turning away.

'Or Mrs Beckles was deliberately misinformed,' Hansard suggested.

It was a sober pair who finally repaired to the Pelican, where we chose to dine at six, a compromise between the country hours we were used to keeping and the more fashionable hours kept here. Turner, apprised of the latest developments while assisting us at our *toilette,* undertook to convey them to Jem, currently visiting his cousin. Between them, he had no doubt, they could establish almost to the hour, certainly to the day, when Lady Elham removed from the city and discover her intended destination.

To my immense pleasure, Dr Hansard had contrived, via the estimable Turner, to procure tickets for a performance at the new Theatre Royal. He assured me he had once unforgettably seen Mrs Jordan act; I fear that this evening's leading lady was no more than acceptable in her skills, but *The Rivals* still provided us with honest entertainment.

Although Hansard had told him not to wait up, Turner was awaiting us with his usual carefully blank expression. Only when asked did he declare, 'It seems true that Lady Elham has scarce been seen in Bath since Christmas. There is a strong rumour that Lord Elham is unwell and that she has been caring for him. But not, I venture to add, sir, at Moreton Priory.'

'Quite so.' Hansard waited while Turner served us some punch he had prepared against our return. 'Thank you. Did Rumour have any suggestions as to their whereabouts now?'

'As to that, sir, I regret that it is entirely contradictory, especially as one story was that she was attending him at the Priory. Her ladyship has an estate in Devon, of course, as part of her marriage settlement. But then, Lord Elham has properties all over the country. And at this time of year, there is the lure of London.'

'There is indeed,' I said. 'And even if we do not find Lady Elham there, perhaps we may find Lady Templemead.'

'Shall we be proceeding to London tomorrow, then, sir?'

'I don't know, Turner. I am loath to career around the countryside on the mere off-chance of running our prey to earth,' Hansard grumbled. 'Imagine getting all the way in London and finding the good ladies had been residing in their far-flung country seats all the time! Cornwall, Northumberland? Where might they not be?'

I stroked my chin. 'On the grounds that one day's labour might save us many, might I make a suggestion? The attempt might be tedious in the extreme, and eventually fruitless.'

'Spit it out, man.' He did not need to remind me that Turner could not leave us till he was dismissed, and that Jem was even now probably awaiting his company. The balmy air had made me tired; how much more fatigued must our trusty retainers be, since it was to them that all the work had fallen?

'To have left Bath on any of the major roads, Lady Elham must have passed a turnpike,' I reflected. 'Ten to one the keeper would recall an equipage such as hers as it passed?'

Hansard shook his head. 'As our friend the crossing-sweeper pointed out, there must be many such – Bath still attracts the beau monde, at least those fancying that they would benefit from the waters.'

Turner coughed. 'I fancy that the Master of Ceremonies in the Assembly Rooms might have some idea as to her movements, provided that she signed the subscription book.'

'I cannot imagine my cousin neglecting any social protocol,' I said.

'Your cousin! I had forgotten you are related.'

'It is a very distant connection, Edmund. She wanted a gentleman as her parson; I needed a benefice. It pleased us both to think ourselves as part of the same family, at least at the start of our acquaintance. She came to refer to me less as "Cousin" and more as "Parson", so I fancy I displeased her in many ways.'

'Not least in your benevolence to the poor,' Edmund nodded. 'But we digress. Turner, I agree that we should make best possible use of our time here, so that we do not set out on some wild goose chase. Pray ask Jem to join us here tomorrow morning so that we make the best disposal of our resources.'

The following morning masters and men foregathered in our private parlour for an early breakfast of ham and cold beef, washed down by ale. The previous day's rain had gone quite away, and the room was flooded with inspiring sunlight. For all Jem insisted that he should hire a horse and make all the enquiries himself, we were united in feeling that a division of our labour was fairest. Accordingly Jem and Turner set out to the nearest livery stables where they might both acquire hacks. Dr Hansard and I, more used to the pleasures of walking than our servants, strode south to cross the river at the Old Bath Bridge, turning first of all west, for the Bristol turnpike, then south to enquire on the Wells road, and finally – having had no joy so far – east for the Widcombe to Bathwick road. Fatigued, perspiring and disheartened, both by the lack of hard information and the readiness of grasping toll-gate keepers to haggle for such as they had, we turned back in silence, the spring sunshine by now really strong.

Finding an agreeable coffee house as we trudged back to the centre of the city – were its roads really so very much harder than those we were used to? – we agreed to cut our losses, hoping that our servants had had better luck. To mask our disappointment, perhaps, we confined our conversation to the excellence of the landscape surrounding the city, and the elegance of the buildings within, truly a sublime blend. Refreshed, I was happy to acquiesce in Edmund's request that we visit the Baths themselves, though he resolutely declined the hot spring water offered to him when we adjourned to the Pump Room. I confess I did but sip at mine, finding it brackish, indeed, unwholesome.

'If you ask me,' he growled, forgetting that he had once wished Lord Elham's old nurse could have the luxury of treatment here, 'the chief benefit of taking any spa's waters is not the waters themselves, but the fact that you separate yourself from the temptation of the groaning table that caused your symptoms in the first place. As for the baths themselves, good God, have you seen the way that no distinction is made between diseases as patients are lowered into the waters? I should have thought you stood a better chance of taking someone else's illness than getting rid of your own!'

But he was in better mood after a late luncheon, taken in our private parlour. Of Turner and Jem there was no sign.

We had not yet signed the subscription book at either of the Assembly Rooms. First we progressed down to the Lower Rooms, and then we made our way back up to the New – or Upper – Rooms, where we had the good fortune to meet Mr King, the Master of Ceremonies, in person. To my amazement, he recognised me immediately although it was nearly six years since I had visited the city with my parents, and at that time I was not in holy orders. It was the work of a moment to tell him my new title, which he received with a generous bow.

I was delighted to present Dr Hansard to him. No one could have been more gentlemanlike in his greetings, or more concerned when we told him we had to take bad news to Lady Elham in person.

'I have to say that I have seen very little of her this year,' he said. 'Her attendance at our entertainments has naturally been limited by her mourning, and one would not have expected her to play cards or attend balls. But even when she has promised to attend a concert, she has cried off at the last minute – she has been quite unlike herself.'

'To what do you ascribe her behaviour?' Dr Hansard asked. 'I speak as her medical adviser, not as a common gossip.' When Mr King hesitated, he added, 'It is for reasons of her health that I am particularly resolved to break this bad news face to face, not through the unfeeling medium of a letter.'

'Your kindness does you credit,' Mr King said. Leaning closer, he continued, 'All I have heard is that her son is unwell – some nervous disorder, I understand. But I do know that her housekeeper here has taken a new post with the Salcombes – perhaps she would know more. You will find them in Laura Place.'

Dr Hansard made a note. 'And her butler? No man knows more of the household, after all.'

'I believe he has left the city. But if you furnish me with your address, I will make enquiries and wait upon you there.'

'Pray – might I be so bold as to make one further enquiry?' I asked. 'Have you news of Lady Templemead? I believe she is a cousin of Lady Elham, and a conversation with her might spare us all time.' For all I knew, of course, the connection between the two ladies might be as tenuous as that between Lady Elham and myself, but I did not share that doubt with Mr King.

'I will make discreet enquiries. Dr Hansard, it has been a delight to make your acquaintance, and, Mr Campion, to renew yours.'

We parted with bows and great satisfaction on our side.

'There is one more matter, Edmund,' I said, as we watched him out of sight. 'John Coachman died here. Since we have time on our hands, I would like to pay my last respects at his graveside.'

'And do you happen to know where he is buried?' he asked, suddenly irascible. 'I confess, Tobias, that all this uphill-downhill walking has brought a blister the size of a guinea on my heel. We still have to call on the Salcombes. We may need to visit every parish church in Bath, and I am too old and too tired!'

'Let us ask the Salcombe's new housekeeper,' I suggested, understanding the problem of the blister all too well, having a very similar one of my own. 'Surely she will know what befell a fellow servant, be he never so lowly. Would you wish me to summon a chair?' I asked hopefully.

He scowled. 'Crippled I may be, but I am not infirm. We will walk, Tobias – we will walk!'

As a matter of courtesy, we agreed to present our cards to the Salcombes, since any gentleman might be pernickety enough to object to two strangers, however respectable, calling on his housekeeper. Lady Salcombe, however, arrived at her house at the very moment we were admitted, and throwing etiquette to the four winds prettily insisted that we join her for refreshments. She could not have been more than two and twenty, a blue-eyed blonde doll of a creature standing not five feet tall. Her husband, a tall man twenty years her senior, with a dark complexion hardly enlivened by alarmingly saturnine eyebrows, soon sauntered into the room, nodding at us, but would rather have been reading his newspaper than even attempting desultory conversation.

As we explained the reason for our call, easy tears filled her ladyship's eyes. 'But of course you will wish to say your farewells to an old acquaintance! Dear Dr Hansard, dear Dr Campion, pray – I have a houseful of servants to look after me—'

'All getting fat doing nothing,' Lord Salcombe observed.

'—And I am sure they would welcome a breath of fresh air, especially in this lovely weather. If you will be kind enough to furnish me with your Bath address, I will ensure that you receive the information by this time tomorrow.'

'A drop more Madeira, Hansard?' her husband asked. Receiving an answer in the negative, he laid down his newspaper and took himself off, without so much as a 'good day'.

Lady Salcombe's simple unaffected kindness, without a hint of the condescension that Edmund endured at Lady Elham's hands, made for a very pleasant half-hour, at the end of which, as we punctiliously made our bows, she rang for a steward to take us to his lordship's bookroom, whither the housekeeper was summoned.

Mrs Prowle was the antithesis of dear Mrs Beckles. Nearer

sixty than fifty, she was a lady much given to black bombazine and sour looks. However such a hide-bound woman had come into the employ of the free and easy Lady Salcombe I could not imagine. It would have been fair to say that obtaining information from her was like extracting teeth, had she had any such dental furniture left in her mouth.

At last she conceded that she had never heard of John, but that was hardly surprising, since she had become Lady Elham's housekeeper only in the middle of January. She understood that the previous incumbent had left under something of a cloud, an incident possibly involving the disappearance of certain silverware, but she had no idea of her current whereabouts, or that of her ladyship. A grim snap of the jaw intimated that she had no interest, either.

We gave her more thanks than she deserved and left, rejoicing in the kindness of one woman, if not the other.

'I confess, my young friend,' Edmund said as we limped slowly back to the Pelican, 'if only the Baths were not such a damned unhygienic place, I truly believe at would go and plunge this old body of mine into them!'

And I might well have joined him. But I had another idea.

'Edmund,' I began, 'when we asked the crossing-sweeper about the activities of Lady Elham, he narrowed his eyes, in a such way that I would like to pose him another question.' In fact he had reminded me sharply of Jem, in his role of the gravedigger in our hayloft *Hamlet*, splitting hairs over who was to be buried. Had we asked him the wrong questions?

My garbled explanation was enough for him to concede that he might accompany me, so off we set with footsteps that might have been slow and painful, but were nonetheless purposeful.

The man might have been a statue, so little had he moved from his original site and indeed posture.

'And when did you last see her ladyship, if not in her own carriage?'

'Ah, that'd be two weeks ago. Maybe less.'

Dr Hansard flashed another coin before his eyes. 'Be precise, man!'

But that he could not or would not be, so we turned away. I would not inflict further pain on my old friend's feet, nor he, I suspect, on mine.

# CHAPTER EIGHTEEN

It seemed that all Dr Hansard and I were now called on to do was to repair the damage to our feet and, casting vanity aside, return them to the comfort of the footwear temporarily laid aside as too unfashionable. There was no sign of Jem or Turner, and it would have been unreasonable to expect a speedy response from those offering to help us, so after literally tending our heels, now we were metaphorically kicking them. It being almost the hour for Evensong, I would have liked to attend the service in the abbey, but felt drawn to Christ Church, a modern building much closer to the Pelican. I admit that my feet were influential in this decision.

To my amazement it had been built with the novel notion of providing pews for all worshippers – no payment was accepted for any of them. To be sure, none of the villagers was ever excluded from St Jude's because almost all of the pews were in the hands of the Elhams, who graciously permitted any of the villagers to use any but their family pew. Others like Bulmer could and did afford a subscription.

Divine Service concluded, I made myself known to the priest in charge, a man whose courtesy was only exceeded by his scholarship. He was kind enough to show me round, indicating items of interest. He assured me that though Christ

Church would have been convenient for such as Lady Elham to worship, he had certainly never seen her. Nor had he buried poor John Sanderson, the coachman. Neither piece of information surprised me. I declined his kind offer of hospitality, and returned to the Pelican, to find Dr Hansard most audibly asleep.

Turner and Jem were in the taproom. Turner, giving the clear impression that a man of his calibre rarely condescended to use such a place, was buried in a newspaper, and Jem engaged in affable discussion with a couple of other grooms, who presumably had not observed a copy of *Pamela* half concealed in his pocket. I had never known him with a taste for the sentimental before. Did he see in the heroine an equivalent of Lizzie, subject to the philanderings of a Mr B? And if so, whom did he suspect of being Mr B?

There would, alas, be no *Pamela*-like happy ending for our Lizzie.

Loath to disturb either man at his leisure, I slipped quietly back upstairs.

However uncomfortable it made them at first, we invited Jem and Turner to join us as we dined in our private parlour. At last they conceded that since they had information to impart, and since it was a shame to waste the good food set before them, they would indeed sit down with us. It seemed, however, a tacit part of their bargain was that they would wait on us, but at last I could say Grace and our meal began.

Turner took to the variety of dishes to the manner born, as if used to the leavings of Dr Hansard's table. His housekeeper was as economical as any, hating waste and preferring to share any bounty with her fellow servants to passing it on to the poor. Jem, whose calling had placed him lower in the pecking order, stuck to dishes that he recognised; though conceding that the wine-roasted gammon was very well in its way, clearly he preferred the beefsteak pudding.

We waited until the cloth had been removed and the dessert was on the table before we filled in the sketchy outlines of our day's doings. Jem and Turner had had the advantage of being on horseback – an advantage for Jem, rather, since Turner had clearly found the unwonted exercise as fatiguing as we had found ours. But their endeavours had at least resulted in some success, and they were able to report several sightings by toll-gate keepers of Lady Elham's carriage on the Lansdowne road. There were even more on the London road, far more than could be accounted for by journeys home to Moreton Priory.

'But any lady would have acquaintance in the area she would want to visit, even if she were in mourning,' I objected.

'Indeed,' Hansard agreed. 'And we can ask Mr King about her ladyship's particular friends. It would be no surprise if she were on calling terms with the Methuen family, whose home lies to the east, the Blathwayts to the north. And there are any number of less well-known families with smaller properties whom she might visit.'

'Of course. And I am sure Mr King will point us to them. Yes, Jem?'

'Begging your pardon, Dr Hansard, we also rode in several directions from both toll-houses—'

'The charges for which I insist on reimbursing you—'

'—And made a list of possible places she might have visited.

But there was one in particular that caught our eye. It seems that one family, coming on hard times, as you might say, has let their home to medical men such as yourself, Dr Hansard, who have turned it into a private asylum – as we found when we happened to fall in with a local man at an inn. Lymbury Park, they call it.' The casual way that Jem dropped the information did not deceive for an instant. The glance he cast at Turner confirmed that they were pleased with what they had found.

Hansard beamed. 'And did you gather information about any of the inmates that might have interested you?'

He did not need to speak Lord Elham's name aloud. All of us about the table nodded our tacit understanding.

'Indeed, sir, we tried our best. But though the man failed to respond to our flattery and other blandishments, we suspect that though it might be higher than a couple of tankards of best home-brewed, the man might well have a price. With your permission, we might try to find him again.'

'Whatever this venial man demands, he must be paid,' I declared.

'He must indeed,' Hansard agreed. 'Do you think that bribery would come best from you two, who managed, after all to scrape acquaintance with him, or from a humble clergyman, or even from a bullying justice of the peace?'

Turner and Jem exchanged glances. 'It is hard to tell, sir,' the former said slowly. 'Perhaps he might yield information to you or to Mr Campion, but his price would certainly be higher.'

Hansard stroked his chin. 'It may be that there is a fellow justice of whom I might make enquiry. Such a man would have power to insist that information were divulged.'

Turner shook his head. 'I might advise the indirect route, sir. Let the force of law be brought in later, if needs be. Should our interlocutor produce no information of note, then we might be wasting our time – and others'. But should a name be of interest, then the law might be involved.'

And so it was concluded. Turner rang for the table to be cleared and for port.

Jem cried off at this point, telling us that his cousins would be in hourly expectation of him, and Turner likewise declined.

'I have no further need of you tonight, mind!' Hansard said. Digging in his pocket, he produced several half-guineas, which he pushed across to the two men. 'For the expenses incurred by today's labours, gentlemen. No, no argument. I suggest we all meet here tomorrow morning at nine to make further dispositions.'

We were still drinking coffee after breaking our fast on eggs far from as fresh as those we were used to when a servant brought up a card. To our astonishment, it was Mr King's.

As one, Jem and Turner rose and cleared the table, disappearing from the room as if by evaporation, before our honoured visitor had climbed the stairs.

Mr King, as immaculate as Mr Brummell even at this hour of the day, consented to accept a dish of chocolate, and sat down, clearly full of news. But not until the courtesies were exchanged did he explain the reason for his call. 'I have just this moment seen Lady Templemead's coach arrive at her lodging in Milsom Street,' he said, 'and since you thought that she might hold all the information you needed, I made haste to come this way.'

We said all that was proper.

But he had not finished yet. 'I understand that Lady Elham's butler may be beyond your immediate reach. I am told that he found a post with the O'Malleys, and is now bound for the West Indies. However, in consultation with some of the servants in the Upper Rooms, I have put together a list of Lady Elham's more intimate friends.' Without saying so, he contrived to suggest that Mr Guynette, Master of Ceremonies at the Lower Rooms, would not have been matched such efficiency.

We spoke for a few minutes longer, promising to put in an appearance at the Upper Rooms as soon as our pressing business permitted, and with another graceful bow he left us.

'Lady Elham's servants seemed to have dispersed themselves far and wide,' I observed.

'They have indeed – though poor John Coachman has done so the most convincingly.' He coughed, and looked me shamefacedly in the eye. 'Tobias, in the blur of the recent days, I seem to have lost sight of our original purpose, which was simply to inform Lady Elham of the death of her former abigail.'

'And to watch her expression as we did so!' I reminded him. 'Had it not been for Dr Toone's calling into question the period of Lizzie's demise, we should never have insisted on that. And it is hardly surprising that unspoken suspicions should have arisen as a result of her peregrinations hither and there. But we do seem to have become ensnared in a web of suspicion and enquiry. Do you think that we should write to the good people back in Moreton St Jude and explain the reason for what may be a protracted absence?'

He flushed. 'I have already done so,' he said gruffly, as if caught out in something shameful.

To whom would he have written but to Mrs Beckles? 'I am glad of it,' I cried.

He retired in silence behind the barricade of his newspaper, and I said no more. Instead, I cast my eyes down Mr King's list of Lady Elham's friends and intimates in the area. There were few, as was to be expected of a lady in the first months of mourning. I looked in vain for people with addresses north and east of the city to explain her many journeys, and could only draw one sad conclusion, that she must be visiting young Lord Elham in the asylum that Turner and Jem had found.

I had always regarded him as an unpleasant young man, of course, with an unruly temper, with no regard for the niceties of social intercourse or respect for the processes of law. Furthermore, if Matthew were to be believed – and I knew of no reason to doubt him, having seen some evidence with my own eyes – he possessed a vicious streak that delighted in not simply slaying but also torturing animals. But was that sufficient to have him incarcerated in an asylum? Were viciousness of temper always thus punishable, then there would be few sons left to populate the upper ten thousand. Dr Toone himself would scarce have escaped. Yet from being a vilely savage youth, he had grown into a responsible doctor, whose expertise Edmund valued above his own. What excesses could Lord Elham have committed – unless he were guilty of murdering our beloved Lizzie? In that case, he should be tried by his peers and hanged by the neck. And how had his mother found out about her abigail's death, and contrived to smuggle her son to a place of comparative safety? What implications did this have for the truth of all her ladyship's letters giving Lizzie's whereabouts?

My head reeling, the last thing I wanted was the announcement of another visitor. When I saw from her card who it was, however, I changed my scowl to a beam of surprised delight and ran to the top of the stairs to greet her.

'Lady Salcombe! How more than kind of you to call!' And how strange of her to risk censure by calling on two men, with only her abigail to attend her. But perhaps such freedom was these days permitted in Bath.

Her bright eyes took in Dr Hansard's ill-concealed newspaper as he struggled to his feet, but she contrived to ignore the slippers still on his damaged feet.

She too accepted a dish of chocolate, sitting primly opposite me and watching me over the rim as she sipped. 'I had to come myself,' she said, 'because I have a terrible confession, which has to be made in person.'

'Your servants have found no trace of John Sanderson's burial?' Hansard prompted her.

She turned towards him. 'But, Dr Hansard, however did you guess? When they came back empty handed, I sent them out again. Only this time I sent them to churches that their fellow servants had visited, lest in their hurry they had overlooked something the next man might easily find. But all report, a second time, that there is no record of his burial, not within Bath. So – and I pray you, tell me if I have done wrong – I have despatched the two most trusted servants to all the parishes within riding distance of the city, and they will tell me this evening what they have found. Can you wait that long? I am sorry if this inconveniences you.'

'My dear Lady Salcombe,' I said, 'you have not inconvenienced, but indeed helped us a very great deal. Imagine the length of time it would have taken two strangers to the city to elicit the information! Pray, may we — ' I had almost said, *may I* – 'call later and speak to your servants?'

She stood up, giving a bob of a curtsy. 'That would be delightful. Mr Campion, Dr Hansard – I fancy you do not have a great acquaintance in Bath, and it would give my husband and me enormous pleasure if you were to dine with us. Shall we say at seven? Nothing formal, of course,' she added, 'just three or four couples.'

Delighted with the invitation, we both escorted her to the door, where we found her dimpled maid whiling away the time by flirting with the singularly ill-favoured Boots.

I was aware of Hansard's ironic eye upon me as we closed the door. 'What a pleasure that will be,' he said, in a tone I did not wholly understand. 'Well, Tobias, I believe we must venture out to the shops again – unless you propose to wait on her lovely little ladyship in your boots and breeches?'

Equipping ourselves with evening dress must be our priority. Fortunately in the elegant emporia of Bath, a gentleman might soon be made presentable. Even if the fit of the coats might not have passed muster in the ranks of the dandies, we felt that we should not disgrace ourselves.

'Your pretty ladyship will think you a fine fellow now, if she did not before,' Hansard observed, as we stood side by side before the tailor's mirror.

'She is not mine!' I said, blushing hot as a schoolboy.

'Let us just say that she finds you agreeable now, and that

nothing in your appearance this evening will spoil that opinion.'

'Nor in yours, provided that you dispense with that damned wig of yours, and have your hair cut properly!'

A gleam of deep satisfaction spread over Turner's face at the sight of his master's new coiffure. It was almost as deep as Jem's as he presented us with a list of the inmates of Lymbury Park, written in some haste in pencil on the back of an old shopping list.

'We were able to find our informant again,' he said, 'and as before found him partial to a drop of heavy wet. But he wasn't so cast away that he couldn't recall all these names, or to hint that some of the people within might be better known by other names. Mr Mortehoe, now, Toby – might not that be the family name of the Earls of Hartland? And as I recall, wasn't that lad of theirs, the one who smashed all the windows in the orangery back home, always a bit of a loose screw?'

'You may be right – well done! But this one here, Mr Dumbrill – I think that might be his real name. I knew him at Cambridge. He tried to jump a horse over High Table and was duly rusticated. Then they found out he was more than just a peep-o-day boy, but a real rum 'un, who would as soon batter and bruise his barques of frailty as bed them.'

'In-breeding,' Hansard remarked, strolling over to read the list over my shoulder. 'Lord Elham has a variety of estates, both great and small, to call upon as aliases. I don't suppose there is anything as obvious as a Mr Moreton on your list?'

'Alas, no.' I passed over the list so that he could peer through or over his spectacles, as the whim took him. 'But there is a Mr Bossingham there.'

'Bossing 'em? Surely a hoax!'

'Possibly not. The Elhams take their name from their main estate in Kent, do they not? Now, I had an aunt living near Canterbury when I was a boy. She was an autocratic old lady, and soon became known amongst us children as Lady Bossingthem. We thought we were terrific wits, because she actually lived in a village called Bossingham. And this village – hamlet, rather – was some five or six miles from Elham. I could send for a map if—'

He shook his head. 'I do not doubt your memory, especially one involving tyrannical aunts. So you think that this Mr Bossingham and Lord Elham may be one and the same?'

'I do not so much *think* as *surmise*,' I said.

'But it need not be a fallacious conclusion. I think it is now time for me to enlist the help of a fellow justice, Tobias. And tonight's engagement may furnish me with a name to whom I may apply. Let us go and prepare ourselves!'

# CHAPTER NINETEEN

When we saw the elegance of the Salcombes' other guests, all bang up to the nines, our guilt at our sartorial extravagance was somewhat diminished. Unsociable though his lordship might be, his good lady's charm and the superiority of her table had attracted the cream of Bath society, and we sat down at dinner with no fewer than six other couples. More came in afterwards and my dinner partner, a remarkably well-read lady near forty, obliged us all by sitting down at the piano and opening a sheaf of music. With a whist table the only other attraction, there was no doubt that Hansard would dance, and I joined in with a will. Perhaps I hankered for a moment after a pretty Moreton miss hanging out for a suitor with no less than ten thousand a year, but all my partners were agreeable and light on their feet. It seemed no more than a matter of minutes before the tea tray was brought in at ten-thirty.

'A most agreeable evening,' Hansard declared, as we strolled home, under the bright light of a full moon. 'And I cannot help commend the Bath habit of early hours. How absurd to think that twenty years ago I should have been setting out for an engagement at this time, not returning from one.'

'But it must be this very respectability that has driven away the majority of the *ton*,' I said, registering as I rarely did the difference between our ages, and wishing I could have enjoyed many more hours in such company. But it was not for me to carp. 'Did you learn of a suitable justice?'

'Indeed I did, and Salcombe was kind enough to dash off a letter of introduction to him. Sir Hellman Dawlish.' He patted his inside pocket reassuringly. 'Salcombe tells me the man is of a gouty disposition, and keeps even earlier ours than our new friends, so we may set out betimes tomorrow morning without fear of incommoding him.'

Perhaps it was the amount of champagne I had consumed that emboldened me to say, 'If we find Lord Elham there, if indeed he seems guilty of the ghastly crime, will not his mother be reluctant to return to the Priory?'

'In her place I would retire to the most remote of her estates, or even seek a watering place abroad,' came his guileless reply.

'In which case,' the champagne and I continued, 'the Priory will be shut up, perhaps even sold. And what will happen to all the staff and servants?'

His pace slowed, as did mine. 'Why do you ask? You were not thinking of establishing a home for indigent footmen?'

'Because, my dear friend – nay, I speak out of turn as a friend, but within my rights as a clergyman,' I stuttered.

'This sounds like a very solemn end to a convivial evening,' he prompted me. Perhaps he had an inkling of what I wanted – what I *had* – to say.

'Mrs Beckles is a very proud lady,' I said, aware I was rushing my fence. 'If she were left without employment, she would see any offer for her hand as an act of charity, not an assurance of love – as the offer of a home, in your own words, for an indigent gentlewoman. Dear Edmund, for God's sake, swallow your pride, if you can, and do not wait until your house is perfect before you speak to her.' When he turned from me, without speaking, I continued, 'Why, a woman of her taste and discernment would positively enjoy making her mark on it. Think what pleasure she would take in choosing paintings and china for her own use, not that of an employer. Consider the pleasure she would take in sitting with you in your library, reading the latest volume of poetry while you peruse your scientific journal.' I confess I was moved almost to tears by my own eloquence. By that, and by the champagne.

Was he offended? His silence boded ill. But at last he turned back to me, a smile on his honest face. 'As a friend, I would tell you to mind your own business. As your parishioner, I admit the sense of what you are saying. I have been stiff-necked, believing I had the luxury of as much time as I wanted to offer the lady the home she deserved.'

'Before you opened my eyes to the reality of country life,' I reflected, 'I would have said the lady would have been happy in a cottage with you, with a couple of hens and a garden. But since I have seen the true state of many of our cottages, I find I cannot recommend life in a damp hovel with a mud floor.'

'Nor shall I ask her to share that sort of existence with me,' he laughed. 'I get out of reason cross when my rheumatism plays up.' Soberly, he continued, 'Do you think she will accept my offer?'

'There is only one way to find out.' But in my mind's eye I

saw the tendernesses that had so often passed between them, the glow on her face as he singled her out. Could a woman of such sense, indeed such sensibility, deny the delights of a marital home to herself and to the man I was sure she loved?

Having explained our plans and told Jem and Turner that they might consider the day theirs to do as they wished, we presented ourselves at eleven sharp at the residence of Sir Hellman Dawlish. It was situated on none other than the Royal Crescent, and was furnished with style and opulence in the very latest fashion, at which we could scarce forbear to gasp. The first-floor parlour overlooked the Crescent's gardens, a view we had a few minutes to enjoy before our host joined us. The room itself was furnished in the antique classical mode, with a fitted carpet and marble fireplace. Pier glasses between the windows added to the general sense of space and light.

Sir Hellman was a man of Dr Hansard's age, but spare of build and with what hair he had left cut most modishly. His coat was clearly cut by Weston, and his cravat was in its own way a masterpiece. He greeted us as if we were long-lost friends, bidding us sit on what proved to be remarkably uncomfortable Egyptian chairs. He took another, giving no indication that he might be suffering from gout. However, he was very ill-complexioned, his skin almost yellow in hue.

Preliminaries over, he sat back, inviting Dr Hansard to open his budget. 'For you must know,' he said, 'that it is not every day that I am asked to authorise entry into a lunatic asylum.'

'Nor do I ask every day. In fact, I do not recall ever having to seek a possible murderer in such a place,' Hansard rejoined. 'But when a young woman has been hideously done to death, and violated *post mortem*, one feels the conventions must be ignored.' He explained poor Lizzie's fate, and had the satisfaction of watching that sallow complexion pale still further.

'Her murderer did such a dreadful thing after killing her?'

'I hope and pray that it was after, not before, she died. But decomposition was so advanced that I could not tell.'

I thought I was inured to all the horrors of my loss, but the idea – one I had not permitted myself to consider before – that Lizzie might have been eviscerated while still alive brought bile to my throat. It clearly had the same effect on Sir Hellman, who walked swiftly to a side table and in silence poured us all a glass of Madeira.

'Surely,' he said at last, sitting once more, 'such an act must be the work of a madman indeed. Not only will I authorise your visit to interrogate the young man in question, but I will also accompany you. I am not unknown in the area, gentlemen, and I fancy my personal authority will open even more doors than a simple letter.'

'It is not just the man himself that we wish to talk to,' Hansard said, 'because I cannot imagine for one moment that he would confess. But his keepers, those in charge of the institution, would be able to confirm or deny whether he was at liberty during the salient periods.'

'I take it speed is essential?' Without waiting for a reply, he rang for a footman, giving orders for his carriage to be brought round within the half-hour.

* * *

Never had I set foot in an asylum before, the fashion for people from the beau monde to while away tedious hours by observing the misfortunes of others having long since passed.

There was no hint of Lymbury Park's function at its gatehouse, guarded by nothing fiercer than an apple-cheeked dame engaged, when we summoned her, in hoeing her vegetable patch. She admitted us with a curtsy and a smile, closing, but not locking, the gates behind us.

'That augurs well, at least,' I said, sinking back against the very comfortable squabs of Sir Hellman's carriage.

Dr Hansard shot me a look. 'In what way?'

'I expected to see Gog and Magog on guard, preventing demented patients from roaming round the countryside. But it seems to be an altogether more liberal regime.'

Hansard laughed. 'Sir Hellman, forgive my young friend. He is a Cambridge man, and it seems they do not teach logic there. He sees no gaolers, so assumes that the prisoners are free to wander at will. I see no gaolers, and deduce that the inmates are so carefully restrained within doors that there is no fear of them ever reaching the gates.'

Sir Hellman, most truly the gentleman, smiled. 'Let us suspend judgement.'

The house dated from Tudor times, with matching wings added during the reign of Queen Anne. The aspect was pleasing, with sheep grazing quietly on a great meadow, separated by a ha-ha from a circular gravelled area quite large enough to turn a carriage. As soon as the coach stopped, liveried footmen appeared, promptly letting down the coach steps and handing us down, and we were welcomed into the house by a grave butler. Everything spoke of civilised normality.

'We are here to speak to the superintendent,' Sir Hellman announced.

'I will see if Dr Brighouse is available, sir,' the butler said, with a perfectly judged bow. He might have been Pemberton's double, so closely did he resemble the butler at my family's London house.

Nonetheless, we sent our cards in with no explanation – however discreet the man appeared, we tacitly agreed to reveal our business to no one except the superintendent himself. After a moment, during which we cast our eyes on an undistinguished set of family portraits, we were ushered into a spacious study, complete with not only a fine set of bookshelves but also a pair of globes. The furniture looked to me like examples of Hepplewhite's craft.

We were soon joined by a round-faced man in his early sixties, soberly enough dressed to be a man of my calling, and with a wig that predated Hansard's in fashion. To my delight, my friend touched his own scalp, in an unconscious gesture of self-satisfaction at having had his hair dressed more fashionably.

'Dr Brighouse at your service, gentlemen. Please be seated,' he said, rather curtly for a man whose business might well be to soothe and reassure relatives that their ailing loved one would be safe in his care.

'Dr Brighouse,' Dr Hansard said, having introduced himself and us, 'I understand that families unfortunate enough to find themselves with an offspring who is – shall we say – unstable, may seek help here.'

'Indeed they can. But I fail to see why you need the presence of a clergyman and another gentleman to discuss my avocation.'

I forbore to glance at Hansard, but surely there had been a

slight emphasis on the word *gentleman*?

'It is not your very noble calling we wish to discuss. Sir Hellman and I are here in our capacity as justices of the peace. But,' he continued, as Dr Brighouse's arm shot to the bell, 'for the time being we merely wish to make the most discreet enquiries about one of your inmates.'

'Which one?'

'I believe that Lord Elham may be in residence.'

A ghost of a smile flitted across Brighouse's face. It seemed that he filed away the phrase for future reference, much as Widow Jenkins did, though in markedly different circumstances. 'He is indeed *in residence,* Dr Hansard. But why should you wish to know?'

'Dr Brighouse, I am sure that you deal in the confidential all the time. So, in this instance, do we. You may rest assured that it as a matter of considerable moment, however.'

The other medical man nodded. 'Do you wish to speak about him or to him?'

'Both, in time.'

An expression of strong reluctance crossed Brighouse's face. 'I cannot think it would improve his health and temper if he were to receive such a deputation.'

'You make an interesting distinction, Dr Brighouse,' Hansard smiled. 'Do I infer that while some of your patients are indeed mad, some are simply bad?'

'You may infer what you wish. Indulgent parents, inadequate nurses and timorous governesses kow-towing to the heir all contrive to spoil headstrong children – and, believing that their wayward children are oversensitive, the parents then decline to send them to school. Some of their waywardness would be beaten out of them at Eton or Harrow for sure,' he added.

Was I the better for all that pain at Toone's hands? At least my subsequent path in life, though far from that my father would have chosen, had not led me here as a patient.

'And in which category does Lord Elham fall?' Hansard asked.

Brighouse stroked his chin, a gesture designed but failing to make him look wise. In fact he looked more like one of my chubbier pupils trying to make sense of simple arithmetic. Any residual apprehension I might have felt in the man's presence melted away.

'It is hard to say,' Brighouse finally admitted. 'Certainly there has been a want of discipline, with no inculcation of morals or manners. But there does seem to be an innate and at times uncontrollable violence underlying his boorishness, which is why, of course, he is a frequent visitor here.'

I was impressed, despite myself.

'And how are you treating him?'

'He is no longer under restraint, though there have been occasions when that has been necessary. Indeed, the lowering diet and regular bleeding I prescribed at the start of his present sojourn here appeared to have done the trick. I am always pleased, gentlemen, when one of my patients can return to his home.'

'Despite the detrimental effect this must have on your income?' Sir Hellman put in.

'There are always others in need of treatment,' Brighouse replied, adding belatedly and rather unctuously, 'alas.'

'Alas, indeed. Is there any likelihood that Lord Elham will ever return home permanently?' I asked.

'I regret that as soon as he returns to his old surroundings, and, I believe, to his several bottles a day, he suffers a relapse, and is compelled to return to our care.'

'He has done this more than once?' Hansard asked sharply.

'Indeed. One might almost describe his visits as regular, were there any set pattern to them. We first treated him two years ago, but his father insisted that his behaviour was simple high spirits, and removed him, despite our fears that he was not ready to return to society. Her ladyship thinks him too delicate for our regimen.'

If only I had spoken more forcefully to my cousin about her son's behaviour! However, I could not imagine her having let me get beyond the first syllable of criticism. 'Would you tell us the dates of his periods here?' I asked.

'Of course.' Removing a key ring from an inner pocket, he selected a key and bent to open a drawer in his desk.

A loud bell sounded. Whoever was ringing it did not stint his energies – or stop.

He paused, removed the key from the lock, and replaced the key ring in his pocket. 'Excuse me, gentlemen.' None of would have said that he hurried, but he left the room swiftly, with an undeniable purpose.

A slight click from the door prompted Hansard to rise also. As he tried the door, he turned to us, hands spread. 'Gentlemen, it seems we are locked in.'

After ten minutes of kicking our heels, I confess that had I been a housebreaker I would have taken a penknife to that tantalising drawer. To do so would at least have ended the speculation that filled the intervening minutes.

At first, with a gasp of shock, we had remained silent, especially when Hansard, still at the door, declared he could hear the footsteps of what he could only deduce must be a very large dog. A baying confirmed this.

'So despite Dr Brighouse's affability and ease, all here is not Paradise,' Sir Hellman had observed. He rose to his feet and, shielding his eyes against the sun, peered through the window. 'Nay, they might be preparing for a fox-hunt, with these hounds and these men on horseback.'

'For a man-hunt,' I corrected him, as I joined him at the window.

It did not take long. A figure – I do not like to say it was a man, though it was mother-naked – fled across the gravel and hurtled towards what he possibly saw as the safety of the meadow. He misjudged the ha-ha, and fell awkwardly, clutching his ankle, from which blood was streaming. There must have been a tripwire, which I had failed to observe. He strove nonetheless to hobble on. As we watched in horror he was floored by two dogs, and gathered into a straitjacket by no fewer than three burly attendants. Even as he lay panting and screaming on the soft grass, Dr Brighouse forced a contrivance into his mouth, and poured liquid inside. When he judged his patient sufficiently calm, he had him loaded on a large handcart and, still surrounded by dogs and attendants, trundled away.

Too shocked by what we had seen to talk, we resumed out seats. After a while, as our pulses slowed, we heard the click of the door being unlocked, and a footman and a maid brought in wine and a laden tray.

The butler, following on their heels, bowed. 'Dr Brighouse's compliments, gentlemen, and he is sure that you will understand the reason for his temporary absence. He hopes you will partake of refreshments while you wait.'

Although he retired, he left the two servants with us, thus inhibiting any conversation we might have wished for – and any unauthorised exploration of that drawer. He also locked us in again.

I noticed with distaste that there was still blood on Brighouse's cuffs when he returned, clearly anxious to reassure us that such behaviour, while distressing to all, was easily controlled by those with experience. At the same time he contrived to suggest it was a rarity in the calm and ordered existence of his establishment.

'Now, may we proceed to Lord Elham's records, and, if necessary, to speaking to the young man himself?' Dr Hansard asked, the servants having been dismissed.

'I cannot think that the latter will be possible,' Brighouse replied. 'After an incident like today's, all our inmates are unsettled and we find it necessary to...to pacify them.'

'You mean by dosing them with laudanum, whether they need it or not?'

'And by bleeding them,' came the even response. 'Dr Hansard, if you know of a better way of dealing with those of such a disposition, pray tell me,' he added, more tetchily. 'Now, to Lord Elham, and whether he will ever be able to take his place in the Upper Chamber.'

'Nay,' said Sir Hellman, breaking his silence at last, with a gust of laughter, strangely out of place in its vehemence, 'put him in there and his strange ways will never be noticed.'

'Quite so,' Dr Brighouse agreed smoothly, as he bent to unlock a drawer and produce a ledger. 'In here I keep the dates of admission and discharge of all my patients.' He ran an index finger along the columns. 'See: there is the date; the patient's alias; the reason for admission; any special regimen; date of discharge. And if the patient has to be readmitted, then we begin the whole process again.'

'You do not list the patients by name?'

'It would not be easy to steal this ledger, but it would not be impossible. You can imagine that confidentiality must at all times be maintained, when information in the wrong hands could lead to...unpleasantness. I am thinking of inheritances, marriage settlements and so on. So full details of the patients are kept separately, under a numerical system.'

'Very creditable. Now, might I just compare the dates that I have in my notebook with those of Elham's *residence*?'

I might have known that Dr Hansard would be so efficient, noting down details I had kept but vaguely in my memory.

His face impassive, he copied information from the ledger into his notebook. 'You are absolutely certain of these dates?'

'Absolutely?'

'I think that we may need to speak to Lord Elham, as soon as you deem him to be fit.'

'In connection with what, Dr Hansard? A criminal offence? Because I must warn you that in a court of law he might not be considered to be fit to plead.'

'Even though he would be tried – as a peer of the realm – in the House of Lords!' Sir Hellman observed.

# CHAPTER TWENTY

If I had had a choice of being treated by Dr Brighouse or by Mrs Brighouse, I would have chosen the former.

We encountered his good lady as we made our way to the west wing of the house, every door being unlocked for us and locked behind us, a decidedly intimidating experience. A soberly dressed female, weighed down by a huge chatelaine laden with keys, was berating a quaking maid for some failure. She made no attempt to lower her voice, let alone desist altogether, as we approached, Dr Brighouse escorting us. At last, when it was a choice between sending the young woman on her way or continuing to block the corridor and prevent our further progress, she abandoned her prey. *Us* she treated with more affability than we would have chosen as her husband introduced us.

'This is Mrs Brighouse, gentlemen, who does me the honour of acting as matron and housekeeper here at Lymbury Park.'

Instead of curtsying, she shook our hands in an almost mannish way, her grip being the equal of any sportsman I had met. In her forties, she had the air of one who had married above her station, but was determined not to be obsequious in any way.

'Good day, gentlemen. You catch us at one of our rare crises, you see.'

'Indeed, madam, the sight of that poor patient being pinioned and drugged was not what we hoped for,' I said.

'You would rather have seen him run, as he was, into the village and ravish the nearest female? Well, that would not I. Mr Brown, as I shall call him, is a danger not just to himself, you see, but to others. If he was not here, I swear you'd see him swing at Tyburn, gentle birth or not.' She lifted her chin in challenge, arms akimbo.

'My dear, I have explained to these gentlemen that we are providing a most discreet and useful service.'

'Good. And little enough reward we get for it too. I'd return these monsters to their families, for two pins, to see how they liked having them wandering round at all hours.'

'Surely you lock them in!' I could not help looking around me in some apprehension.

'Mortal cunning, some of them, you see. But, bless your soul, gentlemen, you've no need to fear. Look'ee here.' Reaching for the nearest door, she lifted a panel that concealed a small barred spy-hole. 'Go on, see for yourself how docile they can be.'

Her husband swiftly closed the panel. 'Nay, Honoria, my love, they are here to meet one man only. Mr Bossingham.'

She pulled a face. 'He's up on the third floor this week. The more restless they are, the higher we put them, you see, gentlemen.' Surely this contradicted her husband's optimistic assurances. 'Now, if you'd be so kind, just step this way.'

We followed her up what would have been, when the house was a family residence, the backstairs, their mundane meanness somehow emphasised in what I increasingly felt, despite Brighouse's earlier optimism, to be a place of despair.

Each pace, moreover, took us deeper into a smell, and then a stench, of human ordure, such as one is most used to in the stews of poor towns and cities.

Mrs Brighouse bustled ahead, banging vigorously on any door behind which an inmate was foolish enough to cry out or weep. No words were exchanged, but it was clear that on other occasions they might have been, and at once the hidden room fell unnaturally silent, with not the movement of a chair or the scratch of a pen to be heard.

At last she stopped, and, with a theatrical flourish, lifted Mr Bossingham's hatch.

Hansard stepped forward softly. As he peered in, his face became inexpressibly sad. He gestured me to take his place. There was the noble lord, the Eleventh Duke of Elham, reduced to a sobbing boy, clutching a child's rag doll for comfort as he lay, wearing no more than soiled small clothes, on a straw mattress on the floor. A stinking bucket in one corner catered for his bodily needs. I was reminded, most horribly, of the cell from which we had plucked young William Jenkins. Never had I liked Elham, nor found him a decent human being, even, but to see him like this was past enduring.

I replaced the flap as quietly as I could, not wishing him to have the further humiliation of knowing he was the object of derision or pity.

'You still wish to question him?' Brighouse asked curtly.

'Indeed I do,' Hansard declared. 'Pray have him cleaned up and conveyed to a more presentable room where he and we may have a little more dignity.'

* * *

We declined the offer of further refreshment, and passed the time calming our souls in the delightful pleasure gardens to the rear of the house. They were laid out in the French fashion, with elegant promenades between weed-free beds. One man lazed in the shade of a tree, while four or five others, all dressed in the same drab blue shirts and breeches, applied themselves with hoes and rakes. None of the latter took any notice of us, but the solitary man sprang to his feet and touched his hat. A large dog, which I had not seen till that moment, was instantly alert, almost begging its master for permission to spring into action. But he kept it firmly to heel, and walked authoritatively towards us, an upright carriage combined with a pronounced limp suggesting an erstwhile military career.

It was clear that neither Sir Hellman nor Dr Hansard felt inclined to explain our presence, but I said mildly, 'I take it these are your trusty inmates? And that you care for them out here, in the open air? We are visiting Mr Bossingham, you know.'

'Waiting for them to make him presentable, are you? If you asks me, there's nothing wrong with him that a spell under Old Hookey wouldn't put right, begging your pardon, Padre. If his father purchased a cornetcy for him, he would have done in Portugal or Spain just as well as here. A few route marches under the sun, a few nights bivouacked under pouring rain, and under a good sergeant he'd soon have learnt to mind his temper and his tongue.'

'And where did you see action?' I made myself ask, despite the familiar feelings of nausea rising in my gorge.

'Back in '08, sir, at Vimerio. We showed them our mettle, I

can tell you. Then they replaced Old Hookey, and we were done for, no argumentation.' He spat, copiously. 'A well set-up man like, you, Padre – I'm surprised you're not in the Peninsula yourself.'

It was time I told someone, however lowly, the simple truth. 'I am too lily-livered. I would have disgraced any army unfortunate enough to have me in its ranks.'

'Well, you've missed out on some good times, Padre. And some bad,' he added, as if he were meeting my frankness with some of his own. He patted his hip. 'But I was lucky enough to find a clean billet, even if it wasn't how I meant to end up. Luckier than most in my position, even if my girl did take it into her head to marry one of them navvies.'

I pressed his shoulder. We both had sorrows to endure, and preferably in silence.

In a hoarse undervoice he added, looking each way to see that we were not overheard, 'It's the drink what does for young Mr Bossingham. Keep him off his port and his blue ruin, make him stick to proper gentlemen's liquor, and he'll be as fine as fivepence before the year is out. God knows what they pours down his gullet here, but it leaves them more than a bit foxed the next day, I can tell you. They comes in *want*ing a drink, and ends up *need*ing something stronger, if you take my meaning.'

I slipped him a couple of coins, and he backed away, knuckling his forehead.

Hansard and Sir Hellman had drifted away from me, and were engaged in a desultory inspection of the borders. But as they neared one of the inmates, we heard a shout from the terrace, and a flustered-looking Dr Brighouse, with more haste than dignity, was summoning us to the house.

Assuming that Lord Elham was ready for interview, we returned briskly, but we were kept waiting in a small saloon for nearly a quarter of an hour. With two servants at hand to pass round yet more unwanted refreshments, we could not have any serious conversation; our ire could not altogether be hidden, however, when at last Dr Brighouse deigned to return, with a miserable-looking Lord Elham in tow. Two male orderlies brought up the rear, and as before there was a click as – presumably – the door was locked behind us.

Elham was dressed in the same shapeless blue shirts and breeches as his gardening colleagues. He had recently been shaved, by none too gentle a hand, and his hair was so dishevelled one hesitated to call it even a Brutus cut. He bowed, but the movement was as rigid as if a rocking horse were mimicking a flesh and blood beast.

We bowed in return; he was, after all, a scion of a noble family.

'How do you do, my lord?' Hansard asked, stepping forward with an outstretched hand. 'I am sorry to find you here. How long have you been unwell?'

The young man – today he looked scarcely more than a boy – shook his head as if to clear it. Slack-mouthed, he turned to Dr Brighouse for guidance.

'Nay, Mr Bossingham, try to answer the gentleman for yourself.'

His eyes rolled with terror.

Hansard took his hand and his elbow to guide him to a sofa on which they sat side by side. 'Surely you remember me, my lord? Your mother's physician, Dr Hansard.'

I swear that if Elham could have shown more signs of terror, he did now. He gripped the arm of the sofa convulsively, and tried to stand. The hands of the two attendants forced him back.

Hansard looked up at them. They quailed before his glance. 'Do you know, Dr Brighouse, I think we might be able to manage without our friends here. And, if I might be so bold, without your good self too.' His smile was steely.

Brighouse stood his ground. 'If you are going to try to question him, I must be present – as his medical adviser.'

'But I am also his medical adviser; Sir Hellman here is a justice; and Mr Campion a divine of repute. I think he will be safe with us, do not you? We will tell you when you may return.'

Elham regarded all this as a child might watch a disagreement between his parents, eyes flying anxiously from one face to another.

At last, Sir Hellman walking compellingly to the door, Dr Brighouse retreated, taking his servants with him. But he did not omit to relock the door behind him.

Reaching gently for Elham's wrist, Hansard checked his pulse. 'There, that didn't hurt, did it, my lord? Will you stick out your tongue for me now? Good. And let me look at your eyes. Very good.' Whatever he observed there tightened his face in a frown. 'We're getting on very well now, are we not? Do you remember my doing all these things when you took a toss one day down by Birchanger Wood? You had a new hunter, a showy bay, and he never did like hedges, did he, though he'd fly over fences and gates with the best of them.'

'Too short in the back,' Elham said, speaking as if from the bottom of the sea.

'That's right. Good lad.' He turned briefly to me. 'He's so full of laudanum he'll take a month to dry out. I would not be surprised if he acquires an addiction to it, just like any Bath tabby. At his age, too. Well, I shall recommend to her ladyship that we remove him from here and place him in the care of Dr Baillie or Sir Henry Halford. I have half a mind to take him with us—'

'But how could we care for him?' I objected, and then wished I could swallow my words. Was I not a follower of Christ, some of whose greatest miracles involved healing the sick?

'Exactly so. Weaning him from his opium will not be pleasant, either for the patient or for the physician. But it must be done.' He patted Elham's hand again. 'I will come and visit you again very soon, I promise you.'

'But you have asked him no questions!' Sir Hellman exclaimed.

Hansard shrugged. 'I will try, but cannot imagine that anything he says will be of any use to us.'

'Please try,' I begged. The living face, piteous as it was, was replaced in my mind's eye by the tragic face of my dead Lizzie.

'Very well.' His glance told me that I was being foolish. 'Tell me, my lord, do you know how long you have been here?'

He shook his head.

'But you remember your home in Moreton Priory?'

A glimmer of the old arrogance showed itself. 'I have many homes now I am a lord.'

'Any one of which would surely provide him with better shelter than this,' Sir Hellman muttered.

'And which one do you like best?'

'Grosvenor Square. I like London best. Better than the country.'

'Do you like Moreton Priory? Do you like the people there?'

'I didn't like him. He was rude to my friend.' Elham pointed an accusing digit at me. 'But I got my revenge! Set some twine to make him take a tumble. Hope he bloodied his nose when he parted company.'

'Do you recall why I was rude to him?' I asked.

'I want to go now. Tell them I want to sup early in my room. Call my valet now!'

Hansard's glance at me spoke volumes. 'Was there anyone you did like at the Priory? Any young lady?'

The response was a decided negative.

'Did you like any of the servants?'

'Didn't like Corby. Too nosy by half. Mama got rid of him.'

The kind old butler! And whence had he been removed?

'Didn't like Davies,' Elham continued. 'Didn't like Mrs Beckles. Sour-faced old bitch.'

At least Hansard now had a taste of his own medicine.

'Liked Lizzie.'

I did not need Hansard's finger on his lips to make me silent.

'You liked Lizzie. Did you kiss Lizzie?'

He smirked, and then made a suggestive movement with his hips. I gripped the arms of my chair. The man was an invalid, or I should hardly have been able to contain my ire.

'Are you saying you were intimate with her?' Hansard asked, with a minatory but sympathetic glance at me.

Elham pointed at me. 'You wanted her, but it was I

who—' He framed a vulgarism matching his gesture.

Hansard put up a hand to restrain him. 'Enough!'

He fell silent. But his smirk became a vile, licentious leer, which spoke louder than a thousand obscenities.

Perhaps sensing that neither Hansard nor I could have spoken, Sir Hellman got to his feet. 'My young friend, I understand that you enjoyed marital relations with the young woman. Were you indeed married to her?'

All too clearly, Elham did not comprehend – but it was the concept, not the words that defeated him. 'Marry a skivvy? As soon marry Haymarket ware.'

'But you begat a child upon her,' Sir Hellman reminded him sternly.

'What if I did?'

'Were you proud of that? Or were you afraid of what people might say? Tell me, Lord Elham, because she had become an inconvenience, did you kill Elizabeth Woodman?'

# CHAPTER TWENTY-ONE

'Lizzie dead? Lizzie dead? No, no, no!'

Although I confess to wishing otherwise, Lord Elham's shock sounded as genuine as Jem's or mine, and no less grief-stricken.

'Alas, Lord Elham, she is,' Sir Hellman insisted sternly. 'Lizzie Woodman has been foully murdered.'

'Who by? Pray, sir, pray, what are you saying? Dr Hansard, what is he saying?' He clutched frantically at the doctor's hand.

Hansard said, with surprising gentleness, 'Sir Hellman tells the truth, my lord, and sorry I am that he does. That is why we are here today. We came to tell you.'

'But who should want to kill her? Pretty Lizzie?' And then, as the horrid truth penetrated deeper into his fuddled brain, he burst into tears. Sir Hellman, revolted, took a step back. I, mindful of my own distress when I had found the sad remains, forced myself to kneel before him, praying that God would give me strength to love him as I ought.

'Lord Elham, I know we have never been friends, but may I offer you any consolation within my power? Is there a chapel here, where we may pray together?' I reached for his hand.

He leant towards me. Heavens be praised! He was going to accept my offer! There was hope yet for his sanity.

He spat, full in my face. And for good measure kicked me between the legs, so that I rolled backwards, crying out as much for the indignity as the pain, which was, in truth, considerable.

Sir Hellman rapped on the door. 'Attendants!'

Clearly Edmund was exasperated by this high-handed behaviour, but, as he saw my continuing acute discomfort, accepted that this must be the end of our conversation, at least for the time being. He helped me to my feet.

Dr Brighouse entered as Elham was dragged away. 'I will thank you, gentlemen, to leave immediately. I cannot have my patient distressed in this way.'

Hansard looked at him coolly. 'Dr Brighouse, *I* cannot have *my* patient distressed in this way. You will prepare him improved accommodation forthwith. When I have seen him installed there, and when you have furnished me with a complete list of the medicines you prescribe and the diet he follows, then we will depart. And not until then. Meanwhile you will not lock us in this room or any other. Do I make myself clear?'

Brighouse blustered.

I stepped forward, suddenly every inch my father's son. 'I do not perceive any reason for argument. Do as you are bidden.' Later Edmund would tease me about this sudden hauteur. For the time being I dare swear he was glad of it.

Brighouse turned on his heel.

* * *

Within fifteen minutes a truculent but mercifully silent Mrs Brighouse presented herself at the door. Indicating with a jerk of her head that we were to follow her, she set off along the corridor where we had first encountered her. Arms akimbo, she stood outside a door but made no effort to unlock it. Nothing loath, Hansard lifted the inspection flap and peered in. He nodded with some satisfaction, but did not suggest that we looked too.

'Good. All that remains is to see what regime he is subject to and we can depart.'

Still in silence, she led us back to the book room where we had started our visit. Her husband was seated at his desk. Taking a sheaf of paper from a drawer, he flung it on the desk. One or two leaves fluttered to the carpet. Turning, I caught Mrs Brighouse's eye and looked downwards. She bent and scrabbled them together, placing them in my outstretched hand with a bob of a curtsy. My father would hardly have acknowledged that sort of service from a menial, simply because he was unconscious that it was a service. However I might differ in attitude these days, quite deliberately I did mimicked my father again.

There was silence as Dr Hansard scanned the notes. At last he announced, 'You will start reducing the laudanum tomorrow. Not by much – he is already far too habituated – but by a tenth. And by a further tenth in three days' time, and so on. As for food, you may continue with this lowering diet, with the addition of a little soup for supper, but he will take no alcohol whatsoever. I shall return shortly to see that my instructions are being carried out. And,' he smiled, 'any attempt to exclude me or either of my colleagues will be met with the full force of the law. And now you may have our carriage brought round.'

We were all too full of diverse emotions to wish for much conversation. Travelling with my back to the horses, I contrived to look out of the window, praying, as the countryside unfolded, that the Almighty have mercy upon all the participants in the tragedy of Lizzie's death. It was borne in upon me that others too were in need of his succour, such as the haggard-looking men we saw trudging along the roadside, hoping, no doubt, for employment in the city.

Reluctant to sit down in our dirt with Sir Hellman, we pleaded a previous dinner engagement. Had he known it was with a groom and a valet, he might not have accepted our apologies quite so graciously, but he engaged us to dine the following evening, so that we could apprise him of any further developments.

The evening having turned suddenly chill after the glorious daytime sunshine, Turner had lit a fire in our parlour, and was mixing a bowl of punch. Jem, resplendent in a new waistcoat, insisted on waiting on us once more, but until we had all partaken of a cup of punch we refused to summon the servants bearing the first course.

'For there is news you must hear, Jem,' Hansard declared. 'First of all, however, a toast. To justice!'

We joined in the toast with a will, but without joy.

'Lord Elham innocent! Never!' Crushing his napkin, Jem threw it on the table and made to rise to his feet.

'On the basis of what we saw this afternoon, Jem, it is true that no jury would find him guilty,' Dr Hansard said gravely. 'My only hope is that when he is less befuddled by laudanum and goodness knows what else is in the patent medicines with which Dr Brighouse has quacked him he will recall events he has all too obviously forgotten and be prepared to confess. But even if he does, it would be hard to prove – given that the Brighouse register affirms that he was on those premises at around the time we now believe Lizzie to have been done to death, that is, in late November or early December. He had no forewarning of our visit and thus no reason to change his records. And there was no sign of them having been changed, either.'

'But what if Lizzie didn't die before the snow?' Jem pleaded. 'What if she died only a week or so before...before Toby found her?'

'Again, Brighouse's records attest to Elham's having been in his custody.'

'They must be wrong! Must be!'

Hansard relented. 'We shall certainly have to look at them again. But we must also speak to Lady Templemead and, if possible, to any of Lady Elham's servants left in her employ – singularly few, I may say.'

'And, according to Mr King, so many departed to places where questioning them would be well nigh *im*possible,' I added. I sank my face into my hands, ready to despair.

'Might one deduce, gentlemen,' Turner began, awaiting only Dr Hansard's nod before ringing for the servants to clear the first and bring in the second course, 'that speaking to Lady Templemead herself might prove easier? Very good, sir.' He pulled the bell.

'First find her ladyship,' I growled, with bad temper ill-becoming a man of the cloth.

'As a matter of fact, we may have done,' Turner said, prim as ever, but with something like a wink at Jem, who responded with a glimmer of a smile. 'We did not like to be idle, while you two gentlemen were careering about the countryside.'

'But—' In vain to point out that they had been given the day off; Jem would be at least as desirous of ending the mystery as I, and had every right to spend his time as he wished. I overrode my own objection. 'What did you discover?'

We were interrupted, however, by the arrival of the servants, bringing in a brace of duck, a râgout à la Francaise, a plate of macaroni and some cauliflowers. Turner received the dishes, laying them conveniently about the table, before dismissing the servants with a nod.

Assured that we were all content, he answered my question. 'We discovered where Lady Templemead is staying. It is, of course, servants' hall gossip, that we obtained by carrying the basket of a kitchen maid sent to buy vegetables,' he added, parenthetically. 'Her ladyship's husband owns an estate near Bristol. He is not one of the *ton*, by any means, sir. A self-made man. Lady Templemead's father was more than happy with the marriage settlement, however, since it paid off his considerable debts. Sir Thomas is a great Bristol merchant, a veritable nabob, who has, according to our informant, made his fortune in the West Indies and retired home to enjoy it. Unfortunately he has the reputation for being a stickler, far higher in the instep than his birth warrants.'

'So a simple morning call would hardly be eligible,' I mused.

'A letter of introduction would be required,' Turner confirmed.

'Which we do not have. I suppose that, failing all else, as a justice of the peace, Hansard, you could simply demand to speak to her,' I said.

'And how cooperative would that make the lady? No, we need a mutual acquaintance, Tobias.'

Jem, never at his most comfortable at our informal gatherings, though he would not have held back had we been having this discussion in a stable yard, coughed. 'The gentleman you were with today, Toby, may well know Sir Thomas. After all, he was a merchant too – at least, his father was.'

Hansard nodded. 'I would rather not have been indebted once again to Sir Hellman. Though his generosity in sparing his time and indeed his carriage were inestimable, there were times when I found his temper too hasty. If we are discussing delicate matters with ladies, then tact is vital.'

He pushed himself from the table and took a turn about the room.

I permitted myself a glance at my watch. 'There is one man who might possibly oblige, and this evening too. But we are not dressed to see him. Mr King,' I explained.

Never had two gentlemen transformed themselves so quickly. Turner had worked wonders, and, despite our protestations that we could walk, Jem had secured the services of two chairmen.

When we arrived at the Upper Rooms, it was clear that Mr King already had the proceedings well in hand. Chaperons had no need to worry that their protégées would languish unnoticed when Mr King had the business of introductions in hand. The ballroom was aswirl with colour and gaiety when we arrived, and Mr King was looking, as well he might, content with his evening's work. He was happy to oblige us in our request; we were equally happy to twirl around the floor while we waited for the note of introduction.

It was agreed that, armed with Mr King's letter, the four of us should set out betimes the following morning. Strictly, Turner was a supernumerary, but we were persuaded that to leave him at the hotel when the rest of us were abroad would have been cruelty itself. With all his sober ways, it was easy to forget that the man was but ten years older than I, and I knew my feelings had I been similarly placed. Kitted out in a borrowed cape, he insisted on sitting outside, blowing the yard of tin at Jem's behest, Jem driving Dr Hansard's carriage.

If Sir Hellman's abode was opulent, Sir Thomas's was little short of palatial, a veritable Gloucestershire Chatsworth. It could have been little more than thirty years old, blending elegance and solidity with beautifully landscaped grounds coming into their full maturity.

'All built on slavery,' Hansard muttered.

I must express my horror. 'Indeed?'

'How else would a Bristol merchant make this much money? When everyone else is making money the same way, moral stances are very difficult, Tobias. My Indian fortune was modest by many men's standards, and to the best of my knowledge not a penny came from dishonest or immoral sources, but there is a part of my conscience that is glad I lost the greater part. At least now I have the satisfaction of knowing that every penny coming into my coffers is entirely untainted.

'Now,' he continued, as Jem tooled us to the huge portico sheltering the front door, 'recall that we are here simply to enquire about Lady Elham's whereabouts, bearers as we are of news of a family misfortune. Only when we have Lady Templemead's trust do we speak of Lizzie and why she may have left Lady Templemead's employment.'

I nodded. 'I will become the very pattern-card of an unctuous clergyman.'

How I wished that I had the benefit of my mother's interest in, and knowledge of, all the families of the *ton*. She would have known all about Lady Templemead, from her antecedents to her alliances, her strengths to her Achilles heel.

A very superior butler, clearly disdainful of our provincial addresses, informed us that Lady Templemead was not at home. On my addressing him as coldly as my father would have done, however, he condescended to accept on a salver Mr King's letter of introduction, and to show us into the library.

This was a room of such exquisite proportion that I declare I could have waited all day for a response, especially when I saw that the quality of the volumes on the shelves lining every wall matched that of the furniture and the silk carpets. Here were all the great classical authors, learned histories, volumes of poetry and what looked like a First Folio of Shakespeare's plays. Dr Hansard, meanwhile, was enthralled by the tomes on the history of India.

The pretty clock on the marble mantelpiece announced that

we had waited a full hour before the double doors at the far end opened, the butler bowing deeply before a lady of Mrs Beckles' age but with none of the warmth of that lady's expression that always suggested that the very sight of you had improved her day. Rather Lady Templemead, if it was she, had made such a habit of disdaining her acquaintance that her face was now set in a sneer. Clearly even our best Bath finery did not impress her. Why should it indeed? She was as elegant a lady as I had ever seen, her dress silk, her hair dressed in the latest mode and covered with the tiniest wisp of a cap. She provided two fingers for us to make our bows over.

'Lady Templemead,' I began, 'as Mr King's letter will possibly have informed you, we are here only to make enquiries as to Lady Elham's whereabouts.'

'So I understand. But I cannot apprehend why you should conceive for one moment why I could help you.'

'Lady Elham has given us to understand that you are cousins,' I said, 'and, moreover, close friends.'

'Cousins? Believe me, it is the most distant of connections. Bosom bows with that woman? Indeed no. We may be nodding acquaintances in Bath, but then, one is with so many people one would not wish to meet elsewhere.'

'So you have no idea where she might be now?'

'None.' Her tone, her demeanour, told us that our interview was over.

'Your ladyship, might I ask if your acquaintance was such that you might employ one of her ladyship's servants?' I asked. Was there an etiquette in such matters or had I simply made myself look foolish.

'That would be a matter of convenience, not friendship.

There are, however, some whose personal recommendations one would give more credence to than others.' She did not need to add, that Lady Elham was not one of those. Her cold smile spoke volumes.

I was about to blurt that Lady Elham was fashionable enough not to have her word doubted, when Dr Hansard stepped forward, with his most charming and conciliating smile.

'Indeed, your ladyship,' he said with a sigh, as if not just understanding but agreeing with her. I had seen my mother adopt just such a tone, when extracting gossip from uncomprehending acquaintances.

'Such waywardness of manner,' her ladyship agreed, dropping her voice and indicating that we might sit. 'One moment in the boughs, the next quite mawkish. At one moment she was talking of remarrying – at her age, Dr Hansard! – the next of taking the veil and retiring to a convent.'

'Is that why she wished to place her abigail with another lady?' he asked, placing himself at right angles to her on one of the sofas. 'Because she herself no longer needed her?'

'Abigail? Abigail? What is this?'

'We understood,' Hansard explained smoothly, 'that Lizzie Woodman, Lady Elham's personal maid, had evinced a desire to live in town, and that you, spending more time there than Lady Elham and being in need of a dresser, had agreed to employ Lizzie.'

She had begun to shake her head even before Hansard had finished speaking. 'I have been faithfully served by my dresser since the dreadful times in France. Marie has talents a younger woman could not dream of.' She did nothing so vulgar as to smooth her hair or dress in order to elicit a compliment for either herself or for her dresser.

I kept my voice as calm as I could. 'So you never employed Lizzie Woodman in your household?'

She looked at me with a thin eyebrow indicating that she preferred to converse with the genial doctor. 'I may have a scullery maid by that name... How would I know?'

How indeed? Benevolent employer my own mother was, but I suspected the staff she knew by name were far outnumbered by those equally essential to her comfort who remained completely anonymous as far as she was concerned. I accepted the rebuke with a bow.

Hansard shook his head in apparent sympathy. But I knew that even as he uttered his bland platitudes, he must be as desperate to confer with me as I was with him.

'And what is the news you must so urgently convey to Lady Elham?' Lady Templemead demanded.

'A family matter only,' Dr Hansard said.

'A matter serious enough to send you chasing about the countryside in search of her?' Lady Templemead observed. 'The very thought gives me palpitations.'

'Palpitations?' Hansard's voice was like honey. 'My dear lady – and spasms, too, no doubt? Permit me.' He took her wrist, and solemnly nodded his head. 'Ah, there is some sign of distress in your pulse. You must not overexert yourself, my lady, or I cannot answer for the consequences. Should the symptoms persist, I must tell you that there is no better man than Sir William Knighton.'

We rose as one, our sympathy for her almost all she desired.

'But I have been so remiss! I have omitted to offer you poor travellers refreshment. Pray, a little wine?' She was ready to ring the bell.

'Alas, my lady, we must decline your kind offer. We must continue our search for Lady Elham. Pray, have you no idea where she might be found?'

She stared. 'In her home at Moreton Priory, I should suppose.'

## CHAPTER TWENTY-TWO

Jem and Turner deduced from our grave faces and unwillingness for conversation that we had serious tidings. However, our news must wait until we could speak in private. Accordingly, they observed the usual master–servant niceties until at last we arrived at a respectable-looking inn. Although Turner tried to bespeak a private parlour, the best the landlord could offer was the taproom, which, he assured, was always empty at this time of day. For all our sakes we were happy to accept this offer and the refreshment he promised.

At last, foaming tankards before us, we could open our budget. They listened in silence until the narrative was complete.

'Lady Elham was lying all along!' Jem breathed. 'There never was a job in London, or a secret husband, or a journey to Warwick or Leamington?'

'There might have been all three, but not while Lizzie was in the employment of Lady Templemead,' Hansard replied.

'Why should Lady Elham lie?' And so wildly? I thought of her words about Lizzie and her babe.

'The usual reason is to protect someone,' Turner said, applying himself fastidiously to the landlord's best home brew.

'But who? You tell us it is impossible for Lord Elham to have killed Lizzie because he was locked up in Lymbury Park,'

Jem said, with such anger that he might almost have been blaming Hansard himself for Lizzie's death.

Hansard, moreover, might have been accepting the blame. 'All I can suggest, gentlemen, is that we return to Lymbury Park to see if I mistook the dates, or if there is forgery that it would take better eyes than mine to detect.' He looked at his watch. 'We are to dine with Sir Hellman this evening, Tobias, are we not? So stop sipping at that glass as if you were a delicate miss straight from a seminary. We have miles to cover, and fast.'

Jem wasted no time, but, knowing the horses had to make the return journey, did not force the pace. Suddenly, however, he brought the carriage to a halt on the main road. We peered out. There was no sign of an accident.

Turner had already leapt down, and was helping someone to his feet.

'I am all for charity, Tobias, and could recite as well as you the story of the good Samaritan, but what the deuce does Turner want with a beggar when he knows that speed is of the essence?'

Turner returned at a run, putting his face to the window. 'It is the man whom Jem and I met that inn, sir!'

'The venial man?' I prompted him.

'Indeed. He has lost his post at Lymbury Park and is walking to Bath to seek employment there. May we take him up, sir?'

At first my instinct was to suggest that Turner relinquished his place beside Jem and joined us inside himself, Turner knowing the art of companionable silence. However, I soon realised both my selfishness and my folly; in his disgruntlement, there might be much more that the dismissed servant could tell us.

It seemed that Hansard had the same idea. 'By all means. Turner, invite him into the carriage, please. We may find he is less venial now. And does he have a name?'

'Sam, sir.'

Sam was exhausted and hungry. Losing his employment as an attendant had lost him access to the servants' hall and also his home.

'Sam Eccleshall at your service, gents both,' he declared with a low as he got into the carriage. 'I was seen speaking to Jem and whatshisname, sir,' he told Hansard. 'And for all I told them I'd been as secret as the tomb, they threw me out. And I'm not used to this walking, sir – I got blisters the size of florins, and I'll swear my stomach's flapping in the wind.'

'Jem and Turner will take you to the inn while we speak to Dr Brighouse,' Hansard assured him, 'and there you can eat your fill. Then, if you still wish to find work in Bath, we can convey you there the moment we conclude our business at the Park. I wonder why they didn't want you to talk to Jem and Turner,' he mused, as if not expecting an answer, which he could in any case have supplied himself. Sam had given away information that his employers had not wished others to know, and by doing so betrayed their trust in him.

'I dunno. I never told them nothing to the purpose, did I? Maybe you kind gentlemen could put in good word for me.'

'Maybe we could. As a matter of fact, we may well be able to do so,' he assured him, duplicitously. 'I'm sure good strong reliable men like you are hard to find. It's not everyone who would care to work in an insane asylum.'

'Indeed, nor would they, sir. The sights you do see would move many a man to tears, I can tell you. But not me, not no more. I'm used to it, see.'

'What sort of thing might move one to tears?' I asked, not seeing why Hansard should have to shoulder all the burden of the conversation.

'Seeing those young lads crying for their nurses – that's sad, that is. And seeing old men, swaddled up like babies.'

'Old men?' Now I came to think of it, all the inmates that we had seen had been young. Even the party working in the gardens had been no more than five and thirty. I had a sudden pang of fear: what if that cordial ex-soldier had been observed as he spoke to me, and he too had now paid the price? There was little enough work for the halt and the lame.

'One or two.'

'And when did they arrive?'

Hansard went too fast.

A cunning look crossed Sam's face. 'I suppose you gents wouldn't have a drop of daffy about you? Or blue ruin? 'Cause I'm fair parched, that I can tell you. No?'

'At the inn, Sam, at the inn. And a good beefsteak.'

'Now, you were telling us about these poor old men—' I leant forward confidentially, receiving for my pains a gust of stinking breath.

'Ah, so I was. Like the others, filled to the ears with laudanum, and such. You'll know the sort of thing, sir, being a medical man,' he told Hansard.

I raised an eyebrow; it was unlike Turner to have been so indiscreet.

'And what else?' he asked.

'They see things. And sometimes they won't give them any laudanum and they see worse things. The screaming and hollering they do make. One old guy, he comes in as sweet as you or me, and they've got him up on that top floor, through all that snow and frost, and you wonder he survived. No fires, you see, in case they harms themselves, or sets fire to the place.'

'And when did this old man come?'

He pulled a face. 'Just as the weather turned cold, sir. A weather-beaten old cove he was, suffering something shocking with his rheumatics.

'And when did you say the weather changed?'

He smacked dry lips. But he knew he had met his match in Hansard. 'A couple of weeks before Christmas, gennelmen. Maybe three or four. No, not so long. Three.'

I could see from Hansard's expression that he was going through the same mental processes as I. John Sanderson – dear John Coachman – was supposed to have died here in Bath. There was no evidence in any of the parish records of his death. Perhaps, praise the Lord, he might still be alive, and incarcerated in the same secretive asylum as Lord Elham.

Hansard rubbed his hands as he caught my eye. 'Thank you, Sam. Now, I wonder how far it is to that inn.'

I have never seen my friend move so fast. Flourishing an entirely blank piece of paper he had purchased from the landlord of the inn where we had deposited Sam, he burst into Brighouse's book room.

'John Sanderson! In the name of the law, where are you

keeping John Sanderson? So help me, if I have to choke the information out of you, I shall have it!' Hansard grabbed the other doctor by the throat.

'I have no patient by that name—'

'Have you that patient by another name? Speak, man!'

Brighouse's eyes were bulging. All he could do was point upwards.

'If he's dead, by God you shall pay for it!'

'Let him speak, Edmund,' I whispered urgently. 'Do not have his blood on your hands.'

'And the blood of how many others is on his hands? Pah!' He suddenly released his hold, and threw him across the room. 'On your feet! Lead the way.' He grabbed him by the scruff of his neck to assist him.

We found what was left of John Coachman in a cell-like room neither better nor worse than the one in which we had found Lord Elham the previous day. The doses of laudanum had left him vacant-eyed, with a severe tremor. What little hair he had was now snow white; his strong frame, prey once to nothing worse than rheumatism, was reduced to skin and bone; as for his head, there was no sign of the kindly but shrewd mind that had once functioned within.

'What is to be done?' I whispered.

Once John Coachman had been moved to a superior room, one adjacent, in fact, to Lord Elham's, we adjourned to Dr Brighouse's book room. Now the personification of the obliging physician, with no more than occasional fingering of what must be a very bruised throat, Brighouse summoned yet more refreshments for us all.

'You will not be surprised if I ask you to eat and drink what you offer before we touch anything.' Hansard smiled grimly. 'Why did you do it, Brighouse? Connive in the living death of that old man?'

Hand still shaking, Brighouse poured three glasses of brandy, and drank deeply of one of them. 'There, gentlemen, you will see there is nothing to fear. What was better, to connive in the patient's living death or to kill him outright, as I was bidden?'

'But die he assuredly will, unless some miracle occurs.'

'He will have the best nursing I can provide – provided, gentlemen, that you ensure that the person who required his death can never come near me to exact retribution for my betrayal.'

'I am sure we can promise you that,' I said easily. 'Especially as we do not know who he is. I think it is time you enlightened us, do not you?'

'I dare not! I dare not!'

'Come, you are being unreasonable. We all know that a most heinous crime has been committed. The miscreant must – will! – be apprehended. Then you will have no cause to fear,' Sir Hellman reasoned.

'No, no! Pray, do not ask me – not yet. I dare not!' Indeed, he was white to the lips with terror. What kind of monster could instil this degree of terror in a rational man?

He held up his hands in supplication. 'Look around you, gentlemen – pray, look in any of these rooms at any of my patients and tell me what could be done better! It is only those who are a danger to themselves or to others who receive the harsh treatment that you have seen. And would they be better treated anywhere else?' He took another sip of brandy. 'Now, I will undertake to reduce Mr Sanderson's doses of laudanum, and to increase his diet, much as you have already instructed me to do in the case of Lord Elham. But you must protect me! Pray, gentlemen, protect me!'

I took a steadying nip of brandy and walked to the window. 'Have you dismissed anyone from your service recently?'

No doubt fearing another burst of fury from Hansard, he nodded. 'Sam Eccleshall blabs when he's in his cups. I cannot risk the identity of my patients being known – you must see that.'

'And the man in charge of the patients who were gardening? Is he still employed here?'

Brighouse dropped his gaze. 'He swore he revealed nothing, but how could I trust him ever again?'

'Reinstate both, Mr Brighouse,' I told him, 'and in future pay them more to keep their mouths shut. You will find Sam Eccleshall in the Pig and Whistle. You will have to run that good sergeant to earth yourself, but I will expect to see him at his post when we return.'

'You are coming back?'

'Very soon. After all,' I said, 'we shall need to return this, shall we not?' I picked up his ledger. 'And now, we will take our leave of you. Good day, sir.'

When we returned at last to the Pelican we had very little time to change for our dinner engagement, one which, I admit, I was most reluctant to keep.

'The man made his money from slavery, Edmund!' I

declared, as Turner eased me into my tailcoat. 'How can we soil ourselves by accepting his hospitality?'

'Because none of us is pure. How much of your father's wealth – which, I accept, you have largely eschewed – comes from his own labour? Your stipend derives from Lady Elham and her family, with which, given all the indications so far, one would prefer not to be connected. The guineas my farming patients pay me are available because labourers are paid so very badly.'

'But slavery! Every feeling must be offended!'

'Indeed. But first let us admit that giving away a fortune made perhaps by his father, even his grandfather before him, is not easy. And secondly, let us see what he does with his wealth. He may have manumitted his slaves; he may be a great public benefactor; and above all, Tobias, he may be extremely useful in keeping an eye on Lymbury Park, both as a justice and as one who has already seen and been revolted by some of the practices of the place. Ah, thank you, Turner – you have once again transformed your country bumpkins into civilised gentlemen.'

Turner smiled. 'And, moreover, sir, I will endeavour to find the truth about Sir Hellman from my colleagues in the tap-room, though I suspect that Jem may be more adept at the art than I.'

There was a knock at the door. The Boots had a letter in his hand for one whom he referred to as a *gennelman.*

It was addressed to me, but in a hand I did not recognise. Hansard clearly did, however; his face tightened and the hand held out for Turner to fasten his cufflinks shook.

I opened it. It was from Mrs Beckles.

*My Dear Mr Campion*

*Pray forgive me for writing to you, but I have information to hand that I believe you and Dr Hansard should know. I have been speaking, as you would expect, to Mrs Woodman, still laid low by the shocking revelations at the inquest. At last, appalled by her constant reiterations that Lizzie was no daughter of hers, I took the liberty of remonstrating with her. But – and you may guess my amazement! – she assured me that this was the literal truth. Lizzie, Mr Campion, is not her flesh and blood. Rather she is the love child of someone whom Mrs Woodman has never met. The arrangements were all undertaken by lawyers, who paid Mrs Woodman a sum to act as wet nurse, and then, Mr Woodman at last assenting, to act as her mother. Mrs Woodman still receives a regular sum of money provided she maintains this secret. I cannot but feel that Lizzie's identity must have a bearing on her death, though what as yet I cannot imagine.*

*Yours, etc.*
*Maria Beckles*

*Post scriptum. I have this instant received a communication from Dr Hansard, but wish to put this directly in the post. Pray assure Dr Hansard that I will respond the instant I have opened and perused it, and do me the honour of passing on my sincerest good wishes.*

Without a word, I passed the open missive to my friend, gripping his shoulder affectionately as I pointed to the ending, surely as open a declaration of love that in all conscience a lady could give. More I could not do, not knowing whether he had taken Turner into his confidence about his intentions towards the lady – though I would have wagered all Sir Hellman's wealth that Turner had known, to put it vulgarly, the way the wind was blowing long before I had so much as an inkling.

We dined *à trois* with Sir Hellman, but clearly could not speak of the matter so important to us all until the servants had cleared the table and withdrawn.

'You are telling me that on someone's orders an innocent man has been kidnapped and kept in a drugged stupor? Gentlemen, have you been reading too many novels from a circulating library? We are living in nineteenth-century England, not in some Gothic Alpine kingdom!'

Dr Hansard sipped the excellent port thoughtfully. 'Do not think that we are unshaken by the idea. But Brighouse has confessed it himself. John Sanderson lives, Sir Hellman. Yet before Christmas we were apprised of his sad death from inflammation of the lung.'

'Who was your informant?'

'None other than Lady Elham, mother of the drug-raddled wretch whom we suspect of murdering Lizzie.'

'Can you still suspect him? If Brighouse's ledger is accurate – and it had the appearance of truth – then he cannot have been involved.'

'We have brought the ledger for further inspection – perhaps it could be fetched?'

'Indeed – and more candles and a magnifying glass.'

* * *

At last, having examined the relevant entries from every angle, we came to a reluctant but unanimous conclusion: they had not been altered in any way.

# CHAPTER TWENTY-THREE

'If Lord Elham did not kill Lizzie, *could not* have killed Lizzie, who did?' I asked, my brain reeling. I did not feel as angry as Jem had sounded uttering almost identical words, but could not perhaps allow myself to speculate further, lest I found the answer unacceptable.

Dr Hansard's response was measured, warning me, I suppose, that while Sir Hellman was a sympathetic host and fellow justice, he was still not a friend. 'My feeling accords with the sentiment expressed by Lady Elham's housekeeper. Mrs Beckles has informed us,' he told Sir Hellman, his face almost insensibly softening as he mentioned her name, 'that there is now some doubt as to the birth of the murdered maid. Her view is that until we solve that mystery, we shall not find why she was killed, and thus by whom. So I believe an urgent return to Moreton St Jude is called for. We have news, moreover, that Mrs Sanderson deserves to hear from our own lips.'

Sir Hellman bowed. 'Of course. Will you be setting out tonight? There is a moon.'

'I think not; even such excellent servants as ours will need time to prepare. But I believe, Sir Hellman, that we must away far earlier than we would wish, and, of course, than you may consider polite.'

Hellman shook his head. 'Not at all. I quite understand your reasons. I would add another. If the servant of whom you spoke has discovered something someone wished to keep hidden, she herself may be at risk. Considerable risk.'

I wished to object – as I was sure Edmund did – that Mrs Beckles was no servant, but a lady, but we both kept our counsel.

'From Brighouse's terror,' Hellman continued, 'we know that we are dealing with a heartless and ruthless man. Even when I pressed him while you were seeing to Sanderson, Brighouse still refused to say who had placed the poor old man in his clutches. I pray you, do not stand on ceremony. My house is your house, gentlemen. In such circumstances, were you to leave it this instant, I believe I would urge you on still faster.'

We almost ran back to the Pelican, where we swiftly located Jem and Turner. One look at our faces and they were on their feet.

'I say we travel at once, Toby,' Jem declared in the privacy of our parlour. 'We would never forgive ourselves if anything happened to that good woman. She's been a real saviour to the villagers.'

Edmund's heart apparently too full to admit of a reply and further moved, I swear, by Jem's encomium, I agreed vehemently. 'And if you believe that an overnight journey is possible, then let us set forth immediately.'

Turner said smoothly, 'I believe that I might deal with your baggage more swiftly than you, gentlemen.'

'In that case we will pay our shot, and be ready when you both give the word,' Edmund said gruffly.

* * *

Whereas we had made a leisurely journey to Bath, our return was much swifter. When he judged a change of horses necessary, Jem hired others, undertaking to return at a later date to collect Hansard's own.

'You must take some rest yourself,' I urged, as he put his head under an inn yard pump to clear his head.

'Truth to tell, Toby, I'm grateful to be properly on the move at last. It's as if a fever has been building and building and is at last about to break. If by pressing on we can make it break the quicker, then I'm not about to call craven. Now, ask them to find me some coffee,' he told me. 'I want to make sure that they give me some halfway decent cattle, not some old bone-setters fit for nothing but the knacker's yard.'

I did as I was told.

Without being asked, on our arrival in Moreton St Jude the following night, Jem drove neither to Langley Park nor to the rectory but direct to the tradesman's entrance at Moreton Priory. He almost fell with fatigue, but, finding his feet, veritably sprinted to the door, where a startled manservant admitted him, a candle wavering in the night air. We followed with less speed, tumbling from the coach with limbs so stiff I was surprised that they moved at all. Somehow we found ourselves in the kitchen corridor, with a covert audience watching, no doubt, through keyholes and round unclosed doors.

It took horrible moments for Mrs Beckles to appear. At least the explanation for her delay was clear. She had been preparing for bed, and wore a fetching nightcap over curl-papers. When she saw who was summoning her, she blushed scarlet and backed away, clutching tighter the shawl she had wrapped herself in.

Hansard seemed unable to speak.

'Pray, Mrs Beckles, prepare yourself for a short stay at the rectory. Go – now!' I urged her.

'Mr Campion, what nonsense is this?' she demanded, with one glance reducing me to a junior pageboy on his very first day in service. 'You wake the whole household! What am I to tell Lady Elham in the morning?'

I would not blush and stutter. Instead, casting my eyes in the direction of the unseen but attentive ears, I said calmly, 'Please do me the honour of permitting me two minutes of your time in private. Absolute private.'

Our eyes met. I hoped that in mine she saw authority and reason, while in hers there was doubt and, at last, acquiescence.

'One moment, sir,' she said, with a bob of a curtsy.

Edmund and I waited like guilty schoolboys, shuffling our feet and preferring not to meet each other's eyes. When her door opened, it was to reveal that she had already slipped on her usual attire and had brushed out the curl papers.

Nonetheless, she had undertaken to admit me alone, and so I left Hansard in the corridor as she shut the door behind us.

'I think I deserve an explanation,' she said, folding her arms in an implacable way that boded no good for Dr Hansard's suit. 'One that will satisfy her ladyship herself.'

'I owe you an apology. There should not have been this drama. But, dear Mrs Beckles, pray understand that, had Dr Hansard and I not believed your life to have been at immediate risk, we would simply have paid a polite morning call on our return from Bath, and would have drunk a glass of your elderflower wine and told you all about our adventures. We would even have shown you the gifts we purchased for you.'

There was no answering smile. 'Why on earth should you think *I* am in danger?'

'Because you have found out that secret of Lizzie's birth.'

'And you think I have told any apart from you? For shame, Tobias!'

I hung my head. But then I rallied. 'If Mrs Woodman is capable of revealing it to you, she is capable of revealing that she has betrayed the information to you. And, lacking any other explanation for Lizzie's death, Edmund and I believe that it may lie in her very birth. If her killer believes anyone else is privy to the secret, that person may be the next victim. We – Edmund and I – would vastly prefer it not to be you.'

'Thank you kindly,' she said, with a dry smile. 'But all this commotion, Tobias – it will be all round the Priory by six tomorrow morning, and thence all over the village.'

'In that case, we must devise an explanation. Pray, Mrs Beckles, please do as I ask – as I implore. Now, as to a post-haste departure, I am sure the reason for that can lie in Mrs Trent. I am sure she will consent to be bed-bound with the influenza and require skilled nursing that only you could provide.'

'I do not like to involve Mrs Trent in an untruth. Perhaps I should visit my sick sister? Augusta lives near Worcester and is constantly asking me to visit.'

'Has Augusta a strong man like Jem constantly at hand? Consider, if this man, whoever it might be, sought you out and attacked you.'

She shot a shrewd glace at me. 'Would not any evildoer be more likely to find me in the rectory here in the village?'

I considered. 'That depends on who else knows about your sick sister.'

'Augusta is hardly a secret! There have been occasions when I have had to ask her ladyship for leave of absence to post down when her end seemed to be approaching. Then many other members of the household have had to undertake extra duties, from the butler to the housemaids.'

I frowned. 'Is there no one else, unknown to anyone belonging to the Priory or to the village, with whom you could seek refuge? Dear Mrs Beckles, Edmund is still outside, pacing, no doubt, in anxiety. May we not admit him to our discussions?'

She blushed fierily. 'Circumstanced as we are—'

'Would you prefer a few moments alone with Edmund?' I asked gently. 'There are matters you might wish to discuss.' Not giving her time to prevaricate, I stepped out and indicated with a movement of my head that Edmund should take my place.

Naturally the person whose company I sought was Jem's. He had returned to the yard. Turner was curled up fast asleep in a corner of the carriage.

'She doesn't want to leave the house, and certainly not to seek refuge in the rectory,' I said bluntly.

'We managed it ill,' he said. 'And I am most to blame. Truth to tell, Toby, I got so wound up thinking about how poor Dr Hansard would feel if anything ever happened to Mrs Beckles that he could have prevented that I never thought about the proprieties. Nothing would have happened overnight. All this could have been done so much better by daylight.'

'By daylight,' I mused, 'Mrs Beckles would have been honour bound to apprise her ladyship of her movements. As it is,' I nodded over his shoulder, 'I fancy she must have left without notifying anyone.'

Like man and maid in the may-time of their years, our friends were walking towards us, Dr Hansard carrying a valise with his free hand.

'Mrs Beckles is not the only one to have an ailing relative,' he said, preventing any comment or congratulation. 'I have an aunt in Derby. Mrs Beckles will stay with her until all has been resolved here. Now, Jem, will you drive us all to the rectory, where we may make more detailed dispositions?'

Edmund and I rode on in silence to Langley Park, leaving Mrs Beckles to be chaperoned by Mrs Trent, with Jem insisting on sleeping in the corridor outside their bedchambers. Travel-weary though he was, Turner had ridden straight to Langley Park to make preparations and to warn Dr Toone of his host's return.

'I ought to be the happiest man on earth, Tobias,' Edmund confessed at last, as our horses picked their way through the moonlight. 'But all I know is that I am the most exhausted.'

'Tomorrow the fatigue will be forgotten,' I assured him, 'whereas your happiness will be yours to savour for the rest of your life.'

'Much as want her by my side, I am glad she is prepared to go away from here. Tobias, do you ever feel there is evil in the world?'

'I am a clergyman, Edmund! Of course there is evil, just as

there is good. But why do you ask? Just to keep us awake with disputation?'

'Not at all. I have seen many things in my life, things that you could not even dream of and hope you never will, but nothing has made me so ill at ease as my present situation. For the first time in my life I can trust no one, excepting,' he amended with a laugh, 'yourself, Jem, Turner and my dear Mrs Beckles.'

I did not laugh as I replied, 'Then we are of the same mind.'

We were still anxious the following morning, even though Mrs Beckles had sent off a lad with a note for her ladyship saying no more than that she had been summoned to a friend's deathbed and would contact her as soon as it was possible. Naturally she gave no hint of her destination. Mrs Trent very kindly agreed to accompany Mrs Beckles on her journey. Susan, round-eyed with excitement, was to go too, never having been out of the county before and seeing Derbyshire as a magic land. The weather being fine, Jem invited her to sit on the box with him, leaving, he said, the two ladies to enjoy their gossip in peace.

That left us with two immediate tasks. The first was to break to Mrs Sanderson the news of her husband's present condition. The second was to have further speech with Mrs Woodman, requiring her, with the greatest authority we could appeal to, to reveal the name of Lizzie's parents.

With Lady Elham's gracious permission, Mrs Sanderson still lived in the tied cottage that many another employer would have given her notice to quit the instant she became a widow. As we had expected, the outside was as immaculate as ever, with the smell of baking telling us that Mrs Sanderson was at home. She greeted us with puzzlement, as well she might, but automatically wiped the seats of two upright chairs with her apron as she invited us to sit. Before we could speak, she bustled off to the scullery to return with cowslip wine and new bread, which she served with butter from the home farm.

'Her ladyship has been so good to me, so very good,' she declared, sitting at last on the very edge of a third chair. 'All through this hard winter I have had as much fuel as I could use, and more food than I could eat, God bless her. And still she tells me I may stay. I thank God for such a benefactress.'

'Amen,' I said solemnly. I cleared my throat. 'What would you say if I told you that you had been misled about John's death, Mrs Sanderson? That he was not in fact dead, but alive, though grievously ill.'

'I should not believe you!' she declared roundly. 'Why should anyone mislead an old woman? And if me, why mislead her ladyship herself? She condescended to visit me herself to speak to me. And she told me all about his illness and the care she had ordered for him, and how she herself had bathed his brow with lavender water.'

I ventured a glance at Edmund. He was as white as I felt I must be.

'Well? Is that all you came for, to drink my wine and tell me my dear good man was alive? Let me tell you to your face, Mr Campion, there are many in the village who say you are a mischief-maker, and by God they are right. And you, Doctor, being taken in! Away with the pair of you!'

I would have argued, tried to correct her misunderstanding, but with a sharp jerk of his head indicated that we were to leave immediately.

When we reached our horses, Edmund spoke first. 'Neither of us has uttered – in connection with this dreadful business – one name. But now I think we must.'

'It is impossible! A dastardly crime like this! How can a woman – a *lady*! – be implicated? She must be the victim of someone's coercion.'

'Let us reserve judgement. Tobias, indulge me in this. Before we go to Mrs Woodman's, let us pay a call on Mrs Jenkins.'

'For what reason?'

'Do you recall speaking to me about young William before Christmas? You told me he had nightmares, and asked me to prescribe a sleeping draught. Thinking if he divulged the content the dreams might disappear, I tried to question him. All too clearly he was too afraid. I thought he feared the return of the dreams. I wonder if he was afraid of something else. Some*one* else.'

I shook my head. 'Of the workhouse master? But he—'

I could feel the effort he was making to be patient. 'Of the person he saw pushing Lord Elham into the water, Tobias. That is who he fears. So we must go post-haste and require him to tell us everything.'

'Are you saying that Lady Elham watched someone murder her husband?'

'For God's sake, Tobias. Everything we have heard implicates her ladyship. I am saying that William watched Lady Elham murder her husband!'

# CHAPTER TWENTY-FOUR

'Why do you stand there like a chicken with the gapes! Surely you understood why I wanted to remove Mrs Beckles from Moreton Priory, and why I was all too happy for Mrs Trent and young Susan to go too? Surely you have seen that everything points to Lady Elham's involvement!'

Still I shook my head in disbelief. 'But the chapel...the paintings...the Bible readings...'

'Even Titus understands the need for urgency more than you appear to,' Edmund said, getting on his own horse and kicking it into motion.

Mrs Jenkins looked the picture of health as she greeted us at her cottage door, and I thanked God for the oasis of normality in the chaos of mind into which Edmund had plunged me. Of course, deep down I must have suspected my cousin of some involvement, but I clung to the belief that she was merely – merely! – attempting to protect her son from justice, something which he would probably have evaded anyway, given his madness. Later, when it was demonstrated that he could not have committed the murder, I thought – I know not what I thought.

But now there might be further, terrible evidence that she was more than an accomplice.

'And how is my young patient?' Hansard enquired as he dismounted.

'Is he still suffering from his nightmares?' I asked, doing likewise.

Her smile faded. 'Seems to me they've got worse,' she said, curtsying at Hansard, then at me. 'And why I cannot fathom, since he's had such a piece of good fortune we'd never dreamt of.'

Hansard did not need to press my arm to keep me silent. 'Indeed? And what might that be?' He chucked the youngest child under a dimpled chin.

'He's going to be a page,' she said.

'Up at the Priory?' he asked casually.

'Bless you life, better than that. At her ladyship's London house. She says he's such a fine upstanding lad he'll look good in her livery. Or maybe he'll become a tiger, if he stays small, like his father, God rest his soul.'

'And how does William feel about this – this good fortune?' I asked.

Her smile faded. 'I fear that he will be a disappointment to you, Dr Hansard, and to you, Mr Campion. He weeps, him a grown boy, and will not eat, and swears he will not go. He says his place is here with us.'

'He is the man of the house,' I said quietly.

'And where is he now?' Hansard looked about him. 'I must give my godson a golden guinea before he sets out on such a journey.'

She nodded doubtfully. 'He's out in the woods on Mr Campion's glebe land, sir, chopping some logs he said we might have.' She looked to me for confirmation I gladly gave.

'You are sure of this?'

'Aye. He took a good length of my washing line to tie them up,' she said with a smile.

'Do you know to which part of the woods he was headed?' I asked.

'The east covert, I do believe.'

'Excuse us, Mrs Jenkins,' I said, already turning from her and ready to mount Titus.

Titus had once been my favourite hunter, and relished the chance to show his paces once more. We left Hansard well behind. Would we be in time? I dreaded to think what mischief a desperate child might do to himself, fearing not just to leave his home and family but to be at the mercy of a woman he had seen either letting her husband drown or indeed murdering the man. As I galloped I found enough breath to call out his name. What did I dread more, finding him gone altogether, kidnapped by a woman who could not afford to leave a witness alive, or finding a sad body swinging forlornly from a noose made from his mother's washing line, rope which, God help me, I had provided myself?

At last the woodland became denser, and I was afraid even the sure-footed Titus might find a rabbit hole. So we dropped to a walking place. Still I called William's name.

Did I hear a sound, other than the twittering of courting birds? Surely that was a sob? I pressed forward the more eagerly, at last coming to a log chopped almost in two. Of the axe and its owner there was no sign.

'William? William? It is I, your friend Parson Campion! I am come to tell you that you do not have to go to London! You will stay here with me! William, I will look after you. And your family,' I added, lest my cousin had threatened the family if he did not acquiesce. 'I promise you that you will be safe if you come out now.'

Where was the rope? Dear God, where was that rope?

I dismounted, tethering Titus, and ranged round on foot, still calling, still assuring him that he would be safe. Soon I heard Hansard's voice, making the same promises.

'William, here are both your old friends come looking for you! Enough of this hide and seek! Dr Hansard has a guinea for you if you come out now.'

Up shot the good doctor's arm, so that the sun caught the gold. We waited in silence.

Never had a minute seemed so long. All I could hear was the pounding of my heart, which seemed to have transferred itself to my ears. Hansard grasped my arm, touching his ear with the other hand, and then pointing to our left. What had he heard?

I strained harder. Had I heard a twig crack, or was it my imagination?

'William,' Edmund called quietly, 'can you not see this guinea? It is only your good friends Dr Hansard and Mr Campion!' But he did not wait for a response. Without warning, he sped off as fast as he could, his breath coming, as mine did, in painful gasps.

A pair of small feet swung to and fro. William had even taken off his boots and put them neatly side by side, climbing in his stockinged feet onto a pile of logs he had kicked clear to launch himself to his Creator. Hansard grasped William's legs, pushing them upwards, his old arms straining over his head in the effort to take the child's weight.

'I am not strong enough to hold him!'

I heaped the logs quickly, clumsily, but managed to gain a foothold, reaching too, and taking the weight of William's body. To my amazement, I heard the thud of hooves. It seemed that Hansard's horse had learnt a trick I had tried in vain to teach Titus, to come when whistled. Standing in the stirrups, Edmund cut his way through the mercifully thin rope, and William sagged into my arms.

I laid him gently on the ground.

Edmund tore away the child's neckerchief and felt his pulse. 'He lives. Barely. He hardly breathes. Fetch the smelling salts from my saddlebag.'

He did not need to urge haste.

The salts had no effect.

'If only I could breathe my own breath into his lungs, *force* his heart to beat more strongly,' Edmund cried. 'We have not saved him from all his travails just to have him expire like this!' At last, in desperation, he put his mouth over William's and did indeed breathe into him, rubbing the child's chest as he did so. All I could do was fall on my knees, begging help from the Almighty.

Whether it was His help or Edmund's more mundane actions, but at last the lad seemed to stir.

I found a feather and laid it on his lips, all the time thinking of King Lear's vain quest to prove that his daughter lived. Perhaps it did move. Perhaps.

'Try again,' I urged Hansard. 'Just once more.'

At last William breathed on his own, but his eyes gave not so much as a flutter.

Edmund lifted him carefully. 'We must take him back to his mother, and I must stay with him. It will fall to you, I fear, to beard Mrs Woodman in her den.'

'Of course. But first I will accompany you. In fact, I will run ahead and prepare her. How much shall I tell her?'

'That he has had an accident. Should he die, that is what I will tell the coroner. That he was playing with a rope and slipped. It may be the truth. But I fear it was not. Whether it was an attempt at suicide or someone tried to take his life, we may never know.'

Leaving William to the best care Edmund and his mother could provide, I set off, my heart weighed down. I could not imagine the despair, the terror, that must have driven a child to end his life rather than face a new one with a woman he knew was capable of killing. Or – would it be worse? – being torn from his homely task and strung from a bough, all too aware of the consequences.

''Morning, Parson! Why the Friday-face? You look as if you've lost a florin and found a rusty button!'

At last I looked up. It was Matthew, axe in hand, shirt open to the waist, epitomising strength and sanity. He, as much as anyone, deserved a truthful explanation of my grim face. I reined in Titus and dismounted.

'Matthew, I believe we are almost ready to identify Lizzie's killer. But there is a little more information to gather. Do you care to accompany me to Mrs Woodman's cottage? I have some questions to put to her, the answers to which you might like to hear.'

'You are telling me the truth, aren't you? And it is a truth you have paid a heavy price for, to judge by your expression. Beg pardon for my earlier jest, Parson.'

'With all my heart. Will you come with me?'

For reply, he fell into step with me. Titus consented to be led. 'Do you ask because you need a witness?'

'I ask because you loved Lizzie.'

For a while, neither of us spoke, both deep in our own thoughts.

It was Matthew who broke the silence, coughing awkwardly. 'Seems I shall have to have the banns read, Parson. For me and Annie. Seems she's in a promising way, and I want to do my duty by her and the babe.'

'Of course. Bring Annie along to the parsonage whenever you care to and we shall fix the day. Congratulations, Matthew. I hope you will be very happy – and that you will bring the babe to be baptised as soon as you can. And that Annie will be churched.'

'It doesn't mean I loved Lizzie any less, Parson,' he pleaded.

'Of course it doesn't,' I said, thinking of the Burke-reading young lady who needed a suitor with ten thousand a year, and the even brighter eyes of Lady Salcombe. 'Lizzie would have wanted you to mourn, but not repine. Matthew! That's smoke!' I pointed. A steady column of smoke, far greater than from a cottage chimney, rose in the woods. There came the ominous crackle of burning wood.

'Ride ahead!' he urged.

I needed no second bidding.

Mrs Woodman's cottage was well alight when I reached it, but, pulling my coat about my head, I plunged in, fighting through the smoke until I found the old lady, asleep in her chair.

I tried in vain to rouse her, even to pull her from it. But she did not stir. In fear of my own life as the fire raged, I dragged the chair and her upon it to the door. As I reached it, a terrible creak told me the lintel was giving way. I dragged with all my might, but failed. The burning timber crashed down on her legs, igniting her skirts.

I ripped my coat from my head and used it to beat at the flames.

And then there was water all over us both. And more. Matthew had reached us and was filling bucket upon bucket from her well, hauling as quickly as he could.

Her dress now a charred heap of rags, we carried the old lady, still on her chair, out of range of the sparks from the blazing thatch.

Matthew took a look at me and fetched another bucket. 'No point in trying to save the cottage,' he said, 'but we might save your hands. Just keep them in the water. I'll see to the old lady.'

'But—'

'Do as you're told, or you'll lose the use of them. Do it!'

While I obeyed, he laid her gently on his shirt, covering her poor burnt legs with what was left of my coat. We exchanged a sad glance. How could she live with such injuries?

I knelt beside her. Matthew thrust my hands under water once more. 'Lie still, Mrs Woodman. Matthew will ride for the doctor. Take Titus, man. Hansard's at the Jenkinses' cottage: seek him there. And bid someone bring a gig, and plenty of pillows.'

'No need for any rush,' she gasped, as he galloped off. 'I'm dying, Parson, and that no one can deny.'

'How did this happen, Mrs Woodman? You must tell me!'

She moaned in pain. It was clearly too late for explanations.

'Shall we pray for God's mercy?' I suggested.

She inclined her head. I put her hands together and clasped them with my dripping fingers. A faint smile told me she found comfort in the words I spoke.

At last, I took it upon myself to refer to the harsh words she had spoken about Lizzie when she first disappeared, letting her know that Mrs Beckles had given some explanation.

She raised tear-filled eyes to mine. 'But, Parson, you know now that they were the honest truth! True, I should not have uttered them, since I vowed by all I held sacred that I would never reveal the secret. I was Lizzie's wet nurse. No more. I never knew her true parents, but I suspected. I suspected... But a woman like me can't make accusations, especially when my mouth is stopped with a golden guinea every quarter, regular as the moon. I was to bring her up like my own, they said—'

'Who said?' My pulses were racing.

'The legal men who brought her to me. I made my mark on their paper, Parson, and as God is my witness I've spoken of it to no one till now.'

'He will surely forgive you.' I moistened her lips with water. 'I suppose the men of law left you no papers?'

'Nothing,' came the sad reply. 'But,' she added, 'my guinea still comes each quarter, so belike they don't know she's gone.'

If I had committed murder, the last person I should wish to suspect that I had committed such a heinous crime would be a man with a legal bent, so probably Lady Elham had not told them that Lizzie was no more. Why indeed should she have done, the pretence being that she had done more than leave her service, and subsequently that of Lady Templemead?

'Tell them, Parson, will you? I shouldn't be taking what isn't mine, should I?' she added with some agitation.

'Of course. I will do whatever you want. But whom shall I tell?'

'He said his name was Bunce. Mr Bunce, from Bunce and Bargate. Up in Birmingham, he do say. But I wasn't to tell. I wasn't to tell. I swore on my Bible.'

'You broke your oath for the best of reasons. Now,' I continued, desperate to hear the accusation from someone else's lips, 'tell me one more thing. Whom did you suspect of being Lizzie's mother? For she too must be told, you know. And her father.'

She whispered something. I bent my head close to her mouth but could make little of it. Leicester? Lempster? Knowing that at very least Mr Bunce, from Bunce and Bargate, should be able to provide details, I gave my full attention to making her last moments more bearable. 'Now, shall we pray once more while we wait for the doctor?'

I had closed her eyes by the time Hansard reached her, with nothing to alleviate her last agonies except the sure and certain promise of the life to come.

He nodded sadly. 'I could not have saved her, Tobias. It was well you were here to offer comfort. What a coincidence that her house should burn down the day tragedy strikes another family,' he added, as he straightened. 'Will you see she is carried back to my cellar, Matthew? Thank you. And then we will see to your burns, Tobias.'

* * *

I woke when the evening sun found a gap in the curtains. I was not in my own room, but a strange one. As I struggled to my elbow, I was pushed gently back.

'Dr Hansard says you are not to stir till he says so, Mr Campion,' Turner said.

'But I'm so thirsty,' I complained, like a sickly child. Edmund had given me something to relieve the pain, and it must have sent me off to sleep.

'I will raise you by lifting the pillow, and then you may take a sip of this saline draught.' He suited the deed to the word, holding a glass to my lips. Laying me back again, he said, 'Dr Hansard said you might have some more drops if the pain is very bad.'

'I shall do very well without them, thank you, Turner. Where is Edmund?'

He tutted disapprovingly. 'Down in the cellar looking at poor Mrs Woodman's body, as is his way, sir. If you can spare me, I will let him know that you are conscious.'

I must have drifted off to sleep again, because the next thing I knew was Edmund feeling my pulse.

'He must have the constitution of an ox, this young man,' he observed.

Toone's voice replied, 'Indeed he must. I beat him sorely when we were at Eton – only for his own good, mind you.'

For the sake of their friendship, that was a myth I must remember to perpetuate.

'So why do you make an invalid out of me?' I demanded, forcing open my leaden lids. 'I may feel buffle-headed, but I am sure that is a result of whatever concoction you made Turner pour down my throat.'

'It is. I had to dress your burnt hands, Tobias, and that gave you pain. Thanks to Matthew's quick thinking, however, there is very little tissue damage, and you will learn to wear your scars with pride. You should – it was no mean feat to rescue Mrs Woodman.'

'Had I succeeded in saving her life, it might be praiseworthy.'

'I think she would have died soon anyway,' Toone said. 'You told Hansard that she was unconscious when you dragged her out. That was because someone had hit her so hard they had fractured her skull. Whoever did it – and I am sure we are all in agreement as to the likely culprit – intended anyone seeing her injuries to deduce they were caused by the fire, were they of course noticeable by then.'

'And have you arrested her yet?'

Edmund laughed, but with no gaiety. 'Would we dare without your presence? If you feel you can get up, and if Turner can make you halfway presentable – the fire has taken half your hair, Tobias – then we will have the horse brought round and sally forth at once.'

## CHAPTER TWENTY-FIVE

I was making my way downstairs when I heard a maidservant calling out to Dr Hansard. 'They do say, sirs, that there's great doings at the big house. It seems her ladyship's taken it into her head to go on her travels all over again. Such a hurrying and scurrying you never did see!'

'Thank God for the nosiness of villagers!' cried Edmund, as she left. 'My good friends, we must be on our way.'

We rode too hard for conversation, grateful for the brightness of the spring evening. Titus seemed puzzled by my handling of the reins, but had he seen the bandages and understood why they were there, he could not have been more biddable.

'Her ladyship is not At Home,' Woodvine, the butler, declared.

'She will see us,' Dr Hansard announced grimly, veritably pushing his way into the entrance hall. 'Where is she? Her boudoir? Do not attempt to announce me – I know my way well enough.'

Even Hansard found himself constrained by years of training to tap on the door before pushing it open. The three of us stepped in, standing shoulder to shoulder. 'I am here not as your physician, but as a justice of the peace,' Hansard said portentously. 'And I believe you know all too well why I am here, my lady.'

Before she replied, she appeared to notice something left lying on the carpet. A servant, not one of my protégées, but a new face, bent, despite an armful of clothes, to pick it up.

'Leave it! Wait in my bedroom!' To my amazement, Lady Elham picked up whatever it was herself. 'And take care not to crease my new grey silk when you pack it!' She gave an odd smile as she turned back to us. 'Some refreshment, gentlemen? No? Forgive me if I take some of my drops, Dr Hansard – I feel my palpitations coming on.' Her back to us, she measured a quantity into a glass, and turned to us, raising it as if in a toast. She swallowed convulsively, gasping a little. 'And why are you all here? You can see it is not convenient.'

'I wish to speak to you concerning Lizzie's death. Murder, I would say. And the murder of Augustus, Tenth Duke of Elham, William Jenkins and Nan Woodman. And the illegal incarceration of John Sanderson and of George, Eleventh Duke of Elham.'

It seemed to me that she paled. Certainly her breath came in ugly gasps. But she did not reply.

'As for Lizzie, she was with child, my lady,' he continued. 'And it seems to me someone wanted to ensure that she bore no more babes.'

'Do not repine over the unborn child's death,' she whispered. 'It would have been a halfwit. Inbreeding, Doctor Hansard – surely a man of your calibre knows the problems it brings. Every great family has members confined to attics or elsewhere. What hope could there be for any child of my son's, especially one begotten of his sister?' Her eyes focused on me, with some difficulty, I thought.

'She has taken something!' Toone declared. To my amazement, he seized her, attempting to put a finger to the back of her throat. With amazing power, she fought him off.

'A purgative, then!'

I knew that he and Hansard would do all they could but that I was superfluous. I busied myself looking round the room. What could it have been that she wished so much to pick up? Where had she put it? There was nothing untoward on the little silver tray that held her drops and the jug of water. I followed the line of the wainscoting.

'If only we knew what poison she has taken,' Hansard groaned. 'Then we might try an antidote.'

I proffered a pellet I had just picked up.

Toone took it. 'Rat poison?'

'She must have told her staff that there were mice here, thus ensuring a ready means of escape. Good God, Hansard, how long will she be like this?'

He shrugged.

Urging her to her daybed, I took her hand and knelt beside her. 'There is still time to make your peace with the Almighty,' I urged.

'No time. No time at all.'

'There is time to confess all you have done and why you did it. Let us make a beginning. Why did you drown your husband, Cousin?'

Her smile repelled me. 'Cousin! Well, I suppose I am. I hope you are spared the family madness, Cousin Tobias. Elham – my husband, save the mark! – was forced upon me by my family, a young man who was so far from knowing the ways of the world that he was unable to consummate our marriage, spending what should have been our honeymoon in an asylum, but one far less charitable to its inmates than Lymbury Park. It was given out that we had gone on the grand tour. I lived in seclusion with his brother's family until Augustus was deemed fit to emerge and breed. Once it was established that I was *enceinte*, I was spared his company, but he insisted on seeing his first-born. Never having seen a new-born before, he was so appalled by the sight that his madness came upon him again and he spent a further spell in the asylum. As you know, he spent longer and longer periods at liberty, but he was never strong in the intellect.'

'Was that reason to kill him?' Hansard demanded, muttering under his breath that if stupidity were a capital crime we would lose at least half the upper ten thousand.

'The reason I killed him was that he gave his niece a slip on the shoulder,' she said clearly. 'Oh, do not look so shocked, Cousin Tobias. Even a clergyman must have heard the expression. He *forced himself upon her*, you ignorant boy.'

'Lizzie was your daughter,' Hansard said, as if it were the most natural thing in the world.

'By Elham's brother. Lord Leominster. She was conceived and born while we were supposedly on the grand tour. Hence *my* seclusion,' she added with a twisted smile. 'She was a taking little thing, so I had her farmed out to a recently widowed woman, who had lost her own baby, on what was then one of Elham's less favoured estates. I thought I would never have to see her again. But then Elham got some maggot in his brain about the shooting being good here, and so it was I saw a great deal of her. You will know that Widow

Woodman was handsomely paid. Provided she kept the secret absolutely, of course. Which she did until a few weeks ago. Where is Beckles?' she asked pettishly. 'Such a deedy woman.'

I clutched Hansard's shoulder to steady him. He nodded in acknowledgement. At last he had his voice sufficiently under control to continue. 'So for that slip of the tongue Mrs Woodman had to die. Did you kill her yourself, my lady?'

'How could I ask anyone else to? I set the place a-fire, too. Widow Woodman's secret will die with her.'

'Not if I run Bunce and Bargate to earth,' he replied.

My cousin wrinkled her brow as if trying to concentrate. 'She did not die?'

'Not immediately. Not until she had suffered a great deal.'

She shrugged. It was as if she knew that she too had a great deal yet to endure. 'And then there was the problem of my son. No sooner did he see a placket than he had to put his hand in it. Lizzie couldn't be sure which man had fathered her child. I told her I would personally escort her to a place of safety. Though she was tall, I am taller, and a great deal stronger. And I had to ensure that she would bear no more babies. They would all have been mad or bad, you see.'

Were these the words of a sane woman? Even the urbane Toone, leaning at a distance on the mantelpiece, gasped with shock.

'And William Jenkins? Why did you kill him?'

'William Jenkins? Who—? Ah, the foolish child who saw me hold Elham's head in the stream. He was poaching, of course, and ought to have been hanged, or at least transported. That was what I threatened him with, if he ever spoke of what he'd seen. I gave an entirely false description to those who were searching for him, contradicting those who tried to recall him. I employed him again, just once.' She smiled reminiscently. 'I hope he did not hit you too hard, Tobias. It must be hard to judge, when one uses a club almost as large as oneself. But I thought it was time to bring you down a peg. And I gather you recovered your health and indeed your watch. He wanted to keep it and your boots, but I insisted he threw them away. And then he found the watch again. Foolish child.'

With great sorrow I said, 'I rewarded him and his family generously! No wonder the poor boy was ever after uncomfortable in my presence.'

She might not have heard me. 'Then I heard a rumour that he was sleeping ill – calling out! – and I was afraid of what he might say. So I told his mother I would turn him into a respectable footman at Elham House.'

'Their Grosvenor Square residence,' I explained quietly to the others.

'There are so many bodies in the gutters of London that one more would not have been noticed,' she said.

'And he was so terrified of what you would do that he tried to hang himself this morning,' I said grimly.

'Did he say that? He lied. Typical of that class,' she said, wincing at some fierce pang gripping her stomach.

I could not speak.

'He may yet tell the whole truth,' Hansard corrected her sharply. 'He is deeply unconscious but by and by he may recover.'

'By which time I will not be here to worry,' she said, with grim humour. 'Where is my maid? I had to have a new abigail, you know, the last being unsatisfactory,' she added in a society drawl. 'Before that there was some blabbermouth of a butler. I forget now where I left his body. And John Coachman too. He would insist he saw me slit that chit Lizzie's throat and bury her. I didn't want to hurt him myself, poor old man, so I had someone poison him. That nice doctor at Lymbury.'

I tried to tell her that he still lived, but her voice grated on.

'Do you know him? A Dr Brighouse. A most charming toady, with a vile mushroom of a wife. She probably steals the inmates' food. Please look into it.'

'We will indeed, my lady,' Hansard said. 'So remind me, why did you have your son incarcerated at Lymbury?'

'He was as mad as his father, and far more vicious-tempered. I was always having to pay off some villager whose pig or hen he had disembowelled. He got worse when he came into the title and the estates. He raped Lizzie, you understand, subjecting her to the sort of practices more suited to the Hellfire Club, I do assure you. So away he goes from time to time.' She clutched her throat, retching horribly.

'Toone, I would welcome your professional assistance here. Pray leave us, Toby – wait outside and let no one enter without my permission,' Hansard told me.

I did as I was told, telling a startled manservant to bring me a chair, a branch of candles, a prayer book and a decanter of wine. From time to time the terrified abigail would emerge, carrying a covered vessel. She did not tell me what it contained. I did not ask. She returned with other, empty receptacles.

A bevy of servants huddle at the far end of the corridor. I sent one of them for Mr Davies, the steward.

'Her ladyship is very ill, Mr Davies. You should ensure that you can locate the next in line of succession and send for him.'

'Not Lord Elham, sir?'

'Do you not know where Lord Elham is?' His face gave him away. 'Although I fear he will have to return for a funeral, he will not be well enough to live at the Priory for many weeks yet. Indeed, he may never be able to. At very least, a trustee must be appointed. I'm sure I can rely on you, Davies, to be totally discreet,' I added, stern as my father.

It was in the early hours when Edmund reappeared. 'I think it is time for you now, Tobias.' He led me through into the bedchamber, where she lay on the bed screaming aloud and writhing in agony but apparently insensible of our presence.

'Good God, Hansard, how long will she be like this? Have you nothing that would help her?'

'As I helped Jenkins out of his pain and into the next world?' He looked me straight in the eye. 'I have not.'

I did not believe him.

I looked on her ghastly features and prayed for a rapid end to her suffering. Then I remembered poor Lizzie's death, and changed my prayer, that the Almighty might in His infinite wisdom suit her punishment to her appalling crimes.

It took her ladyship till noon the next day to die.

# EPILOGUE

*'Bury them in the churchyard? On hallowed ground?' Miller demanded. 'Both of them? Suicides?'*

*I said quietly, 'Her ladyship was clearly deranged when she killed herself. And his lordship was nine-tenths drunk when he crammed that poor hunter of his at the wall.'*

*Lord Elham had been temporarily released from his incarceration to attend his mother's obsequies. Though he was accompanied by two of Dr Brigstock's strongest assistants, he had managed to elude them and fall upon the contents of his cellar. Then, even while his mother lay unburied, he had taken his favourite hunter and ridden neck or nothing across the park – with fatal consequences.*

*'Bad business with the horse, that,' Bulmer said. It was clear he considered the horse far more loss than the rider, and I could not have argued. 'Imagine, having to have it shot, when he'd paid three thousand guineas for it, they say.'*

*If ever there was madness, it must be paying so much for horseflesh when so many of the Priory tenants still went unshod.*

*'I have put the question of the burials to the bishop,' I reminded them, 'and he insisted that we hold the funerals here.' In Christian charity, I should have agreed with him, but*

*there were days when, looking at the green mound containing poor Lizzie's mortal remains, it was hard to remember the forgiveness that was the cornerstone of my faith. 'Now,' I continued briskly, 'Mr Clark cannot be expected to dig both graves—'*

*Bulmer sighed. 'Not with his wife likely to occupy the next, and that all too soon, I hear.'*

*I smiled sadly at the man. Was he at last becoming my ally? 'Can I rely on you to find someone who will dig deep but with reverence?'*

*Bulmer nodded. 'I'll set one of my best hands on to it.'*

*'Mr Davies will see him well paid for his pains.'*

*Miller put in sharply, 'And that boy – what about him? They do say he tried to top himself. And I can't see no bishop saying a thieving little pauper lad like him should be buried with decent folk.'*

*Was he a thief? I believed that Lady Elham had spoken the truth when she had told him to throw away my watch. How had he come to find it again? And if he had somehow smuggled it past Bulstrode, would he indeed have shown it to me? Perhaps he himself did not know: he was only a child, after all.*

*I shook my head firmly. 'He may yet recover.' Dr Hansard had summoned many distinguished colleagues to confer over poor William's treatment. 'In any case, should he die, William's death will not be suicide. He was the victim of a murderer – her ladyship,' I added. 'You remember the evidence at the inquest.'*

*'The coroner didn't say she'd strung him up with her bare hands,' Miller objected.*

*'As good as,' Bulmer said. 'Is that mother of his all right for meat and vegetables, Parson? Because I could get one of my men to take some up – aye, and do any digging needful in that garden of hers.'*

*I felt tears rising. 'You are a good man, Mr Bulmer.'*

*He looked shamefaced. 'It was Dr Hansard told me it might be called for.' He grinned. 'And when will you be reading his banns, Parson, his and that lady of his?'*

*Was it not dear Mrs Beckles herself who had warned me against gossip? 'Mrs Beckles is busy about the Priory, as you can imagine, helping Mr Davies set everything in order. All the silver and china is being packed in straw, the pictures taken down and furniture stowed under Holland covers. The servants are all working very had.'*

*'They do say the new heir's promised them a whole year's wages, and God bless him for it,' Bulmer said.*

*Miller nodded gloomily. 'After that, then – tell me what'll happen after that. They say the new Lord Elham won't live in the place.'*

*'Would you if you had any choice in the matter?' Bulmer demanded with a shudder. 'They say he's got a big place of his own in Surrey or some such,' he added.*

*He waited till Miller took himself off and leant to touch me confidentially on the arm. 'Seems my daughter-in-law is in a promising way, Parson. You don't suppose the Lord would mind if I asked him to keep an eye on her, do you?'*

*'I'm sure he wouldn't, Mr Bulmer. And if you'd like to come into the church, I will gladly add my prayers to yours, for her babe too.'*

*We knelt side by side. I knew not the details of his*

*entreaties, but they were long and I dare swear deep felt. For myself, I also commended to the Almighty the future of William. If he lived, might it be as a healthy child; if he had to die might the ending be swift, with no more suffering. Only then would Mrs Jenkins be free to mourn and care properly for her other children. She had not been unsupported, of course: Jem was among several kind souls who insisted on watching the invalid while she snatched what little sleep she permitted herself.*

*Did Jem perhaps begin to feel tender sentiments for the young widow? It was impossible to tell from his behaviour, and I respected him too highly to pry. In any case, was any man on this earth blessed with finer judgement of right and wrong? All I knew was that as yet he showed no sign of quitting the parsonage or the village. Whatever he did, God would guide and support him.*

*I prayed too for my dear friends Edmund and Maria, soon to be man and wife after their unorthodox betrothal. Not all the tragic events around them could dim their obvious delight in each other now that their relationship was in the open, and there were very few who begrudged their happiness. The moment they judged that their marriage would not offend the sensibilities of their friends, I would marry them by special licence – God knew that they had waited long enough not to bother with the tedium of banns. They insisted that the ceremony would be private, with very little white satin and very few lace veils; in spite of these deficiencies, no one would doubt the perfect happiness of their union.*

*I asked for God's blessing on Susan, now aware of the full horror of her sister's fate. She was still in her own opinion brown and squat, but several of the young men in the neighbourhood clearly found her not unattractive, and perhaps her eyes followed Jem less than they were wont to do.*

*Farmer Bulmer prayed on.*

*Not wishing to disturb him, I dared to add a prayer for myself. My mother had written imploring me to be reconciled with the rest of the family and take up a benefice within her gift near their main country seat. I could do as much good in the wilds of Derbyshire as I had done in lush and leafy Warwickshire, she urged. What should I do? Where could I be of most use? Perhaps I was even called to serve as a missionary in far-off India?*

*At last, torn in so many ways, I could only utter the words of the prayer that Our Lord Himself taught us: Thy Will be done.*